CRITICS PRAISE C. J. BARRY!

UNRAVELED

"Hot new author C. J. Barry serves up more adventurous fun. This is a talent that is definitely on the rise."
—*Romantic Times*

"Loaded with action and plenty of sizzling romance. . . . C. J. Barry [is] a writer who is destined to be a superstar."
—*Midwest Book Review*

"Once again C. J. Barry has outdone herself. . . . Another winner from up-and-coming author C. J. Barry, *Unraveled* is sure to capture the attention of all."
—*Romance Reviews Today*

UNEARTHED

"A hot new futuristic voice has landed and her name is C. J. Barry. This interstellar roller-coaster ride blends just the right amount of action, passion and humor. A smashing debut."
—*Romantic Times*

"C. J. Barry provides an exhilarating science fiction romance that readers from both genres will enjoy. . . . Loaded with action, plenty of humor and romance . . . fans will savor this delightful novel."
—*Midwest Book Review*

BEAMED UP

I must be dreaming, she thought, watching colors appear and dissolve before her. Fallen asleep at the computer again. Wouldn't be the first time. However, the out-of-body experience was something new. A rainbow of light exploded, flooding and overwhelming her senses. And as abruptly as everything had started, Lacey landed on her feet with a jerk. The world spun around her, focusing in a dizzy rush.

She breathed. Prickly warmth and pale beige walls surrounded her. Something smelled like it was burning. She hoped it wasn't her.

"How do you feel?"

The deep voice jarred her from any thought she may have been forming. Slowly and with great dread, she turned to face the source.

It was a man. A gorgeous man. The kind darn-good fantasies were made of, in fact. He had chestnut hair pulled back into a short tail and piercing dark eyes like a black bear. He filled out a taupe crew-collar shirt, tan pants, and brown knee-high boots nicely, with a body as broad and powerful as a Mack truck. Although he was smiling at her, there was something in his stillness, a glint of danger in his eyes that set him apart from any man she'd ever seen.

And he stood there like he'd been expecting her, waiting for her and only her.

Other *Love Spell* books by C. J. Barry:

UNRAVELED
UNEARTHED

C. J. BARRY

UNLEASHED

LOVE SPELL NEW YORK CITY

*To my terrific agent, Roberta Brown,
for her fearless and unconditional
faith in my brave new worlds.*

LOVE SPELL®

May 2004

Published by

Dorchester Publishing Co., Inc.
200 Madison Avenue
New York, NY 10016

ISBN 0-505-52573-9

The name "Love Spell" and its logo are trademarks of Dorchester Publishing Co., Inc.

Printed in the United States of America.

Visit us on the web at www.dorchesterpub.com.

ACKNOWLEDGMENTS

I'd like to thank my great editor Chris Keeslar and everyone at Dorchester Publishing; the infamous Purple Pens; the CNY Romance Writers; my dedicated critique partners Patti, Joyce, and Stephanie; Romance Writers of America; and every one of my loyal readers. Special thanks to Catherine Spangler.

As always, I am forever grateful to my beautiful family: Ed, Rachel, and Ryan.

UNLEASHED

Chapter One

"That's one dry rock, Reene," Zain said to his computer as he surveyed the horizon over planet P254-334-5 through his ship's viewport. Below was an endless monotony of sunburned sand dunes broken by an occasional rock outcropping.

Reene replied, "An astute assessment, sir. Eighty percent desert, twenty percent water. No detectable human or alien populations. There is a viable atmosphere. However, significant terraforming would be required to place a water-based populace here."

Good, Zain thought. The fieldwork of mapping a new planet was easier when it had no people. "Include that in our report to StarNet."

"Yes, sir."

Zain checked their progress in the planet's holo-image on the console. Reene had divided the planet surface into equal sections forming the typical grid pattern. As they passed over the next section, the sensor readings scrolled up beside the holo-image displaying surface maps, climate, electromagnetism, geochemistry, gravity. Zain scanned them. Nothing special. Another routine survey.

He leaned back and closed his eyes, letting Reene take care of the survey grid. Lately, charting star systems and the planets therein had become downright monotonous. Not that he was looking for excitement. He smirked. Well, maybe just a little.

"Sir, I am getting an unusual reading over grid A5501," Reene announced.

Zain opened his eyes and noted a significant anomaly in the stats. He moved forward for a closer look. In one pinpoint within the grid, the energy readings were off the scale. What the hell was that?

"De-orbit and bring us down," he commanded, the first whispers of adrenaline unfurling in his gut.

As Reene took the ship down, Zain continued to monitor the readings and the planet surface. The terrain remained constant. No breaks and nothing to explain the kind of energy the sensors were picking up.

"We are directly over the site now," Reene announced.

"Any idea what this is?" Zain asked.

"We have never encountered this phenomenon before. Therefore, I cannot offer an accurate explanation."

Zain smiled at Reene's flawless logic. "A guess, then?"

"Sir, you may recall that I am not very good at

guessing. Intuition is a trait I have not yet mastered."

Zain had to agree with his computer there. The last time he'd let Reene guess, they'd nearly made inadvertent first contact with a new species. Always a bad thing. Besides, it had been a while since he'd stepped foot on land. A little hands-on data investigation might be just the thing he needed to mitigate the restlessness he'd felt over the past few cycles.

"Bring us down for a landing," he ordered. "Let's see what's making all the noise down there."

His ship responded immediately. The planet's energy readings continued to climb the closer they got to the surface, but Zain couldn't detect the source. He'd never seen anything like this in five years of space exploration.

The earlier excitement he'd felt changed to concern as they neared the planet's surface. Zain waited for touchdown, but it never happened. Something wasn't right. "Reene, pull up," he ordered just as they slipped below what had appeared to be solid earth.

At the same instant, Reene reported, "Sir, I have encountered an energy field."

A flash of light crossed the viewport, striking the ship's hull full force. Another flash simultaneously hit the starboard side and sent a surge of current through the main systems.

"Evasive action!" Zain yelled above the alarms.

His ship jerked hard to the right just as another laser streamed above them, striking the left wing. Reene dropped altitude so fast, Zain's stomach roiled.

All the bars on the console panel flashed and alarms sounded from nearly every system.

"Get us out of here now, Reene!"

"Unable to comply," the computer responded. "Navigation systems are compromised."

Another laser shot took out the shields completely and the holo-images scrambled and then vanished on the console. The spacecraft began a slow, surreal spin.

Zain reached for the stabilizers. No response.

"Stabilizers not functioning," Reene verified. "Shields are down. All systems rebooting."

"Shit," Zain growled. The console went black, and he gritted his teeth as the ship spun out of control, rotating wildly. Distant canyon walls and a desert floor half a klick below flashed by the viewport. The laser fire had stopped, but his ship was coming down hard. At this rate, they wouldn't survive impact.

"Reene, bring up the landing jets first," he ground out through the G forces. The floor of the canyon angled into view just below. Ten meters to contact, he clutched his chair arms and braced for what might very well be his final landing.

Panel lights flashed on and the ship heaved slightly as the landing systems took hold. The final seconds slowed in his mind before the sickening collision of machine and land. Red sand sprayed over his ship as it nosed into the ground. Zain jerked forward, his harness preventing him from going through the viewport.

He shook his head, and it reeled to a stop a few minutes later. The last-second landing jets had saved them from total destruction, but the panel lights were flashing at low power and it was very quiet.

"Reene?" he asked in concern. "You still there?"

Static filled the ship's interior before his computer responded. "Here, sir. Are you functional?"

Zain rolled his neck with a grimace. "I think so."

"Would you like me to run a scan on you?"

Zain watched the ship's systems come back up one by one. They didn't look at all healthy, especially the energy levels. Nearly every system was damaged to some degree, either from the energy surge or the laser fire. "No thanks, Reene. I'm more worried about you at the moment. Release the nanos to start system repairs. What happened?"

"We breached an energy field acting as a camouflage over this crater and triggered a laser attack emanating from multiple locations around the rim."

Zain peered outside at the sheer rock cliffs enclosing them. Above, he could see the sky through the shimmer of the energy field that covered the basin. It was obviously meant to kill anything or anyone who breached it. Why? Who put it there? What were they protecting?

"Scan the area, Reene."

A few seconds later, the ship replied. "There is a single domed structure approximately eight kilometers from our present location. Once the nanos have repaired navigation, I can attempt to move closer."

Zain eyed the ridge above. "Let's wait on that. I don't want to trigger another attack. I'll take the speeder out to investigate. Any sign of a greeting party?"

"Negative."

And no wonder, Zain thought. A normal ship would never have survived such an assault. Luckily, Reene wasn't a normal ship.

"Looks like we aren't getting out of here until I deactivate either the field or the perimeter fire. We need to find the controls for that energy field. They may be in that domed structure."

"Sir, I am also detecting a large mass below us."

Zain stilled. That didn't sound good either. Obviously, this planet wasn't as boring as he'd originally thought.

"Let's hope we don't have to find out what it is."

Chapter Two

T minus five days and counting . . .

Lacey watched the clock on her computer flip from 11:59 P.M. to midnight with the kind of anticlimax that pretty much summed up her existence to this point.

"Happy New Year," she murmured above the theme music to *Gunfight at the O.K. Corral* playing on the TV beside her. A blank Excel spreadsheet sat on her computer monitor with the header, "Lacey Garrett's New Year's Resolutions."

Hell of a way for a woman to ring in the New Year—with her computer and an old Western.

She took a deep, slow, deliberate breath. It was time to get serious and set some goals. Specific, achievable, and sensible goals in a logical order, just like a software program. If she followed the master plan exactly,

7

she wouldn't take any more wrong turns.

So she flexed her fingers and typed, "New Year's Resolution #1: Rebuild career trashed by lying, stealing, scum-sucking, two-timing ex-fiancé/partner from hell, Robert E. Gwyn."

There. Definitely concrete and feasible. And she could almost type his name without twitching now. A definite improvement over the past two months.

Rebuild her career. How long could that take, she thought, considering she was completely broke with one tenuous programming contract to cling to. But if it was anyone's fault, it was hers for taking on an applications partner in the first place. Making him her fiancé was her second mistake. More followed, but a woman could only handle so much humiliation in one sitting.

Besides, the career was the easy part. Reinventing herself was going to be the real challenge, but this was a new start in a new place in a new year. She was finally taking control of the threads of her life.

Exit: Lacey Garrett, Wishy-washy Doormat.

Enter: Lacey Garrett, Warrior Programmer.

Speaking of which. "#2: Control own destiny and fight to the death anyone who stands in my way."

She smiled. Good one. Xena would be proud. What else could she do to stay out of trouble? Ah, yes.

"#3: When in doubt, play it safe."

She nodded firmly. No more taking chances, no more unnecessary risks. From now on she was going to think about her choices and, after careful consideration, make the *right* decision. Her decisions, her way.

She jumped when the window above her desktop rattled on its old hinges and the January winds of Virginia's Shenandoah Valley tried to come inside. The farmhouse shuddered around her, and somewhere in the belly of the hundred-year-old structure, the furnace cranked on with a low, prehistoric groan.

It was a small miracle every time the heat came on. In the two months since she'd moved in, she'd discovered that the place needed serious work—from the damp basement to the leaky roof. Her Aunt Glo had finally succumbed to the winters and wisely opted for a condo in Florida, leaving the place empty and rent-free, which happened to be Lacey's exact requirements. Unfortunately, Aunt Glo had let a lot of things go in her golden years, and tackling roofs and basements was definitely out of Lacey's realm of expertise.

Her gaze traveled from the cracked ceiling to the horse wallpaper to the weathered flooring that had lost its true colors long ago. Aside from the questionable decor, it wasn't a bad house. It had good bones. She liked the handsome varnished woodwork and the way the rooms felt comfortable and cozy once the furnace caught up.

Maybe some paint would help. She could paint. Probably. Heck, she designed software applications for a living. She could figure out how to paint. And some new wallpaper. She nodded to herself, warming to the vision of single-handedly wielding a paintbrush. Do-it-yourselfers did it all the time. How hard could it be?

Bravely, she typed. "#4: Restore this old house."

9

Hmm. On the other hand, those four little words sounded pretty expensive for a woman with no savings account. And it wasn't as if she were going to be here forever. Just until she'd regrouped. Yeah, the place needed work and someday someone would do it. Just not her. She was already on a mission.

She backspaced and retyped. "Repair this old house enough so I don't freeze to death this winter." There. Much more manageable.

Her E-mail binged. She pulled it up and saw a reply from Zainman, the same one who'd posted the *UR-GENT: Can anyone read this? Need help. Please.* message on the Tech-Nest board a few days ago.

Normally, Tech-Nest was used by geeky programmers—and other faceless souls with no real lives—to trade tips, tech updates, and solutions; it wasn't unusual to see *HELP* messages on a regular basis. But this one had been different. This guy had included a series of jumbled images with his E-mail. It had taken Lacey a while to realize that the clutter was actually many layers dumped on top of each other, Magic Eye style. Besides some incomprehensible patterns and codes, one of the images looked exactly like the Stonehenge layout on the poster that hung over her computer. Lucky for Zainman, she had a strange fixation with Stonehenge.

So, instead of concentrating on her one remaining applications contract, she'd dropped him a long private E-mail on the layers and the Stonehenge similarity. Day before yesterday. No reply. No why-thank-you-ma'am. Nada. For a guy in trouble, he hadn't seemed too interested in her reply. Obviously, Zainman was a computer geek with no manners.

She opened his E-mail.

Yes, that's perfect. When was the last time you looked at the stars?

"Oh, brother," she mumbled. What kind of reply was that? Stars? She'd probably hooked a Trekker. She really needed to stop hanging around with nerds. In fact, she was signing off Tech-Nest for a while. It would take all of five days to finish the Marquet project and she didn't need to be losing her only viable income in the foreseeable future. Food and heat had a way of changing a woman's priorities in a hurry.

She deleted his reply, reopened her goals page and added, "New Year's Resolution #5: Don't talk to E-strangers."

Just as she finished typing, she heard Oliver meowing outside for at least the bizillionth time today. She groaned aloud. Yup, she wasn't going to let anyone push her around—except for her cat. Though technically, the cat wasn't even hers. Damn Robert. Not only had he dumped her, he'd ditched his pet too. Poor little Oliver. It wasn't as if he could pick his owner. Lacey, however, had no excuse.

Which brought her to the most important resolution of all: "#6: Absolutely no relationships due to being TSTL—too stupid to love."

She sat back and reviewed the list. Looked good. Yes, this year was going to be different. She was going to get it right.

Oliver meowed again with real conviction and Lacey frowned in concern. He sounded off-key.

Floorboards squeaked under her feet as she walked through the dark house to the kitchen that led to the backyard. She muscled the outside door open and peered out.

In a clear, star-studded sky, a full moon poked through trees that swayed in the wind. Her aunt's house was a far cry from the city of Baltimore where she'd lived with Robert. She wasn't sure if she liked it yet, since solitude and quiet were new concepts. But she loved the country air—crisp and clean and thick with scent. It smelled like freedom.

In a narrow shaft of light from the kitchen, the tiger cat sat in the center of the yard staring up at the roof.

"Oliver!"

He didn't look at her.

Itty-bitty kitty brain, she reminded herself.

"Oliver, come in."

He meowed in her general direction and she rolled her eyes. Heaven only knew what he was looking at. Probably a leaf or something equally fascinating.

Grudgingly, she accepted the fact that she'd been relegated to being a cat-door attendant and pulled open a drawer to find the flashlight. The cabinet teetered on its base, and she had to prop it up with her knee. One of these days, she'd have to get the outside lights working again, and also fix this disaster of a cabinet.

The drawer shut with considerable effort. The rest of the outdated and predominately orange kitchen stared her in the face. Avocado appliances, flooring that was probably asbestos, and cabinets caked with fifty coats of paint—it was a quite a fashion statement. Maybe a little demolition would do her good. Almost like therapy, but cheaper and much easier on the ego.

The skimpy knit tank top and light pants of her pajamas did little to protect her from the cool winter night as she stepped outside to fetch the cat. Her slippers shuffled through a mat of fallen leaves. It occurred to her that no self-respecting Warrior Programmer owned a pair of fuzzy purple slip-ons. Next trip into town, she was going for the faux leopard pair.

"What's the matter with you? Didn't you hear me?" she said, picking up the ten-pound fur ball and rubbing her face against his soft head. "It's a good thing you're cute."

Oliver's little body tensed in her hands as she turned back to the house. She heard a hum above her and froze. Something *was* on her roof. She raised her flashlight to the twenty-one-inch satellite uplink dish attached to the roof. It was rotating in complete circles as if trying to find a signal. She glanced to her bedroom window where her computer sat, alone and unattended. So, why was the dish moving? It always pointed south; that's where the geostationary satellite sat in orbit. That's how she connected to the net in the middle of God's country.

Then she heard a low, teeth-chattering hum above her and looked up into a million winking stars. Nothing unusual there, so why was the hum getting louder and closer? A bassy vibration buzzed her nerve endings and made her ears ring. With growing dismay, she watched a big black hole glide by ever so slowly. When it was directly above her, a tiny light appeared dead center and, as she gaped, it grew bigger. She froze in place, knowing she should run but too mesmerized to move. Then a blue beam blinded her.

The flashlight slipped from her fingers as invisible arms gripped her and threw her into a rolling vortex. She had the sensation of being stretched out, but there was no pain, just a strange feeling of detachment. Far away, she heard Oliver's plaintive meow and her own helpless cry. Lights flashed before her.

I must be dreaming, she thought, watching colors appear and dissolve before her eyes. Fallen asleep at the computer again. Wouldn't be the first time. However, the out-of-body experience was something new. A rainbow of light exploded, flooding and overwhelming her senses. And as abruptly as everything had started, she landed on her feet with a jerk. The world spun around her, focusing in a dizzy rush.

She breathed. Prickly warmth and pale beige walls surrounded her. Something smelled as if it were burning. She hoped it wasn't her.

What the heck had just happened? Oliver was in her arms and appeared perfectly comfortable. She was still wearing her pajamas and sissy slippers, but everything else had changed.

Her gaze traveled around the stone walls of a tall dome-shaped room. Towering arches formed doorways and between them were rows of images she vaguely recognized.

"How do you feel?"

The deep voice jarred her from any thought she might have been forming. Slowly and with great dread, she turned to face the source.

It was a man. A gorgeous man. The kind darn good fantasies were made of, in fact. He had chestnut hair pulled back into a short tail and piercing dark eyes like a black bear. He filled out a taupe crew-type shirt, tan pants, and brown knee-height boots nicely, with a body as broad and powerful as a Mack truck. Although he was smiling at her, there was something in his stillness, a glint of danger in his eyes that set him apart from any man she'd ever seen.

And he stood there as if he'd been expecting her, waiting for her and only her.

Well, that clinched it. She was definitely dreaming.

His eyes narrowed. "I assume you speak English?"

She nodded, too impressed to answer. He crossed his arms and the thin fabric stretched over mounds of hard muscle.

Wow, she marveled. This fantasy dream was a keeper. She wondered if she'd ever seen a man like him before or if her brain had built him of its own accord. Must be those new vitamins she'd started taking.

Of course, any minute now he'd turn into Robert, the fiancé-from-hell, and start stealing pieces of her brain. Her dreams always ended that way.

"Are you CyberQueen?"

She hefted Oliver to one side to concentrate on her newly created fantasy.

"CyberQueen is my screen name," she said. Then she admitted, "Actually, I'm not much of a queen. You can call me Lacey."

He nodded like a good manifestation. "Nice to meet you, Lacey."

Oooo, she liked how he did that. This was kind of fun. He played coy; she could practice being plucky and sexy. He'd never know that she was far from sexy or plucky, and she could wake up whenever she wanted. This beat reality by a mile.

"The name is Zain."

Zain? Her mind made the connection. "As in Zainman?"

"The same," he said.

She gave his powerful body a once-over. "Huh, now that's really weird. I can't believe my brain would have put your body to his . . . vocation. Then again, there was that Bill Nye the Science Guy dream." She nibbled her lower lip and shook her head. "I need a date. That's all there is to it. Some nice guy who just wants me for sex and nothing else. As soon as I wake up, I'm checking the personal ads."

He eyed her with a dark, steamy look. She grinned at him and petted Oliver's soft fur, feeling his warmth against her chest. Everything looked and felt so real for a dream. She wondered what Zainman would feel like.

He was saying, "You are probably wondering why you are here."

"Well, it *is* my dream. I just can't figure out where you came from." She stepped over to him and studied his face. His cheekbones were high and strong, his eyes intense, his lips full and sensual. A short stubble covered his square jaw and she reached out and touched it. Warm and soft. It was as if her mind blended together the best parts of all the men she'd ever met, or wanted to meet, into a single perfect package.

"You are one beautiful man," she said with fearless and heartfelt conviction. "Well, maybe not beautiful, but sexy and rugged in a Wild Wild West kind of way. Like the *Magnificent Seven* gunslingers all rolled into one."

"Is that right?"

She raised an eyebrow at his smooth drawl. Definitely a cowboy. "Do I know you from somewhere?"

A smile played on his lips. "Don't think so."

"Huh," she said. "Well, it doesn't matter. I've sworn off men. It's one of my New Year's Resolutions. That, and new slippers."

He eyed her feet for a moment and then lifted his gaze to hers. "What's wrong with men?"

As if he didn't know. She explained patiently, "Nothing—except that they suck the life out of women, steal their brains, and then leave them for dead." She waved her hand around. "Not that it bothers me anymore, you understand. Therapy took care of all that."

"I can tell," Zainman observed intently. "So, do you kill your mates off all at once or just shred their egos a little at a time?"

She frowned at him. "I hope you don't turn into Freud. I really dislike his theories."

He paused. "Freud is your mate?"

She burst out laughing. "Hardly. I prefer to live alone these days. But if I had a 'mate', he certainly wouldn't be a psychoanalyst who blamed all of man's problems on sex."

"Interesting theory," Zainman remarked with a thoughtful nod. "He might be right, you know."

She speared him with a disgusted look. "*Please.* I know where all my problems stem from, and it has nothing to do with sex. That's about the only thing I know I can do right."

His eyes focused on her. For a second, she was riveted in place. Under his powerful gaze, she felt the heat rise in her body—no small feat for a woman who had sworn off men.

"I believe you," he said at last.

Ah. So, this was going to one of *those* dreams. She'd never had a good sex dream, before. Okay, so she'd banned men. *Live* men. Technically, this was safe territory. She licked her lips. And since she was reinventing herself anyway . . .

He moved away from her and waved to the walls. "Do you recognize any of these images?"

Darn. She wrinkled her nose. Why did all her dreams have to be so puritan? Just once she'd like to know that the dark interiors of her mind could unleash something more exciting than a guy interested in a bunch of blobs on a wall. Freud was probably laughing his ass off in his grave.

Distracted and disappointed, she muttered, "Unfortunately, yes. I just sent you an E-mail about them, remember? You could have at least said 'thank you.' Instead, you just blew me off with some pathetic pickup line about the stars."

The guilty party's eyebrows rose. "I do appreciate your reply. In fact, I'd like you to tell me what the rest of these mean."

She scanned the room covered with hundreds, possibly thousands of Zainman's blobs. What was he talking about? How was she supposed to know what all these mean? There was no way . . .

Then it occurred to her what was happening. "This is an endless loop dream," she muttered. "I knew it. I always get them when I'm stressed and overworked. This new app is going to kill me."

Zainman only stared at her, so she twirled her hand around in the air. "You know, endless loops? I just keep walking through a million lines of code until I get to the exit routine, which happens about 6 A.M. in the morning and I wake up exhausted."

He pursed his lips. "This isn't like that."

She shook her head. "Forget it. Once one starts, I never get out."

"I'd like you to interpret these," he repeated coolly. His serious tone surprised her. Something dark flashed in his eyes and she noticed just how sharp they were. Intelligent, hard, and black. *Dangerous.*

"I don't want to," she replied, growing uncomfortable under his stern gaze. Even Oliver had perked up and was wriggling in her arms.

19

Zainman stepped closer, invading her space. "It's really important."

"Stop that," she snapped, backing up. Oliver started as a chime rang, and everything in the room shivered except for Zainman.

He glanced at the ceiling and said out loud, "Reene, what's wrong?"

A dry monotone replied, "Sir, Cell Three has just ruptured. We are experiencing a primary systems power failure. Auxiliary activated. VirtuWav power dropping below acceptable levels."

Zainman frowned deeply and gave Lacey a look that chilled her to her bones. Oh, she had a feeling this dream was turning nightmare on her.

"Can you compensate?"

"Negative, sir."

"Is there enough power to return imported subjects?"

Lacey blinked. *Imported subjects?* Why didn't that sound good?

"I can initiate a transfer of one life-form within the next ten seconds."

Zainman stepped up to her menacingly and eyed her cat. "Give me the creature," he ordered bluntly.

She clutched Oliver to her chest. "No."

"We don't have time to argue. Let go of it."

He reached for Oliver and Lacey twisted away. "Don't you dare order me around! This is *my* dream, cowboy."

The voice overhead chimed. "Time has expired. Initiating automatic shutdown."

20

Zainman muttered something low that didn't sound at all appropriate in mixed company. Then his formidable gaze met Lacey's as if seeing her for the first time.

A split second later, he faded away and Lacey was floating in midair, holding poor Oliver in a death grip. Finally. It was about time this bizarre dream ended. She reached one hand out and touched the smooth surface of the glass tube she now bobbed inside. Through a blue haze, she could see that she and Oliver were in another place, with metal walls, panels, flashing lights, and odd pieces of equipment. Then she noticed another tube identical to hers a short distance away. It looked like a giant test tube and there was a shadowy body inside it.

Maybe her nightmare was just beginning.

The haze cleared and she drifted down. The tube disappeared into the floor just as her slippers landed on a small blue circle. Her legs gave out. Strong hands grabbed her around the waist and steadied her. What the hell was happening? She regained her equilibrium and looked up at the face attached to the hands.

Zainman?

"What are you still doing here?" she asked.

"I live here." He released her and stepped back, looking highly displeased. "You should have given me the creature."

She covered Oliver's head with her hand. "Are you still on about the cat?"

Zainman glared at it. "It's just an animal."

"He's my pet," she retorted. "More or less. I'm not

handing him over to you, I don't care what kind of dream symbology you are supposed to be." She shooed him away with a flick of her hand. "I don't like you anymore. You can go now."

He didn't say anything, his eyes regarding her with frustration and annoyance. Just like Robert. She hated this stupid dream. It was bad enough living with that look for two years, but to still be dreaming about it was downright pathetic.

"I hope your animal likes space rations." Zainman turned and stepped up to a door that opened automatically for him. He disappeared through it and Lacey was alone with Oliver.

She shook her head in utter confusion. "Maybe this is one of those dreams where you think you are waking up but you really aren't, Oliver."

Silence descended as she waited for the dream to end. Closed her eyes to help things along. Opened them. Still here. Curiouser and curiouser. She stepped around the small room and didn't see a thing that looked familiar.

That's when she noticed the stack of thin boards: paintings. Created in dark, tortured colors, they were a sharp contrast to the gunmetal walls they were leaning against. She peered through the stack. Oddly warped trees surrounded serene lakes and covered low mountain ridges. Reds, blacks, and grays were mixed up in a nightmarish swill. They were very good, almost lifelike in their twisted renditions, Salvador Dali style. Maybe a dream like this was how old Sal got his ideas.

The materials were strange, not quite paint and not quite canvas, but even to her untrained eye she could tell that whoever painted them had tremendous talent and technique. Why would such paintings be in her dream? She didn't paint, had neither the desire nor the talent. Very strange, but then again, nothing about this dream had been normal so far.

A mix of voices and mechanical noises came through the open doorway. Against her better judgment, she walked over to investigate. Beyond the door was a short corridor flanked by doors on each side and a single bed attached to the wall on the right. Past that, she spotted the back of Zainman's head.

She made her way down the corridor. It opened onto a horseshoe-shaped space lined with banks of panels and wide windows. Zainman sat in one of two bucket seats, tapping at a sleek black panel in front of him. Little holographic images popped up and disappeared on the surface, and Lacey watched them with captivated wonder. Colored bars and boxes covered the panel marked with strange writing. Fascinating. It amazed her how an overworked mind tossed things together and made a dream.

Her gaze shifted to the windows with their 180-degree view. Spiky brown plants spread out in all directions across a flat plain. A burnt-orange sun hung just over the dark red cliffs in the distance. Red, she thought. Didn't most people dream in black and white?

Outside, two strange squirrel-like creatures hopped around sparse trees that were right out of a Dr. Seuss book. It all looked very, very vivid. Almost as if it were real—in a creepy kind of way.

"Reene, how long before we recover enough to power the VirtuWav back up?" Zainman said aloud.

"Cell Three has fully discharged. Without an infusion of ancillary power, the VirtuWav is inoperable."

Lacey glanced around the cabin at the voice seeming to come from everywhere. "Who was that?"

Zainman replied dryly, "Lacey, meet Reene."

She looked around. There wasn't anyone else there. She took a tentative step away from Zainman and his invisible friend.

"It is a pleasure to meet you, Lacey," the omnipresent voice said.

She looked at the ceiling, completely baffled. Maybe she was dead. After all, she *had* seen those lights. "God?"

"I am not a god. I am a product of artificial intelligence. It is a pleasure to meet an Earthling," the voice said.

Lacey gave a little hysterical laugh of relief. "I knew it. Too many hours on the computer and too many bad sci-fi movies—a guaranteed recipe for weird dreams."

Zainman interjected, "This isn't a dream, Lacey."

She rolled her eyes. "Will this end already? Joke's over. I have work to do, a cat to feed, and I would like to be awake now."

He eyed her for a very long time before saying, "You already are."

Chapter Three

Zain watched color drain from the woman's delicate features and wondered if she'd pass out on him. As if he didn't have enough problems at the moment.

"You might want to sit down," he suggested and turned the seat beside him to face her.

She didn't move, just stared at him with those incredible blue eyes. Ivory skin paled against soft red lips and shiny, straight black hair that brushed past her shoulders. Little shoulder straps held up a flimsy purple top that hugged her breasts. Darker pants hung from her hips and around her bottom. Outlined were the dangerous curves of a lean, petite body.

She'd been a hell of a surprise when she'd come through the VirtuWav. A classic beauty with a body to match. Unfortunately, she couldn't take orders worth a damn. If she'd only given him her animal, she'd be back home already.

"I'll be going now," she said, sounding dazed. And with that, she turned and wandered back down the corridor to the cargo area and VirtuWav banks.

"Damn," he muttered. All his ship's power levels were in the red, and his one chance at deliverance was trying to walk out on him. He said to Reene, "See what you can do about repairing Cell Three. I'm going to try to pacify our . . . guest."

"Yes, sir."

Zain got up to follow Lacey before she strolled outside and hurt herself. On the way back, he mentally calculated what another live body and a half were going to do to his food and water supply. Normally he carried enough supplies, but only for himself. It had been a long time since he'd had to figure another person into the equation. He didn't even want to consider sleeping arrangements.

He found her standing in the middle of the VirtuWav circle with her eyes closed, clutching her animal in one arm. The creature blinked at him with golden eyes and gave a small cry.

Lacey's eyes flickered open. He caught a flash of fear in them. So, she wasn't as tough as she tried to be. If she was afraid now, she was going to terrified when she found out what kind of mess she'd landed in.

He reined in his frustration. She couldn't realize what her reluctance in the VirtuWav had cost them both. If anything, it was his fault for even attempting the transfer. Now she was his responsibility. Her and her creature.

26

He reached out and ran his fingers across the top of the animal's head, which the creature seemed to genuinely like. It looked very similar to the cat that his friend Tess had brought back from Earth with her. Different color, same indifference.

"What's your cat's name?"

"You tell me," she replied, an edge of desperation in her voice. "I created you, so you should know."

Zain took a deep breath. "This isn't a dream."

She pointed toward the forward cabin. "Yeah, well that's not Kansas out there either, so the only explanation is that you"—she poked him in the gut—"are my imaginary friend and I'm sleeping."

He rubbed his belly where her sharp nail had stabbed him, and she looked at her finger.

"That hurt," she said with a frown.

"I know. You could use that finger as a weapon."

Her face lifted to his and he took the full brunt of her wide, blue eyes.

"Who are you?"

He paused, his ingrained self-preservation conditioning kicking in. A hunted man had to be careful. Then he decided it wouldn't hurt if she knew who he was. She wouldn't be around him long enough for it to matter. "Zain Masters. I'm a being from another part of your galaxy."

Her lips formed a skeptical pout. "Right," she said slowly. "And I suppose this is the USS *Enterprise*."

He scowled. "What?"

"You can tell Scottie to beam me up now," she said,

looking around. "How do I get out of here? There must be a way."

He watched her walk around the cargo space, pushing on the walls and looking behind his survey, exercise, and training equipment.

"My ship isn't very big. You've pretty much seen it all."

Ignoring him, she disappeared to the front cabin. He crossed his arms and waited. He heard her opening and closing doors and cabinets, and let her. It was the only way she'd believe him. The sooner she realized this was real, the sooner he'd convince her to cooperate. She'd recognized something in those jumbled images he'd sent to every information network in the quadrant, and if she wanted to go home so badly, she'd help him figure out what they meant. But first, she needed a little orientation.

"Sir, she appears to be in deep denial. Would you like me to talk to her?" Reene asked quietly.

Zain shook his head. "I don't think it'll do any good—but you might want to protect all your vital equipment."

Lacey reappeared through the door, looking rather frantic. Then she spied the air lock behind him and her face lit up. He moved to block her.

"You can't go outside."

She tried to sidestep him. "Bullshit, I can't."

"It's too dangerous."

"No, dangerous is being trapped in this nightmare with you." She raised her chin. "So move it or . . ."

She looked around and then lifted her cat toward Zain's face. "Or my cat will attack."

Zain's eyebrows went up. The cat blinked lazily at him.

"Really?"

"He's a tiger, believe me," Lacey said, her voice rising in warning.

The cat yawned. Zain didn't move. Lacey gave a growl of frustration and shoved the cat into his arms, startling the cat and surprising Zain. It came alive in a flash, sinking its sharp claws into his skin. He swore as he tried to use two hands to control four sets of crazed feet and all that fur. In the meantime, Lacey scrambled by him and the air lock opened.

He finally freed himself of the hissing, biting, scratching beast and it scampered away. Zain turned just as Lacey jumped through the door and outside.

"Damn it!" He pulled a laser pistol off the rack and went after her.

The escape had seemed like such a good idea. Running had always worked before. She didn't even feel bad about leaving Oliver behind since none of this was real. Because if it was, then that would mean that she had finally gone insane and this would be the Home for Wayward Programmers.

Everything made perfect sense until she lost her stupid purple fuzzy slipper. Then everything went right to hell.

Because that's when she looked back and saw the ship. The one she'd just run away from. *Ship* as in spaceship, USS *Enterprise* and "Houston, the *Eagle* has landed."

And even *that* wouldn't have been so bad if one really attractive, really pissed-off man weren't bearing down on her with a gun in his hand.

"Oh crap," she said and hopped around trying to pull off her other slipper so she could run faster. With both of them in hand, she bounded between the spiky plants and little critters scattering before her.

Any minute now, she'd wake up. Yup, if she ran hard enough and maybe screamed . . . She screamed, just in case. Yup, real soon she'd wake up in her bed in her little house in the country.

But it occurred to her as she heard Zain bearing down on her while her lungs burned in the arid heat and her feet were getting cut up by rocks, that maybe, just maybe, this wasn't a dream and he was a male nurse with a straitjacket.

He grabbed her arm from behind and dragged her to a halt. She couldn't fight him if she wanted. Hell, she could hardly breathe.

"Stop it, Lacey," the man growled, his grip like steel.

She pushed him away. "I want out. I'm not kidding."

"There's nowhere to run and"—he ducked as she swung a fist over his head—"no one around to rescue you." He shoved his gun in his belt, gripped both her wrists and yanked her chest to chest with him. And then they stared at each other for a real long time.

Lacey's teeth hurt from breathing through them with her jaw clenched.

"Let me go."

Zain looked down at her, holding her close, and waited for her to stop struggling. He stood like the peaceful center of a hurricane, giving her something she could cling to as her world spun out of control.

"You can run until you die of dehydration or you can come back to the ship with me and I'll explain everything," he finally said. She stared into his face and he met her gaze straight on. Her out-of-control feeling slowed, along with her heartbeat. Beneath the seriousness, there was sincerity in his expression. But Robert had seemed sincere at first, too, and look what he'd done.

She glanced around. On the other hand, the man had a valid point: there was nowhere to go. No buildings, no roads, no people. Only a desert with plants and disturbing little animals and tall mountains in every direction. It looked like the set of an old Western movie, complete with the gunslinger.

Suddenly, Lacey was very tired. Not only that, her feet hurt and she had to use the bathroom in the worst way. She stilled. Wait a minute. That meant . . .

"Oh no," she whispered and stopped struggling. "It's true. I've gone psycho."

He released her hands and she swayed without his support. He held her arm and guided her back toward the spaceship. Yes, it was definitely a spaceship. It was only about forty feet long—definitely not along the lines of a Death Star, which should be good news but wasn't. The shape reminded her of a giant silver tear-drop that had solidified and tumbled to its side on the ground. Black metal webbing covered the surface, from the tip where she could see the front window to the tail where barrel-like engines jutted out, partly buried in the sand.

And all that was fine with her since she was now officially certifiable. It had been only a matter of time, she supposed, before her mind decided to take a small vacation from reality and dump her into her very own Western fantasy. She slid a glance to the cowboy who now seemed quite substantial. Noticing the gun was drawn and the way his eyes scoured the landscape, she realized that she might have more to worry about than losing her mind.

Zain dropped into his seat and rubbed his face with his hands. Who knew one woman could be so much trouble? He'd been shot, stabbed, and attacked in high-risk military operations under dangerous conditions in hostile territory surrounded by bloodthirsty enemies—with less difficulty. Life was much easier in the military. You told people what to do and they did it. Apparently, this woman hadn't heard of that protocol.

He glanced at the killer cat curled up on one of the consoles. "You are one brave animal," he said, garnering a new respect for the species. The cat simply stretched and closed his eyes.

"Stay away from him, Oliver," Lacey said sharply.

The cat blinked a disinterested acknowledgment and promptly went to sleep.

Zain turned to find Lacey standing just inside the lav door where he'd left her. She watched him with intense suspicion as she settled into the copilot chair across from him. Her color was better now and she appeared markedly calmer.

She laced her fingers together in front of her and took a deep breath. "So where am I? At an institute somewhere?"

"You aren't on Earth anymore, Lacey."

"Ah," she said. "Well, that explains a lot."

He frowned at her tight smile. "That's okay with you?"

"I'm on vacation," she replied simply. "So if we aren't on Earth anymore, where exactly are we?"

"On a planet I was mapping in the Bogeeta Region. I'm a stellar cartographer. I chart new star systems and then sell my information to StarNet Survey, a galactic mapping center."

She nodded as if she understood exactly what he was saying. He took a breath. Good. She was orienting better than he'd expected.

"Where in relation to Earth are we?"

"Approximately three hundred light-years. Not far."

She blinked once. "And this is a spaceship."

"Yes, my ship. It's a Class Twelve Trulhian cruiser, retrofitted with specialized survey equipment and weapons. The VirtuWav you came through in the back has been modified for teleportation. And you already met Reene."

"Teleportation." Her lips curved slightly. "I see. And what is a Reene?"

"He is an integral part of the ship and an intelligent computer. He runs off the ship's power supply but is also capable of evolution and human interaction."

Her gazed shifted around the ship warily. "It's alive?"

"In a way," he admitted.

She nodded, deep in thought, and her nails drummed rapid-fire on the chair arms. After a few long seconds, she asked, "So what are we supposed to be doing here?"

He squinted. "It's kind of complicated."

"Oh, try me."

He noted her forced smile and decided he'd better do just that. "We entered this solar system twelve days ago and had mapped most of the bodies. I always leave data collecting on the hospitable planets for last, since they require a longer, in-depth analysis."

"That makes perfect sense," she added, crossing her arms.

He paused warily. "Right. So two days ago, I was running planetary geological scans from orbit. Some unusual readings recorded over this area and I decided to check it out. However, when we tried to land, we encountered a digital camouflage concealing this crater. As soon as the ship crossed the camouflage, we were shot down. It was—"

"Like a big bug zapper?" she offered helpfully.

He eyed her carefully. "Possibly. More like laser fire. We were lucky to land in one piece but it knocked out most of my navigational systems, weakened the power cells, and damaged some ancillary equipment—"

"My guess would be a rift in the space-time continuum," she suggested. "Happens all the time."

Irritation gnawed at him. "Lacey, you wanted the truth and I'm giving it to you."

"Oh, I believe you," she said. "I'm just fascinated that my mind could conjure all this up. When I go insane, I do it in a big way."

For a fleeting moment, he contemplated telling her about the real seriousness of the situation—the wrecked ships he'd found, the nasty dust storm they'd already survived, the ominous orange glows that popped up intermittently several kilometers away, and the feeling that he wasn't alone on a planet that was supposed to be devoid of life. Then better judgment weighed in.

"You aren't insane. You aren't dreaming. You aren't even hallucinating."

She held a hand up to stop him. "The only reasonable explanation is that I've lost touch with reality, which is fine." She took a deep breath. "I can handle that. I just hope this is a short nervous breakdown because I have a New Year's resolutions list to tackle and an application to deliver. So, if we can just move this along, I'd be grateful."

His patience was gone, leaving raw frustration and very little tact. She backed up as he leaned forward.

"This is your reality, Lacey. We have a serious problem. You're trapped here on this damn planet with me and neither of us is going anywhere for a very long time if we don't work together."

Lacey gaped at him. Maybe they were both nuts, because he wasn't making any sense at all. "Are you an orderly or a patient?" she asked.

"I'm an alien."

She laughed and crossed her arms. "Oh really. You don't look like an alien."

He pressed his lips together. "We have similar DNA."

"I bet all the crazies use that line."

"I know this isn't easy for you but—"

"Sir, we have a problem," the computer interrupted. The ship rattled.

Zain glanced over her head, muttered something she didn't understand, and spun his seat around. He tapped away at the panel madly.

"There is one other problem I forgot to mention," he said, casting another quick glance outside. Beneath her bare foot, the floor trembled. As much as she hated to, Lacey turned her seat around until she could see what he was looking at.

About one hundred feet away, what looked like a fifteen-foot-tall cross between Godzilla and her ex-fiancé on a bad manicure day, was bearing down on them with slashing claw hands, a protruding jaw, and some nasty teeth.

"Oh my God," she whispered. "It's Bobzilla."

Chapter Four

Zain armed the plasma scatter guns as Lacey scrambled past him and grabbed Oliver off the ship's console.

"Reene, give me as much power as you can."

"Complying," Reene replied promptly. Zain watched the energy levels spike as everything in the cabin dimmed. Always a bad sign.

"Zain, do something," Lacey said, clutching her cat as she backed to the far side of the ship.

"I'm working on it. If you have any suggestions, I'll take them now."

She covered Oliver's eyes with her hand. "Just work faster, or Bobzilla is going to flatten us like Tokyo."

The power leveled off. "Lock on target and fire one," Zain ordered. A ball of plasma streaked toward the beast and exploded in a burst of light before it.

The creature stopped its progress and staggered blindly.

Energy levels on Zain's weapons systems dropped, but the beast recovered rapidly and charged them once again. Slashing claws filled Zain's mind and old memories threatened to subvert his control. Only ingrained warrior training kept him focused on the battle.

So much for subtlety. Zain raised the power level. "Fire two." The second blast flooded the landscape with light and the creature lurched to one side and stumbled away.

Zain checked the ship's dwindling power levels. How long could they last at this rate? He ran some calculations, didn't like the answer, and reran them. Didn't like the second answer any better, but accepted it.

They had five days at best. For self-preservation, he decided to keep that little detail to himself.

"Reene, do what you can to bring power levels back up as fast as possible."

"Yes, sir."

Lacey moved up next to him and surveyed the desertscape. "What *was* that?"

"Local wildlife."

She speared him with an apprehensive look. "Wildlife? You are joking, right? That thing looked like it came right out of the Jurassic Era. Do you think he has friends?"

"I can't imagine why," Zain muttered and looked at

her. She was staring out the viewport frowning. "Bob-zilla?"

"Trust me, it fits." Then she turned her gaze to his and slowly genuine apprehension registered in her eyes. He could tell that orientation was just about complete when she began edging her way to the back of the ship. He spun his chair around to face her and crossed his arms.

"It won't do you any good to run," he said. "As you can see, it's not any safer outside than it is in here."

She shook her head. "What are you?"

He frowned at the fear in her eyes and the way she looked at him as if he were dangerous. She had no idea how right she was.

"I already told you."

"What are you going to do with me?" she asked as she shot a glance down the corridor to the back.

"I need you to decipher those images you saw in the VirtuWav. I found them on the walls of the only structure on this entire planet—an ancient stone dome. There's a console in the middle of the dome that I think controls the energy field and the automatic weapons system. If I can figure out how to shut down the energy field or the weapons, we can get off this rock, repair the ship, and send you back to Earth.

"Send me back to Earth," she repeated, looking skeptical but interested. "How would you do that?"

He pursed his lips. "The same way I got you here. Through a transfer portal orbiting your planet, then a few relay accelerators and into the ship using the VirtuWav as a portal receptor."

She laid a hand to her head like it hurt. "The tube thing in the back?"

"Correct."

"But I was in a room—"

He nodded. "Besides being used for teleportation, the VirtuWav can create a virtual image of anything. You were transported directly into a virtual replica of the dome. Don't worry. It was perfectly safe."

She gave a short, cynical laugh. "Safe? I don't think you are qualified to define safe." Then her eyes widened. "Wait a minute. The big black hole in the night. And that's why you sent the note about the stars. To lure me outside."

"Obviously, that wasn't what did it," he muttered, seeing her expression. "So why *did* you go outside?"

Her gaze dropped to the cat, sleeping peacefully in her arms. Zain almost felt sorry for it, but he had his own problems at the moment.

"This is impossible, all of it," she said, anger rising in her face. "Because that would mean you just screwed up my life, maybe for good. And I'm not letting anyone do that anymore. So you get your Virtu-whatsit working and send me and my cat back where you found us."

She moved toward the back room and flinched. That's when Zain noticed her bare feet and the blood on the floor.

"Damn it," he muttered. "Sit down."

"Go to hell." Her entire body trembled with barely contained rage and fear.

He stood up and towered over her, saying softly,

"Sit down or I will strap you down myself so I can clean you up."

Her jaw set but her eyes gave away the pain. Just when he thought he'd have to make good on his threat, Lacey sat with a huff.

Frustration and panic rumbled in her belly as she watched Zain grab a metal box and sit across from her. She held Oliver with one arm and gripped the chair with the other, trying desperately to keep from flying off. Either she'd completely lost control of her faculties or Zainman was telling the truth. Neither option appealed to her, but she'd really hate to lose her mind. She'd kind of grown attached to it.

If she was insane, then this nightmare wouldn't matter. But if she wasn't nuts, then he was telling the truth and she had a lot more to worry about than being broke and losing her client.

She took in the talking space ship that looked like nothing she'd ever seen before. What did Sherlock Holmes always say? If you eliminate the impossible, then what remains must be the truth. No matter how improbable. The E-mail, the blue light in the night sky, the strange room, the attacking monsters, Zain's story. Oh God, she thought. Maybe this *is* real.

As he opened the box, Zain said, "I didn't intend to strand you here, Lacey. Trust me, that's the *last* thing I wanted to do. I just needed you to tell me what you could about those images and then I was going to send you right back. It should have worked. I didn't anticipate losing a power cell."

He ripped open a pouch and withdrew a moist cloth. Her blossoming panic attack was abruptly sidelined as Zain's big hands lifted her left foot carefully. He inspected it and then checked the right one, using the palm of his hand to cradle it. The gentleness and level of concentration he gave her foot made her squirm. A strange man—no, scratch that—a strange *alien* had her foot on his lap and it felt a lot nicer than it should. Long, warm fingers caressed the arch, sending tremors through her and starting a chain reaction her body had no business contemplating. She shifted in her chair.

How long was he going to stare at it like that?

"We have enough food and water for approximately three weeks," he continued. "So the only real problem is power. Normally, the ship can repair and recharge itself, but one cell is dead and the other cells aren't recovering like they should."

"So what happens if the cells stop working altogether?" she asked, realizing what he was saying. "We die?"

He looked mildly annoyed. "It won't come to that."

"But we *could* die," she repeated, leaning forward. "And you brought me here knowing that? Why?"

"Because you answered my message."

Her mouth dropped open. "Your post? On Tech-Nest? I'm here because I was a nice person and replied?"

He had the decency to grimace. "I was desperate. Obviously, it was a bad idea and I'm not any happier about the situation than you are."

Then his hand skimmed up under her knit pants to her knee. Another shock ran through her at the intimate invasion, and Lacey pulled her foot away.

Dark eyes caught her. "I need to make sure you don't have any other scratches."

"Why bother? We're going to die anyway."

He ignored her and latched on to her foot, drawing it back to his lap. "Are you always so pessimistic?"

She bit her lip. "Only when I get digitized across the galaxy without permission. I'm funny that way. If you could suck me through space and into your Virtuwhosit, then why didn't you just shoot yourself off this rock?"

"I'm not leaving Reene behind," he said with finality.

"It's only a machine," she argued.

He looked at her pointedly. "And your cat is *only* an animal. Reene is more than my computer or my ship. He's my assistant and a good friend. I'm not going leave him to die on some forsaken planet all alone."

She blinked, his logic and unexpected loyalty momentarily stunning her. His steady gaze told her that he meant every word. He wasn't going to leave his computerized ship any more than she would desert her pet. Bob's pet. Maybe the alien was more human than she'd thought.

"But it's still just a machine. A computer. If it shuts down, you can bring it back up. If it breaks, you can fix it."

He shook his head. "Reene is more complicated

than that. If the power cells drain completely, he loses most of his working memory."

"He loses his mind?" she asked.

"A good percentage of it. I'm going to make sure that doesn't happen." After a few seconds, he returned his attention to her foot. "The cuts aren't serious. No sutures, but I want to kill any bacteria you may have picked up," he told her.

He swabbed her foot, down the arch, around the heel and back up the side. The solution soothed the pain immediately and his warm hands took care of the rest. He finished the left foot and lifted the right one. She sat, mesmerized by her foot resting in his thick thigh and what he was doing to it. This must be real because not even in her wildest imagination could she conjure up such disturbingly sensual care. Then he stopped and she just stared at his large hands on her skin.

Her eyes met his and he said, "Are you going to help me or not?"

The reality of the situation returned, and she glared at the man responsible for ruining a perfectly good resolutions list. "Why me? Can't you just call Galactic Triple A for help or something? Don't you have any little alien friends that can give you a lift?"

He scowled. "Any ship landing near here will be destroyed. The only reason I survived was because of Reene's integrated navigational systems. Until we shut down those weapons, I can't risk bringing anyone else in."

"You didn't have any problem stranding me here," she observed.

"I only brought you because you seemed to recognize those drawings. You could have gone home if you hadn't argued with me about the damn cat," he snapped.

Anger and indignation surged through her as she nailed him with a glare. "Don't you *dare* blame this on me, Zain. I was sitting at home minding my own business when you sucked me through space and time and God knows what else. The only crime I committed was taking a look at those stupid images."

After a few seconds, his expression softened. He set the box aside and leaned back in his chair. "You are right. Unfortunately, we don't have a lot of choices." He crossed his arms and watched her. "So what will it be?"

She looked out the window at the strange world he'd dragged her into. If she wanted to get back to Earth, she was going to have to help the alien. But dammit, she wanted some ground rules. "I won't be a silent spectator."

He gave a short laugh. "Believe me, that never even crossed my mind as a possibility."

"Is there anything else on this planet that I should worry about?" she asked.

He hesitated just long enough to make her worry. "Your Bobzilla seems to be our biggest threat."

She narrowed her eyes. "I assume you have a plan. Preferably one where we *don't* die."

He nodded. "Since the VirtuWav is inoperable,

we'll have to visit the actual dome." He cast a quick glance out the window at the darkening sky and frowned. "First thing tomorrow."

Sitting in the dark with only his console casting light on the forward cabin, Zain checked Reene's vital signs again. Nominal energy cell change in the past two hours. Not good. He'd hoped the ship would recover faster.

Zain leaned back in his chair and fought the need for sleep. Not yet, not until he was sure they had enough power to protect the ship all night. The short-range proximity alarm didn't need much juice. Another half-hour recharge should do it.

"How are we doing, Reene?" he whispered.

The computer responded. "Do you want the truth, or do you want to sleep tonight?"

Zain gave a short laugh. "It doesn't matter, I still won't sleep well. Give me the truth."

"Recovery rates have slowed by ten percent. I expect that trend to continue or worsen in a relatively short amount of time."

"So, what would you have told me if I didn't want the truth?"

"That things are dandy."

Zain chuckled at his longtime companion's new-found terminology. "Where did you get that from?"

"It is American cowboy lingo. I noted that Lacey has a marked interest in the Cowboy Era on her home planet. Therefore, I downloaded that historical period and am attempting to ease her fears by communicating in Old West dialect."

Zain shook his head in wonder at Reene's capabilities. His computer had better people skills than he did.

"Would you care to review those files, sir? They are most interesting."

"I suppose it can't hurt," Zain admitted. He stared out into the shadows, looking for nocturnal wildlife.

"Any sign of Bobzilla?"

"Negative."

"Can you tell if it's the same creature from yesterday?"

"I do not have enough data to give an effective response. However, it is highly unlikely that only one such creature would exist on the entire planet."

Zain nodded and crossed his arms. He couldn't help but wonder why was he still alive. Not that he was complaining, but that laser fire was deadly accurate. Whoever was shooting did not want company. If it weren't for Reene's superior reflexes, they'd be in a crumpled heap—like several downed spacecraft he'd discovered.

He eyed the communications controls, and for the hundredth time, considered contacting two old friends he knew he could trust—Cohl and Rayce. He would, as soon as he figured out how to deactivate the laser fire. He knew if he told them his current predicament, they would be here in days, whether or not it was safe to attempt a rescue. He wouldn't drag anyone else into this death trap until it was safe. It was bad enough he'd trapped Lacey.

He glanced back at his bunk to where she slept. It was a terrible feeling when he realized he couldn't send her back. A sickening and all too familiar realization that he'd doomed her. Five long years ago in another place in his life, he'd tasted failure and he didn't like it any more now than he had then.

But she'd handled it well, through all that sting and sass she hid behind. He'd seen the way she protected her cat, and the fear that clouded her blue eyes when she felt lost. She couldn't fool him; behind that wall was a woman who cared, maybe too much. Compassionate. Soft. Vulnerable. He scowled. And she was damn stubborn.

Up until a few days ago, all he'd had to worry about was charting this system and staying one step ahead of InterGlax and the bounty hunters. Every minute he stayed in one place was a minute closer to danger for him and anyone in the vicinity. The good news was that no one would land on this planet except in a flaming ball. Not a bad fate for his enemies. Of course, the challenge was leaving it—alive and quietly. A hunted fugitive could never be too careful.

"You have just received an encrypted and secured holo message from Rayce Coburne. Would you like me to play it?"

Zain nodded. "Please."

Rayce's brash face and shoulders appeared clearly atop the control panel. Black hair, blue eyes—he could have been Lacey's brother.

"Zain, where the hell are you? I've been trying to hail you for days. What happened? Find yourself a nice soft woman to settle down with?" Rayce grinned.

Not quite, Zain thought.

Rayce cast a quick look over his shoulder and came back with an uncharacteristically serious look. "Your sister Torrie was here. She said it's urgent that she locate you." He paused. "She made me promise not to say anything, so you owe me for this. Apparently, your father is very ill. I don't know how bad or with what, but your sister seems in a damn hurry to find you."

Zain froze. His father?

Rayce shook his head. "I know you want to protect your family and you aren't exactly on a first-name basis with your father, but I have to tell you that sister of yours is stubborn and downright determined. The family resemblance is uncanny. Sooner or later, she *is* going to track you down." He took a breath. "Personally, I wouldn't want to be on the receiving end of all that red-headed wrath." He raised a hand. "No, I didn't tell her where you are, because hell, I don't even know that. But if you need a place to meet up with her, you'll be safe here or on Yre Gault with Cohl." He leaned back in his chair. "Just think about it. Send a message when you can. Out."

The image vanished and Zain was left in the darkness alone. His father was ill. It was hard to believe that stubborn man would ever allow a microbe to penetrate his rough exterior. Galloway Masters didn't take kindly to being put off his work schedule, not even for family—a family Zain didn't even know anymore. He needed to protect them from his past, and Torrie knew better than to endanger them all by contacting him. It had to be serious for her to sneak out unescorted for a sprint across the galaxy looking for him. Well, she wouldn't find him here. At least, he hoped not—for her sake.

"Would you like to reply, sir?" Reene asked.

He could send a secured message back to Rayce, but he'd already transmitted too many communications from this location and teleported Lacey in. He couldn't take any more chances. Someone might be homing in on him.

"No thank you, Reene."

The power levels flashed into the black for the first time in hours. With relief, Zain switched on the proximity alarm. At least he'd have some warning when someone or something entered their vicinity.

"I'm going to get some sleep," he said.

"Yes, sir. You are below your minimum quotient of rest."

When wasn't he? He stood up, stretched and noted his occupied bunk. The ship had originally had double bunks but he'd removed the second. Why would he need it? It wasn't like he was ever going to have another partner. He could sleep on the corridor floor, but not with Lacey right above him. Much too close for his comfort. The rear cabin would have to do.

He walked by her, catching a glimpse of her sweet face turned toward him, deep in sleep. He stopped, mesmerized by thick black eyelashes, soft lips, fair skin. She looked so . . . demure.

He had to smile. She was anything but demure. Fierce, outspoken, obstinate maybe. Demure was pretty low on the list. Sexy, however, was right near the top.

Lying across Lacey's chest, Oliver spared him a lazy look. Zain stroked its head. His fingers stilled in the cat's thick fur, feeling its body vibrate accompanied by a throaty purring. Must be nice to have no cares, no worries, no regrets. To rest in such peace and contentment. To be able to forget.

He scratched the cat's throat and realized his fingers were centimeters away from Lacey's breast. He held his breath as she gave a great sigh and shifted. Slowly, he withdrew his hand, feeling like an intruder.

Oliver nestled into Lacey's warmth.

"No wonder you're so happy," Zain whispered. Then he shook his head. He was envious of a cat. Now, *there* was a first.

He walked down the corridor and through the door to the cargo area and the VirtuWav banks. As it closed behind him, he said, "Reene, lock the door. Open it only on my command."

The ship's computer chimed. "Accepted. Door locked."

"Secure the rest of the ship. Feed the proximity alarm through the ship's external sound system. Unlock the door and ready all weapons if the alarm triggers." He could be in the cockpit in a few seconds. That would have to be enough. He paused and then added, "And if Bobzilla returns, set to Kill and start firing."

"Accepted," Reene responded. "Good night, sir."

Zain grabbed a mat from a wall bin and spread it on the floor. He pulled off his shirt and pants, leaving on a pair of shorts. Normally he didn't wear even this much but then again, he usually didn't have company.

From the rack, he retrieved his laser rifle, laid it next to him, and stretched out on the mat. For a long time, he stared at the ceiling, battling the memories that always haunted him when sleep drew near. Then he closed his eyes and accepted the inevitable. If this was Lacey's nightmare, at least she had a way out. There was no escape for him.

Chapter Five

Lacey awoke with a start, followed closely by paralyzing panic. Oliver purred on her chest, his little face inches from hers. Above, a dark ceiling loomed like a coffin lid. She'd just had the most bizarre dream of her life, about an alien and a spaceship and . . .

She turned her head. Instruments and panels flashed silently amid all the metal and windows. A long, despondent groan escaped her. No dream. Here she was, stranded in a spaceship on an alien planet with Bobzilla and an extraterrestrial. Now there was a scenario that didn't happen every day.

She wondered how her life back on Earth was faring without her. It occurred to her, quite pathetically, that no one would miss her until at least next Sunday when her mother would make her weekly call. One of her three sisters might call, but they wouldn't worry if she didn't pick up; they were used to her ignoring phone messages and E-mails when she was in project mode.

And her friends . . . She pursed her lips. She'd forsaken most of *her* friends for Robert's friends, who had promptly vanished when he'd left. He hadn't approved of any of her friends therefore, he'd shut them out. For her own good, of course. Everything he did was for her own good. And it was her fault that she'd let him.

And then there was her database, waiting to be finished and delivered by the end of the week. If she missed that deadline, she'd never recover professionally. And Robert would succeed in ruining her. She clenched her teeth, fresh humiliation rolling over her. She had to get back home, no matter what it took. As much as she hated to admit it, she would have to help the alien.

A loud thump at the back of the ship surprised her, and she sat up a little, much to Oliver's disapproval. What was that? She looked around the empty cabin. Zain told her he'd stay nearby while she slept. So where was he?

"Zain?" she said into the night. No answer.

Another hard thump. She glanced toward the closed door to the back room and the Virtu-thingies. Then she remembered she wasn't entirely alone. "Reene?"

The computer answered promptly. "Yes, Lacey."

She frowned at its unnerving likeness to HAL. "Where is Zain?"

"He is in the rear cabin."

With the Virtu-thingies? Alarm set in. Was he leaving? Had he found enough power to send himself somewhere and leave her behind? She moved Oliver aside and hopped off the bunk. A pained groan came from the rear of the ship.

"Zain?" she called, making her way down the dark corridor.

As she stepped up to the back door there came a flurry of activity on the other side—banging, thumping, thrashing noises. She heard Zain's grunts and growls. What was happening to him?

"Are you okay? Is someone in there with you?"

One final loud bang and then terminal silence. Her heart beat in her ears as she shoved at the door desperately, but it wouldn't open.

"Zain, answer me!" she yelled.

There was a faint rustle and then he rasped, "Go back to sleep, Lacey. I'm fine."

She stared at the door in disbelief. He sounded awful. Why wouldn't he let her in?

"You don't sound fine. Open the door."

"No."

"Well, I'm not moving from this spot until you open this damn door." She crossed her arms and planted herself.

Seconds passed. On the other side, she heard Zain mumble something. The door slid aside.

She gasped. His eyes were bloodshot and swollen, his face drawn and damp, his expression grim. There was a sadness in his eyes, a total devastation that rocked her to her soul. It was like she'd yanked him directly out of Hell.

"Happy? Now, go back to sleep," he said as he

brushed by her. Walking to the front of the ship, he dropped into the chair and activated the main panel in the darkness.

"Display current stats, Reene."

Lacey moved up behind him quietly, sensing annoyance and tension like a cloud around him as images popped up on his console.

"I don't suppose you want to talk about it?" she ventured.

"No."

For a whole second, she actually considered shutting up, but something really terrible had happened to him and she couldn't very well leave him like this.

"Bad dream? I happen to have a lot experience with those."

"I'm fine." His voice was hoarse and not at all sociable.

Tempting danger, she slipped into the chair next to him, facing his faint profile against the black of night through the viewport. He didn't even look at her, working instead with utter concentration. Then she noticed his hands in the glow of the panel lights. Blood oozed from his knuckles.

She reached forward and grabbed his hand. "You're bleeding."

He pulled away. "I'll clean up later."

"No. You'll clean up now," she said, fumbling around in the dark to retrieve the kit he'd used on her feet a few hours before.

"Bullshit," he muttered, mimicking her earlier response.

She finally located the kit, sat back down, and opened it. "My, my. What a grumpy cowboy. Now where are those wipes?" She rummaged through the kit's contents until she found a packet and ripped it open.

"As a matter of fact," she said, grasping his hand. "How is it that you and the computer conveniently speak my language?"

"Reene downloaded your dialect, and I did a neural language-translation interface," he said, sounding a little more civilized as she swabbed the blood from his knuckles.

"Which would mean what to us mere Earth mortals?" she asked. His hands weren't bad, but she could make out old scars. Had he been through this before?

"I underwent a few hours of intense language education, a common procedure. I figured it was easier for me to learn your language than for you to learn mine."

Darkness masked his features, but she could feel his tension easing as she washed his hands, fingers, and palms. Much to her dismay, he felt absolutely human.

"So, there are a bunch of human-looking aliens flying around out here in space?"

"Trillions, from one end of the galaxy to the other."

She gave a short laugh. "That's going to be a huge blow to all the Earth men who think *they* are the center of the universe."

He had beautiful hands, she decided. Big and warm and strong. His fingers were long and callused, a little rough. She remembered Robert's hands—perfectly manicured and neat. No strength. No character.

"I think that one's done," he said softly, saving her from her memories.

"Sorry," she mumbled and reached for his other hand. Just as she touched him, he wrapped his fingers around her hand, engulfing it.

"You don't have to do this," he said in a hoarse voice. "I've been taking care of myself for a long time."

She could feel the heat radiating from his skin into hers. It moved through her like a slow, crackling fire, igniting her senses one by one. He was relaxed now. She could hear his steady breathing, feel his eyes upon her. But there was more—a sensual hum radiating from him. She didn't want to let go, drawn to him like a solitary fire in a dark forest. The ridges of his fingertips imprinted her skin, branding her with his heat.

Fear accompanied an unwelcome tendril of desire that wrapped itself around her belly. She recognized it instantly. Every man she'd ever been drawn to was trouble. She had a better chance of winning the lottery than picking a good man.

She freed her hand from his warm, sexy, and totally promising hold, and blew out a silent breath to cool her inner flames. She definitely needed a date.

As clinically as possible, she cleaned his knuckles. "I know you're a big boy. Must be my maternal instincts kicking in."

"You have maternal instincts? I wouldn't have guessed."

She could hear him grinning and grinned too. "I don't get to use them much."

"That's too bad. You're good at it."

She squinted at his darkened face to see if he was mocking her, but there was no hint of sarcasm in his statement.

"Thank you. We're even." She gave him his hand back.

He withdrew it slowly and returned to the ship's control panel. "You really should get some more sleep, Lacey. Tomorrow is going to be a physical day."

She closed the kit. "And what about you?"

He turned his face slightly. "I got a few hours, that's all I need."

She had so many questions about him and his world buzzing around in her head, but she was suddenly beyond exhausted, too tired even to try to get him to talk about the scars on his knuckles or the episode in the back room. She rose and stowed the kit. Besides, he seemed over it, whatever "it" was. At least, she hoped he was. She'd had nightmares before, but nothing like that.

As she crawled back into her bunk, she wondered— what kind of nightmare made you bleed?

Morning broke warm and clear on planet P254-334-5. In the corridor, Zain stuffed another food ration into his pack. It had been a long night and he would have liked more sleep, but that was impossible with Lacey so close. It was bad enough she'd heard him and seen the injury to his hands. But at least she hadn't seen the angry and unhappy man he could become, and he vowed she wouldn't.

He heard her in the lav, singing something that sounded like *O.K. Corral* at the top of her lungs, and despite his grumpy mood, he smiled. She'd made such a fuss over a few bloody knuckles from flailing around in his nightmare. He could still feel her small hands on him, gentle but firm. Warm caresses, tender care, a soft voice. He had to pause in the middle of loading his pack to take a deep breath. Evidently, it had been too long since he'd been alone with a woman.

She hit a horrendous high note with gusto and he chuckled. Not only was she a major visual distraction, she had spirit. And a way of smiling that made a man want more. Unfortunately, he wasn't in any position to even think about it. Both their lives depended on him not getting distracted.

"Reene, while we are gone, work on figuring out how to stop the power drain from the ship. If we lose the cells, I lose you." He paused and then added, "I don't want you shutting yourself down to route power to the critical systems either."

"I can be reactivated if I discharge," Reene reminded him.

"Forget it. And that's direct order."

"Order accepted."

"And watch Lacey's cat, too."

There was a hesitation. "Sir, what does that entail?"

Reene had an excellent question. "I have no idea. Just don't piss it off." Zain glanced over his pack to find Oliver sitting at the end of the corridor staring at him. "So what is it you do?" he asked. The animal yawned for an answer.

"He catches mice," Lacey said from behind him.

He turned. She looked bright and fresh and sexy as hell. She wasn't doing a thing for his sleepless nights.

"What are mice?" he asked, trying to divert his mind from more entertaining thoughts.

Lacey gave a shudder. "Little furry rodents that eat my food and mess in my cupboards." She nodded toward the viewport. "Kind of like those things out there."

He sealed a bag and handed it to her. "They're harmless. He pulled another pack over his shoulder and walked to the rear cabin. "I've already scouted the entire basin and had no problems."

"Yeah, well, I don't think Bobzilla is harmless."

He laughed at her name for the beast. "No, I'd say Bobzilla is hungry."

From a cabinet, he grabbed his rifle and checked the charge. At least he had firepower. When he looked up, Lacey was watching him.

"Tell me you know how to use that."

He nodded grimly. "I know how to use it."

"Good answer. I like a man who can take orders." She smiled at him, taking his breath away. He wondered if she knew how amazing her smile was.

"That's one of the reasons I got out of military. Too many people telling me what to do."

Lacey batted her eyelashes. "Well, never fear. You only have me to worry about."

He patted the pistol in his holster and the laser blade strapped to his calf. "Is that all? I'd rather take my chances with Bobzilla."

She looked clearly offended. "And what does that mean?"

He leaned toward her, grinning. "I can *shoot* Bobzilla."

She wrinkled her nose. "I had no idea aliens were so funny. You should go on tour."

Zain moved toward the door, and Lacey stopped him. "Will Oliver be safe here alone?"

"Safer than we will. I don't think Bobzilla is as interested in the ship as he is in us."

"Great. I feel tons better now," she muttered. "How far do we have to go?"

"The dome is only eight kilometers away."

"Only?" She gazed down at her feet. "I hope my slippers hold out. It would have been nice if you'd sent along an itinerary for this little adventure. You'd make a lousy travel agent."

"Don't worry, we aren't walking. Reene, stay in communication."

"Understood." Reene paused. "Adios, amigos."

Zain chuckled at Lacey's stunned expression.

The air lock opened and they were blasted with the planet's hot, dry ambiance. An early-morning sun hung red in the sky. The desert terrain stretched all the way to the surrounding mountain ranges. Zain lowered his visor over his eyes. Distance and topographical statistics popped up along its edge and multiple distance ranges displayed.

He jumped out of the ship and scoped the vicinity. Satisfied it was clear, he turned back to help Lacey. Her eyes darted around the landscape in search of the beast, no doubt.

"I can take care of Bobzilla," he said as she stood next to him.

She peered at his visor. "I hope so. I'm only here for brain power, remember?"

"I doubt I will ever be given the opportunity to forget."

"Be nice to me, or I'll tell all Earthlings how positively tyrannical aliens are."

He palmed his datapad for bearing. "And here I thought I was just another beautiful man." His gaze flicked to hers. "In a Wild West kind of way, of course."

Her eyes widened in horror as he repeated her own words. He explained, "Reene downloaded some of your American History information for me last night while you were sleeping." He tipped his goggles and drawled. "Ma'am."

"Oh great. Now the aliens know," she muttered and followed him around the back of the ship. She'd unleashed a space cowboy. The universe would never be the same again. "So, you said we aren't walking. How are we getting there?"

He pulled the survey speeder off the ramp that Reene had lowered, and mounted it.

He smiled. "Ready to ride?"

Chapter Six

They hadn't been riding for very long, and already sweat and sand stuck Lacey's tank top to her breasts. She was sure she looked like death warmed over. Goggles protected her eyes from the sting of wind and sand, but her hair had become a disaster.

Zain, on the other hand, looked magnificent—in a Wild Wild West kind of way. The man had an excellent memory. She'd have to remember that. Anything she said could and would be used against her.

It was a smooth, quiet ride, since the speeder was something like a hovercraft. The functions were the same as a motorcycle though—seat, steering, and—she hoped—brakes. It didn't go very fast, but it sure beat walking. Besides, wedged between Zain's rock-hard body and the back of the seat on a speeder built for one wasn't necessarily a bad place to be. She could feel the six-pack abs beneath his shirt where she

gripped him and had the strongest urge to feel around
and see if the rest of him was so well . . . defined.

But since sex was definitely not on the agenda for
this year, she surveyed the landscape—or what she
could see of it beyond Zain's broad back. Red desert
stretched around her in all directions, ringed by im-
posing maroon cliffs. She was on an alien planet.
Well, as far as she knew. What had Zain said? Three
hundred light-years? How far was a light-year again?
Darn. She should have paid more attention in high
school astronomy class. This is what she got for
ogling Paul Watson for an entire semester. Who
would have ever guessed someday she'd actually need
that information?

She licked her lips and adjusted the goggles Zain
had given her. "So, does this planet have a name?"

He glanced over his shoulder. "Just a catalogue
number. You want to name it?"

"How about Death Valley?"

She felt a laugh rumble through his chest. "Let's
hope not."

Ahead of them, a break in the landscape caught Lacey's attention and sunlight flashed off a solid object.
She squinted her eyes. It looked like . . .

"A ship!" she blurted out. "Zain, stop!"

He replied over the engine noise, "You don't want
to see it."

"If it's a ride home, I do. Pull over!"

Zain brought the speeder to a halt, and she vaulted
off the seat. But as she drew closer, she realized this
craft wasn't going to be her ride home. Metal ribs

poked out of the sand like a carcass picked clean. The skin had been ripped and shredded and was streaked with deep gouges. She slowed, taking in the crumpled, charred wreckage scattered over the ground. Zain came up beside her.

She whispered, "They crashed."

"At least a year ago," he concurred. "Brought down the same way I was. I found three more crash sites around the basin."

"Survivors?" she asked with very little hope, and glanced at him. His visor was up, his eyes concerned.

"The crew was dead before they hit the ground."

She could only imagine their last moments. "I don't suppose anyone came looking for them?"

Zain scanned the wreckage. "I doubt any of them had a chance to get emergency messages off. Besides, no one can see this place." He looked up. "An energy field creates a cover that camouflages this entire basin, concealing it. From the atmosphere, it looks like part of the normal landscape. When a ship hits the cover, it triggers the perimeter laser fire."

Lacey noted the unnatural sheen to the sky above them, and the great distance it covered. There was some serious technology at work here. "Why would someone do this?" she said, thinking aloud.

"I don't know, but now you see why I don't want to call anyone else in."

She had to admit he was right. She turned full circle. They were completely enclosed by cliffs. "Have you tried climbing out?"

"The walls are too sheer to scale without special equipment."

Just as well, she thought. She didn't do heights.

Sunlight glinted off the scars on the metal as she walked around the crash site. "Bobzilla was here."

"I'm afraid so. Bad for us."

"Why?"

"Because now Bobzilla knows what we taste like. And apparently they don't care if their food is dead or alive."

"Oh crap," she said with a sigh. "It doesn't feel so good being the creamy filling."

He pulled a cylinder from his pack and uncapped it. "Water?"

She didn't realize how thirsty she was until cool water soothed her lips and throat. She moaned in relief when she'd had enough, and wiped her mouth. Her hand froze as she caught Zain watching her, then quickly looking away. *Oh no, don't be doing that*, she thought. Men were trouble, and this one was alien trouble. She probably didn't even *know* how much trouble he could be. The last thing she needed was a wildly sexy man to add to her problems.

She shoved the bottle back at him. "Thanks."

He stowed it, and they headed back to their speeder. Out of the corner of her eye, Lacey caught movement and glanced at a sudden puff of sand. *Now what?* She was used to the little critters that scurried in the sand around them, but this was bigger. As she walked, she noticed another puff.

"Zain?"

He swung onto the speeder easily, looking for all the world like a cowboy mounting his steed. "They live in the sand."

Lacey slid behind him. "How do you *do* this all the time? Don't you run into things that want you for lunch on a regular basis?"

His mouth curved into a smile. "Mostly, they keep to themselves and ignore me. You'd be surprised how few planets I survey have discernible life."

She donned her goggles and took one final, dejected look at the carnage. Then their speeder moved out again.

"So, what happens if you run into another, well, alien?" she asked, shaking her head at the sheer absurdity of the conversation.

He shrugged. "I leave."

"Not even a 'Hello, I'm from the planet Neptune and I come in peace?'"

"I don't want to be the first alien encounter a planet has. That's someone else's job. Mine is to collect geographical data and pass it along."

"Don't you get lonely?"

His masked gaze turned to her with amazing speed. "You live alone, too."

She blinked, then looked back out at the expanse of sand before them. "I have Oliver to keep me company."

His lips twisted cynically beneath his visor. "And he's such a conversationalist, too."

"Hey, at least he's alive. You talk to your computer," she snapped. "And, frankly, my social life is none of your business."

She didn't like having to defend her self-inflicted solitary confinement. So what that she worked all the time and owned the DVD for every Western known to man? There was nothing wrong with that. And who the hell was he to say anything about her life? What kind of life was *this*? Flying around, collecting data, getting shot at by heaven-knew-what and attacked by Bobzillas? No people, no friends, no fun. Her life looked like a damned party compared to that.

"Welcome to town," Zain announced. He slowed the speeder in front of a single domed rotunda ringed with tall archways. Thirty feet high and nearly as wide, it looked strangely at home in the desolate landscape. Scrawny vegetation hugged its foundation in the only shade available. A few stray shrubs rolled by in the wind.

"Tombstone," she murmured. An uneasy eeriness came over her.

"Excuse me?" Zain asked, looking at her.

She slid off the seat when the craft had settled to the ground. "It's from a movie. A classic. Tombstone looks just like this. Well, except for the red sand and the dome, and there's no one here but you and me. Other than that, it's dead-on."

"A movie. Entertainment?" Zain deduced, dismounting.

"Right. I have a weakness for sappy Westerns. In fact, Bobzilla was in the movies, too. Well, sort of."

"Another classic?"

"I think so, but not a lot of people do," she admitted with a chuckle. "Bob didn't." She flinched. Damn. Where did he come from? Maybe Zain wouldn't catch it.

He looked at her. "Bob?"

No such luck. Really, she needed to think more around this man and talk less. Discussing Bob was definitely off-limits.

She waved a hand carelessly. "No one important." She braced herself, knowing what was to come. The old sinking feeling swamped her as it had numerous times in the last two years. But Zain didn't press, and she let out a slow breath of relief as he removed his goggles and grabbed their packs. It occurred to her that Robert would never have let it go like that. He'd have needled her and followed her around the house and humiliated her until it finally culminated in a huge fight that solved nothing and left her feeling wholly inadequate. Those memories alone still had the power to drain her.

She noticed a large ringed area a short distance away that looked oddly familiar. Then she realized the hundred-foot-wide circle was actually raised in the sand—a henge—and inside it was a definite pattern of stubby stones. They weren't as tall as the monoliths on Earth, and there were no horizontal ledges, but the likeness was still unmistakable.

She turned to find Zain watching her. He said, "There are three other rings surrounding the dome, all identical. Do you know what they are?"

"They look just like the Stonehenge layout, which

is utterly ridiculous. What would Stonehenge be do-ing on an alien planet?"

He surveyed the area. "I don't know. There must have been a purpose for them at one time. But there are no active signs of civilization . . ." He stopped and glanced behind her. She spun around to see another puff of sand.

He pressed a hand to her back. "Let's go."

They walked the last few yards into the shadow of an arched corridor and stopped. Lacey pulled her gog-gles off and leaned against a warm wall, thankful for the shade. She was really out of shape for alien planet exploration.

New Year's Resolution #7: Never underestimate the value of a good exercise program.

Zain leaned against the wall in front of her, his broad shoulders filling it. She liked the way his shirt stretched across his chest and the bulge of biceps through the sleeves. Nice gene pool. He was big for an extraterrestrial, she'd guess. Maybe not. Who knew?

Zain checked the tiny screen of the personal data device he'd used back at the ship. The geek in her asked, "New toy?"

His eyes lifted to hers and she sucked in a breath. Even at a distance, she could feel a hypnotic draw. It was like boarding the *Titanic*. And her without a life jacket.

"This is a survey device," he said. "A combination of technologies rolled into one: communications, data storage, short-range sensors, scanners, processing power."

"I'm sufficiently impressed," she murmured. "So, why do you need me when that thing does it all?"

"Some mysteries only a human mind can decipher."

He stared at her with those intense eyes. She'd originally thought they were black, but in the daylight they were deep brown, like a good strong brandy. But it wasn't the color that held her attention. It was their keen intelligence and ruthless focus.

"Your mind appears to be one of a kind," he added.

Well, that burst a perfectly good moment. Apparently, she was the only one obsessing about gene pools. "Wonderful," she muttered to herself. "My mind. When I die, I'll donate it to science and everyone can say, 'My, what a lovely mind that woman had.' "

He chuckled and pocketed his datapad. "Let's take your lovely mind inside."

She peered into the inner sanctum. "Is it safe in there?"

"I've been here before. No problems yet."

However, she noticed he pulled out his gun and stepped into the room with great deliberation. Maybe he'd had no problems, but he was a careful man. She liked careful. Careful was good. Careful would probably keep her alive. He might be an alien, but she felt a helluva lot safer with him and his techno-weapons between her and whatever might want to eat her.

She stepped quietly behind him into a large circular domed space. It was the same room as in the Virtu-

thing Zain had beamed her into. Center stage was an immense, solid-stone, half-moon-shaped counter six feet across. Around the outer walls, blocks upon blocks of images squeezed between four arched doorways. The blocks stopped about twenty feet up, where the domed roof vaulted high above, covered with a smattering of small black dots. Columns of light from the outside streaked in through the giant archways.

Lacey walked over to the center counter. It was perfectly flat, polished black stone covered with a thin layer of red dust. No markings or writing. She didn't know how Zain thought this could be controls for anything.

He came up beside her and nodded to one square on the wall. "That's where I pulled the samples from."

She moved closer and realized that the image he'd sent was one of thousands that covered every inch of the outer wall. Scanning the room, she shook her head at the enormity of the project. "There must be a thousand of these."

"Reene counted 2,280."

She looked at him as if he were insane.

He smiled patiently. "You can do it, Lacey. You understood one of them."

"I didn't *understand* it. I thought I saw a map of Stonehenge in it. I never said I understood what it meant or what the rest of the layers were."

"Layers? You mentioned those in your reply to me."

She blinked at him. "Can't you see them?"

He walked up beside her and stared at the block for a full minute. "No. Describe them."

Lacey stood in front of the image and concentrated, letting her eyes relax. The tiers separated for her. "Maybe four or five layers. A bunch of lines, some kind of funky lettering and little boxes with pictures in them."

Zain reached out and touched the image. "Are they all the same?"

She moved to the next block and focused. "No, different. Except"—she paused—"for the circle with the dots. The Stonehenge map."

He handed her his datapad. "Draw the layers for me."

She frowned. "You're joking, right?"

His grim expression said it all. "I need to be able to see what you see."

"I didn't bring my secret decoder ring with me, Zain. This is going to take close to forever!"

"Let's start with twenty in the same vicinity. That should give Reene enough to work with."

She grabbed the datapad. Obviously he wasn't taking 'no' for an answer. "Doesn't your computer already have all this from the Virtu-whosit?"

"Yes, but for some reason, he can't see the layers either. If you can identify the individual elements, he can take it from there and decipher the entire room. I'm hoping that he finds something that will point us to the master controls for the laser cover."

She stared at Zain. "And what if we lose Reene to the power drain?"

A deep frown lined his face. "We have five days. After that, the ship won't sustain itself, Reene will deactivate, and we'll be stranded."

Lacey nearly choked. "Good grief. You could have just lied to me."

"You wanted to be partners," he said with a casual shrug.

"I never said that," she corrected him with an involuntary shudder. "Partners are for fools and square dancers. I said I wasn't going to be a silent party. Big difference." Very big difference, in fact, and she was keeping it that way.

"That's good, because I don't do partners either," he said. "So the sooner you solve this, the sooner you get rid of me and go back to your wild social life."

Again with her social life. "My social life . . ." She stopped. Something had moved around the side of the circular counter behind him.

Zain held his position but raised his gun, watching her eyes. She started talking again as a crimson, crablike arm slid around the center island about a foot off the floor.

". . . isn't what I'm worried about." Her voice squeaked a little.

A bony leg appeared.

Zain wrapped both hands around his gun and kept up the conversation. "Describe what you are worried about, Lacey."

A little round head appeared, and Lacey focused her eyes on Zain. Her heart was beating so loud, she could hardly hear herself talk. "Company?"

Zain spun, putting himself squarely in front of her, and pointed his gun at the creature.

Lacey grabbed his shirtsleeve and felt his muscles tighten. "Don't shoot, Zain. I don't think it's going to hurt us."

She peered over the gun. A little head swiveled slightly as it seemed to look from her to Zain, cocking its head like a puppy.

"It looks as if it's thinking," she whispered against Zain's shoulder. He moved a step closer to the creature. Then it slowly withdrew around the corner and was gone.

Zain sprinted around the counter and out the doorway. He had mentioned that he was in the military, and she could see it by the way he moved. She wouldn't want to run into him in a dark alley. Then she remembered the broad-shouldered gene pool. Well, maybe if he didn't have a gun.

He came back and she asked, "What *was* that?"

"One of your sandpoppers." Zain scanned the room. "It disappeared into the sand."

She could tell something else was on his mind.

"What's wrong?"

"Besides everything?"

"I'm serious."

"I think he was . . . spying on us."

Her jaw dropped. "Spying? It's a sand crab, for crying out loud. The only fear it has is being caught and dipped in butter."

"Haven't you noticed that they're everywhere, watching us?"

She crossed her arms, feeling mildly triumphant. "Well, well. And I thought only Earthlings were paranoid of being spied on by aliens."

"Paranoid works for me. It would really help if you could decipher these images. That's our only hope of figuring out what's happening here."

"Or happened," she reminded him.

He glanced out the door. "Right now, I'll take whatever I can get."

Chapter Seven

T minus four days and counting . . .

At 1650 hours on the planet of Kree, a gentle chime interrupted Major Schuler's sleep, and he glanced at the bedside console. One light glowed indicating that a transmission had been received on his private line. Normally any messages could wait until morning, but access to this line was restricted to a select few.

He rolled to the edge of his bed, careful not to wake his sleeping mate. She snored lightly as he left their sleeping chambers and made his way through the house to his private office. Once inside, he took a seat at the circular desk and ordered up the computer. The security program scanned his retina and cleared him.

On the miniature holodeck, an image of a hulking man appeared and gave the briefest of bows under the weight of several weapons strapped to his chest and waist. Schuler raised an eyebrow in surprise. He rarely heard from his hired assassin unless it was urgent. This message could only be about one thing.

Ferretu's gold helmet gleamed, and the man patted the weapon on his hip. With his usual brusque style, he wasted no time on pleasantries.

"There is activity in the Zain Masters case. I have intercepted messages to him from his sister on Dun Galle. She has been attempting to make contact for the past twenty hours. No response from Masters. However, the sister departed her planet and met with one of Masters's associates, Rayce Coburne. I am tracking her movements now." He nodded. "Out."

The transmission ended, and Schuler was left to sit in the darkness of his office. For five years, Ferretu had monitored Masters's family and friends, and waited for a break. Every passing day brought Schuler an equal measure of frustration and relief. Even with a multitude of bounty hunters and all of InterGlax searching for him, Masters had seemed to disappear from the galaxy like a dead man. But InterGlax operatives as good as Zain didn't perish easily or quietly.

Schuler mulled the poor timing of this new development. Why now? Just when his scheme was so near execution. Why did the ghost of the only man who had ever come truly close to discovering his operation have to appear?

He leaned back and pondered the disturbing turn of events. The monitor in front of him displayed the remaining days and hours until the galaxy would finally know what he'd worked on for twenty years: plotting, waiting, and double-crossing InterGlax—his employer and his enemy.

Using Ferretu's gun, Schuler had left a trail of blood behind him: people who got too close, asked too many questions, or couldn't keep quiet. With that blood, Schuler had brought InterGlax to the brink of collapse. One more blow was all it would take. And that blow was finally days away.

All the pieces and operators were in place, and the countdown had already begun. Nothing was going to stop him from unleashing the most deadly force in the galaxy, not even the ghost of Zain Masters.

Zain watched Lacey work. He should be concentrating on finding what that little spy crab was up to but distractions abounded.

To be precise: Lacey. She rested her small hand against the wall, absorbed by a tangled image that only she could see. A little crease formed between her eyebrows as she concentrated. He wondered if she knew that. He wondered what that sleek, heavy hair would feel like in his hands. He wondered who Bob was, and what Bob had done to become the namesake for the biggest, baddest beast on the planet. But it was none of his concern. She'd made that clear. Everyone had a right to their secrets.

Still, the company was nice. It had been a long time since he'd had someone to talk to—and spar with at every possible opportunity, he added grudgingly. But then again, it had been a long time since he'd smiled, too. Perhaps it was worth the disagreements.

He surveyed the room again. There was more to this mystery than lasers, a few shipwrecks, and some odd little creatures. Something big. Something he'd really rather not get involved with.

Like a shadow, restlessness haunted him. This was the longest he'd ever stayed in one place, and he could feel the growing threat. Besides the trapped physical energy that he'd normally be able to vent on his now inoperative exercise equipment, he could also sense another urgency: the same intangible foreboding of danger and entrapment he had when he worked for InterGlax, usually just before all hell broke loose. And with that foreboding, guilt crept in, overshadowing all other distractions. Zain closed his eyes, trying to ward off the image of Crista's lovely body, shredded and battered, floating in a swamp of blood. But it was futile; those visions were his penance.

Crista. Her name alone still had the power to resurrect painful memories with violent clarity. He'd cursed the day that InterGlax had given him a partner, and a woman at that. But Crista had proven herself almost immediately, matching his drive and ambition and yearning to explore with equal measure. Their shift from partners to lovers was seamless—no arguments, no discussions over what needed to be done. She's been a good partner and understood that he was her senior, he was in charge. Right up until he'd got her killed.

Lacey started humming badly and Zain jerked back to reality. He shook off the past and the tension in his body that remembering always left. Why was he thinking about Crista again? He'd thought he had those memories under control, at least during his waking hours. His eyes settled on Lacey and he knew why.

She didn't have Crista's auburn hair or her tall, powerful body, and she didn't take orders worth a damn. She was petite and soft—vulnerable. She didn't have the body of a warrior. Didn't possess the skills of a woman who could hold her own.

She wasn't his type at all.

Right.

The last rays of daylight filtering through the arched doorways reminded him that time was slipping away. He pulled out his comm and activated it. "Status report, Reene."

"Nothing significant, sir. Power levels are holding steady."

It was the best he could hope for. "And the cat?"

"Has not moved in the past hour. I still have yet to determine its purpose or function."

Zain chuckled. Reene was developing a sense of humor. "Just make sure it doesn't escape. Lacey will have your circuits. I'll check in before we head back." He disconnected.

Lacey straightened and arched her back, presenting a distraction no red-blooded man could ignore. Zain looked away in self-preservation. He doubted she'd find his attention amusing.

"I need a break," she announced, rubbing her eyes. "Decoding alien script is hell on the old Earth brain."

He watched her walk over and hop up to sit on top

of the counter. She handed him his datapad. "You sure know how to show a girl a good time, cowboy."

He grinned. "I try. You're not the traditional type, and I didn't want to bore you."

"Next time, try dinner and a movie." She pulled her legs up, folded them, and wrapped her arms around them. "I have fifteen of those designs sketched. I'm not sure if that's enough, but I can at least tell you that each image has the same number of layers and the same types of layers."

Zain nodded. Time was going to be a problem. He didn't know how to tell her without scaring her to death. Beside him, she sighed and rested her forehead against her knees, leaving her slender neck bare. His hand itched to reach out and massage the ivory skin. Of course, then he'd have to figure out what to do with the other hand.

Instead, he paged through her drawings on his pad, looking for anything familiar. Dots and lines, a jumble of codes, something that resembled a language he'd never seen before. Maybe Reene could identify it. Suddenly, he stilled. One code set looked like . . . "Map coordinates," he said aloud.

Lacey lifted her head. "To where?"

"Don't know yet. Could be local, planetary, solar system, galactic. Very unusual."

"That's not the only weird thing," she said. "Why does every one of these have a Stonehenge map? That part is just too bizarre to fathom."

She turned to him. The last bit of daylight filtered through the haze of sand dust inside the dome, illuminating her like a goddess. The soft light on her cheeks heightened the blue in her eyes and shadowed the pout of her lips. With one look, she had the power to chase everything from his mind. Almost.

Behind her, one of the images slowly lit up. Zain looked around and up to find that a dot above them had also come to life. The ground trembled, and from outside a bright light flooded through all four doorways. His senses went on full alert in direct proportion to the torrent of energy that suddenly surged into the room.

With eyes huge, Lacey took in the changes in the walls and the bright lights. She jumped off the counter.

"Wait!" he yelled as she dashed to the door. She reached it before he did and stopped dead. A tall, digital arch of light had filled one of the ground circles surrounding the dome.

Chapter Eight

Inside one of the rings, a huge arch rose out of the sand until it stood about fifty feet high, casting shadows across the darkening desertscape. Lacey gripped the doorway behind Zain and held on for dear life as the ground rumbled beneath her. The arch glowed white and began to rotate faster and faster until it turned into a giant bubble half-buried in the sand.

"Zain, what is that?"

He had his rifle aimed at the arch. "A first-class transportation portal."

She glared at him. "Like I said, what is that?"

Before he could respond, there was a flash inside the sphere, and a giant metal capsule appeared out of thin air. It hovered, bathed in an orange glow, then lowered into the ground and was gone.

"Whoa," Lacey whispered. Then she gasped at another burst of light, another capsule, and the sequence continued. She looked behind her. Light blasting through the other doorways was probably from the other three rings. She noted a distinct pattern as they seemed to flash in a clockwise rotation.

Her eyes adjusted to the strobing lights, and she spotted thousands of sandpoppers scrambling away from the spheres. A few disappeared into the bubble and never came back out. Then another sound drew Lacey's attention: a discord of roars, followed by the unmistakable pounding of big feet.

Bobzilla was back. And he had friends. Three of the creatures charged around the circle of light. Lacey watched a clawed hand swoop into view of the doorway and scoop up a small sandpopper. Bobzilla tossed it into the air and then swallowed it whole. Lacey screamed, covering her mouth in horror. Zain pushed her back against the wall.

"Don't make any noise," he said, his rifle pointed out the doorway. Helplessly, she watched Bobzillas capture and eat sandpoppers like bears scoop fish out of a stream.

"Stop them, Zain," she begged.

"I can't," he replied. "I don't have enough firepower to hold off more than one. If they know we are here, we'll be next on the menu."

She knew he was right, but the slaughter was too horrible to witness. She buried her head against his big shoulder. Minutes passed and then, as suddenly as it had started, the floor stopped trembling. Lacey looked up just as the glow disappeared and the giant sphere dissipated.

To her relief, the remaining sandpoppers all burrowed into the sand. The Bobzillas roared in frustration as they swatted at the ground for sandpoppers. After a few minutes, the sand was quiet and the trio of Bobzillas lumbered away. That's when the other desert creatures scurried out and cleaned up any bits and pieces of dead sandpoppers. Within minutes, the carnage was gone. The wind picked up and swept the surface until the desert looked as if nothing had happened. Night took full possession, yielding to a starlit sky.

Zain disappeared outside. Numbly, Lacey made her way back into the dome, rubbing her arms. The glowing image on the wall was fading, along with one of the pinpoint dots on the ceiling. Good God. Bobzillas, sandpoppers, bizarre images that flashed on and off, and giant teleportals? This had to be real because her imagination wasn't *that* good.

Zain came up behind her. "Are you okay?"

She let out a semihysterical laugh. "Why wouldn't I be?"

He retrieved his pack. "I guess this must be a little overwhelming."

"It's turning into a regular *Twilight Zone* episode." She massaged the bridge of her nose. "What just happened?"

"Four teleportals opened up. Those were storage units being teleported in. *Shippers*."

There was something about the way he said that which worried her, but she had so much to worry about at the moment that it didn't really matter. "Teleported from where?"

"Using relay accelerators, their range is galaxy-wide. Portals that size are usually reserved for large shipping operations."

"Underground shipping operations?" she asked.

"Not usually," he admitted, and he didn't look happy about it. He activated his little communications gizmo. "Reene, come in."

"Sir. There was substantial activity in your vicinity—"

Zain interrupted. "I know. Teleportals activated around the dome. I need you to run some deep subterranean scans."

"That will require significant power," Reene replied after a brief pause.

"I realize that." He kept his eyes on Lacey. "See what you can do in the next thirty minutes. We're on our way."

"Howdy, sir," Reene chimed as they entered the rear hatch.

Zain noted the steamy interior of the ship. Reene must have had to cut the climate controls to conserve power. With each passing hour, he felt the danger of their situation increase—and their options decrease.

Lacey entered behind him and scooped up a waiting Oliver.

"Howdy, Lacey," Reene said.

"Uh, you too. Wow, it's warm in here."

Zain took her pack. Beneath it, her clothes were covered with sand and clung to her like a second skin. He failed miserably at not noticing the fine line of her collarbone and the way her small breasts stretched her shirt's knit fabric.

"Why don't you wash up first? Give me your clothes, and I'll have them clean by morning."

Her eyebrows rose delicately. "And what will I wear until then? I didn't exactly bring an overnight bag."

He opened one of the wall compartments where he kept a stack of shirts—some heavy, some lightweight. He paused, eyeing the lighter shirts, his imagination taking over. Well, it *was* hot in here. He withdrew one and handed it to her.

"This should do."

She unfolded it and held it up. It was nearly sheer, sleeveless, and hung to her knees. He tried not to appear the least bit interested.

She frowned skeptically. "This is the best you can do?"

He shrugged and picked up her pack. "It's probably going to stay warm in here until the outside temps drop."

She squinted. "It wasn't hot in here before."

He shoved fresh rations in her pack for tomorrow. "The internal climate controls were shut down to save power."

For a while, she didn't say anything. "So the ship is losing more power?"

He paused and looked at her. He could give her

some technobabble, but he was pretty sure it wouldn't help.

"Yes. You might want to make your cleanup short."

She nodded fatalistically and threw his shirt over her shoulder. "If you need me, I'll be washing the stench of doom from my body." She turned and wandered into the lav.

He made sure the door was shut before he spoke. "Reene, how bad is the power situation?"

"Levels are down another twenty percent. Two out of our three cells are no longer functioning and require complete replacements. The third will be done in approximately thirty-five hours."

He swore softly. Time was running out and once it was gone, they were as good as dead. This was not going as he'd hoped. The answer was in that dome, and tomorrow they had to find it.

"Reene, when you get down to ten percent power, I want you to initiate a Mayday signal to Cohl and Rayce. Include our coordinates and a sit-rev so they know what to expect."

"Would you like me to send it now, sir? It may be safer."

"We still have tomorrow." Dragging someone else into this mess was going to be his very last resort. He didn't want the crater littered with the shot-down ships of all his friends.

"Understood."

Fifteen minutes later, Zain had finished. The packs were restocked, rifle checked and fully charged. He also stowed the sleeping pads and blankets. He wanted to be ready in a hurry. Just in case his danger sense was screaming for good reason.

He headed to the front cabin, past the lav where Lacey was singing dreadfully. "Reene, let's see what you've got from those scans," he said.

He hadn't even made it to his seat before a miniature holographic image rose from his console. A gridwork of massive tunnels several levels deep appeared, loaded with thousands of capsules like the ones teleported in.

"Damn." He sat down slowly. "Reene, give me a scale on this." A human body appeared in one of the levels, dwarfed by the size of the tunnels.

He heard Lacey behind him, just before she slid into the copilot chair. "Ooooo, cool. A holographic image?"

He glanced at her and then did a double take, torn between the holo-image and his shirt on her body. Two perfect nipples pushed through the thin material.

He forced his mind to behave. "It's a similar technology, but a bit more sophisticated in its integration and cognizant capabilities."

"You have the best toys," she said in awe.

"No, you can't take it home with you."

She replied in a huff, "I could recreate it. I'd just need about fifty years and a couple billion dollars."

He didn't doubt that for a minute. He had a feeling Lacey Garrett could do whatever she put her mind to.

"Reene, any idea what we're looking at?"

The computer responded. "The structure has a diameter of approximately ten kilometers, with its center directly beneath the building. It is at least twenty levels deep, but I am unable get specific enough information about the contents of those levels."

"Holy smokes," Lacey said. "That's under us?" Her blue eyes were wide and worried. And she didn't even know what he knew.

"Could be a storage facility," he said hopefully. He told Reene, "Storage containers were teleported in. Teleportal transport shippers. No markings."

"My scanners cannot examine the containers. Perhaps they have security liners."

Zain stared at the tunnels. Security liners. An interesting development and very unsettling. "We need to go down there."

"Sir, I would not recommend that particular plan."

Lacey's jaw dropped. "I wouldn't recommend that particular plan either."

He smiled. Did she *ever* agree with him? "We aren't getting much accomplished up here."

Hurt flashed on her eyes. "I'm doing the best I can, Zain."

"I know that," he replied softly, trying to stop her subconscious flinch. Bob had really damaged her. "But I'm beginning to think the dome is irrelevant. The real clues must be underground. I'll also guess that's what the energy field and lasers are protecting. And if I'm right, the controls are down there, too."

Lacey crossed her arms. "Do you know what happens whenever you go into deep, dark places in a horror movie? Bad things. I say we put this underground exploration idea up for vote. I vote 'no.' "

He shrugged. "Fine. You can stay up here with Bobzilla."

She narrowed her eyes. "I can *shoot* Bobzilla."

A grin tugged at his mouth. "Aren't you curious about what's down there?"

She glared at him. "You obviously haven't seen *Aliens.* Curiosity kills."

"Not if you handle it right." He leaned on his console. "Reene, where's the entrance?"

"There is no detectable entrance."

"Of course not," Zain said with a sigh. "I don't suppose we could make our own?"

"The ceiling of the first level is fifty meters down. Our weapons will not penetrate that far."

He was running out of options. The answers were underground; he could feel it.

"Keep looking. There must be a way in," Zain said.

There was a pause. "Yes, sir."

"I'm transmitting sketches of the dome images to you," Zain told Reene as he downloaded Lacey's work from the datapad. "One of the layers may be coordinates. Also, I think the dots in the ceiling are a type of star map that matches the coordinates in those images. See if you can verify."

Lacey gaped at him. "When did you figure that out?"

"When the portals went off," he admitted.

Reene replied, "I will do the best I can, sir. I used significant energy to run the scans. I no longer have recharge capabilities."

"Damn," he whispered. He couldn't lose Reene. "I'm sorry."

"It is not your fault."

Zain shook his head. Yes, it was. Reene took orders from him. Just like Crista had. Blindly, they trusted him to make the right decisions to keep them safe.

"I won't let you shut down, Reene."

"I appreciate that, sir."

Lacey looked at Zain, real concern in her eyes. He wished he could tell her everything was going to be all right. But that would be lying.

Chapter Nine

A chorus of sirens tore through Lacey's sleep. She bolted awake, her mind struggling to put order to the blaring alarms, the shaking ship, and Reene's techno chatter. Oliver scrambled off her as she fumbled with her covers and twisted around to find Zain sitting at the controls. Dawn filtered through the viewport.

"We have nine targets . . ." Reene was saying just as the ship took a hard lurch to the right.

"Zain?"

"Fire at will, Reene," he shouted. The ship took a vicious blow and shifted sideways.

Lacey pulled herself over the edge of the bunk and onto the floor as the ship rattled and shook. A large scaly black face filled the viewport, and Lacey screamed. The Bobzilla opened his mouth and tried to take a big bite of the glass, giving them an up close and personal look at a nasty set of teeth. When that

97

didn't work, it swung its big head and rapped its jaw against the glass, leaving a saliva swipe across it. The window held, and Bobzilla roared in displeasure.

"Sir, they are too close," Reene said over the sound of firing guns and bellowing Bobzillas. "I can't protect the—"

The ship leaned hard to the left and stayed there, suspended in time for what seemed like eternity. Oliver skidded across the corridor in front of Lacey, appearing unharmed but none too happy.

"Lacey, hold on to something," Zain yelled over his shoulder. Then the entire ship rolled and Lacey's world turned upside down. She tumbled over the bunk, hit the wall, and landed on the ship's ceiling in a heap. She heard Oliver's yowl as she grasped for something, anything solid and safe. The ship was upside down now and doing a slow rock and roll.

Seconds later, Zain helped her to her feet. "Are you okay?" he asked, standing over her wearing nothing but shorts. Three thick scars lined his beautiful chest. Damn. That must have hurt. She latched on to his solid biceps for support as the ship lurched again.

"I'm fine. What's happening?"

Before he could answer, the ship did another pitch and roll. Zain grabbed her by the waist and threw her down under the bunk, landing on top of her. The warmth of his bare skin was lost in the disorientation of the ship rolling all the way back over again, tossing them between the wall and bunk before landing with a shudder.

"Sir, we are sustaining considerable damage to the

fins, the hull, power cells, all weapons systems . . ."
Reene's voice distorted, then faded out.

Loud thumps reverberated through the inside of
the ship as the Bobzillas used the ship for drum practice.

"You stay here," Zain yelled, rushing toward the
back of the ship. "Reene, open the rear hatch."

Lacey stared after him in disbelief. "*Do not* tell me
you are going out there," she shouted over the nonstop banging. When he didn't answer, she stumbled
off the bunk and into the back room. Equipment and
paintings littered the floor, and the hatchway was
open. She could hear gunfire outside.

"How many Bobzillas, Reene?"

"Four are still . . ."—more static—"attacking."

She cringed, remembering what Zain said about being able to hold off only one. She didn't want to think
about what would happen if he couldn't handle all
those Bobzillas. For a second, she stood in the center
of the mayhem clenching her fists, listening to buck-
ling metal and the battle outside.

"I don't want to do this," she said to no one. And
no one answered because she was it, and no matter
how scared she was, no matter how much she wanted
to run, if anything happened to Zain . . . Oh, hell. He
might be an alien but dammit, he was *her* alien.

"Reene, where are Zain's other guns?"

"Com . . ."—static—"partments.

She popped open a few nearby cabinets until she
found a rack of long rifles. Grabbing the biggest she
thought she could handle, she checked the firing

mechanism. Trigger control. Apparently, guns were guns everywhere.

"Leave the door open, Reene. We'll be right back." She hit the sand running.

Zain fired a salvo into the closest Bobzilla's groin. That should bring the bastard to its knees. It did, but not for very long. Only a few remained after Reene's guns gave out, but damn, these were persistent predators. Zain used a dead carcass for cover and fired everything he had at the three Bobzillas bearing down on him. Another one was trying to flip the ship again. Reene couldn't take much more.

A flash of white caught his eye, and a second stream of laser fire joined his. Old memories flashed back, déjà vu so strong, he nearly froze up. The bad odds, the guns, Crista . . .

"Lacey, get back inside!"

She stood out in the open, wearing nothing to protect her except his sleeveless shirt as she fired on the Bobzilla clawing at his ship.

"I don't think you're in any position to order me around," she yelled back.

Damn stubborn woman.

"Get in the ship!" he ordered again, trying to control his raging anger as he fired again at the beasts. She was going to get herself killed, and he wouldn't be able to stop it.

"Tell me you don't need the help." She sidestepped a swooping claw, and he gritted his teeth against the visions that flashed in his head. Unfortunately, he was too busy fending off three relentless and hungry Bobzillas to argue. He spared her another glance. She wielded the rifle with ease and surprising good aim. Maybe she wasn't as vulnerable as he thought. And as much as it killed him to admit, he *did* need the help.

"Go for the eyes and groin," he called just as a claw sliced through the air with a whoosh. He tucked and rolled to a new position. The creatures took turns coming at him, roaring and swatting at the lasers slicing through their thick skin before backing off once more.

In his peripheral vision, he saw Lacey's Bobzilla stumble away. Relief eased through him. One more down.

"Get in the ship, Lacey. I can handle these three," he called to her.

Then her laser fire joined his at the remaining Bobzillas. Dammit, he was going to have a little conversation with the woman on the importance of following direct orders. Not that it would do any good, but at least he'd feel better. The Bobzillas flailed in the cross fire, tossing their heads and clawing the air. After a few more seconds of unrelenting attack, they retreated, roaring and giving angry growls as they went.

Zain stepped from cover and scanned the perimeter for activity, but found no new attackers. Five dead carcasses littered the hot sand. It was going to smell real nice in a day or two.

"We did it!" Lacey shouted. She ran up to him waving her rifle. She stopped in front of him, eyes wide and slightly unfocused, energized from adrenaline. He knew she'd crash hard when she came down from her rush. Then she would realize what she'd just done and how foolish it had been.

"What the hell do you think you were doing?" he barked.

She flinched, stunned; then anger hardened her expression. "You are very welcome."

He stepped up to her, hissing through his teeth. He was out of control and he didn't care. "You could have gotten eaten."

"As opposed to getting rolled to death inside Reene?" Her body vibrated with anger as she stabbed a finger at him. "You get this straight, Zain: This is my life and I'm going to have some say over what happens to it. If you think I'm going to let you order me around, you're dead wrong. You got yourself a partner, so deal with it."

Oh great. Now they *were* partners. He growled with frustration and turned to walk away before he said something rash. He was a warrior. He was supposed to maintain control at all times.

A partner. Just what he needed.

Zain looked at his battered ship and then down at his diminishing rifle ammo. "I hope you're ready to be my partner when they come back."

"Come back?" she repeated.

He scowled and gave her a long, menacing look. "Of course, now that they know what tasty morsels are inside the ship."

Fear flickered briefly in her eyes before she raised her chin. "I'll be ready."

He stared at her for a long moment. She surprised him at every turn. So much for fragile.

"Let's go check on Reene." He paused and cocked an eyebrow. "If that's okay with you, partner."

Her blue eyes drilled into him. "See, that wasn't so hard, was it?" She rested her rifle on her shoulder, tossed back her hair, and walked toward the ship.

He shook his head. What had happened to his simple life?

He followed her, taking in Reene's condition. Dawn had given way to full morning and as he drew near, the seriousness of the situation became apparent.

"Reene? Are you still with us?" he asked as he noted the buckled hull and bent landing gear.

"Yessssssssir," Reene said with some difficulty. "I have released the repair nanos. However, power is below crucial levels, so their capabilities will be limited. We also sustained additional injuries that will require full replacement parts."

Zain closed his eyes. "That could be a problem."

"Affirmative," Reene replied, matter-of-factly.

Zain put his hand on the hull of the ship and leaned against it. Everything was falling apart on him, just like it had before. And again, it all was his fault. He was a curse to everyone he touched.

New priority list: save Lacey, save himself, save Reene. Hell, at this rate, he'd be happy to save the damn cat.

"How long before Reene shuts down?" Lacey asked behind him.

He lied. "A day, maybe two."

"That doesn't give us much time," she noted.

He turned to her.

She blinked back. "What? Do you expect me to just lie down and die?"

He gave a short laugh and shook his head. Definitely not fragile. "Where did you learn how to use a rifle?"

She shrugged. "Summer math camp."

His eyebrows went up. "Math camp?"

She propped a hand on her hip. "You got a problem with that?"

"No. It just sounds a little—"

"Watch it," she warned. "I've got a gun in my hand."

"—aggressive," he finished carefully.

"Well, it wasn't exactly part of the curriculum. I used to sneak over to a private camp full of boys across the lake. They played with guns," she added, grinning. "I still stop by the shooting range now and then. I guess you could call it a hobby."

"And what did Bob think of that?"

Abruptly, her expression dimmed. "He didn't like it at all."

"Why am I not surprised?" Zain muttered.

Then her gaze dropped to the ground behind him, and he watched the whites of her eyes grow. The hairs on the back of his neck prickled.

"Zain, we have company."

Chapter Ten

Lacey stood dazed as the sand burst open, sprouting creatures like the one she'd seen inside and around the dome. They popped from the dunes in unison, hundreds of them rising on skinny legs. Some big, some small, all rust-colored and bony, they surrounded Zain's ship and scrambled over the dead Bobzillas. A few rose on four of their six crablike legs and unfurled their muscular thoraxes to stand like giant praying mantises. Two independently moving eyes peeked out from under each small cap head to peer at the ship and its crew.

"Uh-oh," Lacey whispered.

Zain spun around, his weapon ready, but he didn't shoot. What was the point? Lacey didn't need a military background to tell her there were just too many.

"If they had any weaponry, they would have used it against the Bobzillas," Zain said quietly, as if that would make her feel better. He turned his head toward his ship. "Reene, do you recognize this species?" he called.

A few seconds clicked by. "Negative."

Sand whipped around the creatures' spindly legs and all was silent.

"Try to talk to them," Lacey urged.

Zain cast a glance over his shoulder. "Do you happen to know how to say 'don't eat us' in sandpopper?"

She wrinkled her nose. "Well, it won't do us any good to stand here and stare. Say Hi."

Zain shook his head and then raised his hand. "We come in peace."

Lacey rolled her eyes. "Well, good grief, that's the oldest line in the book. They'll never believe that."

He frowned. "It's *your* line, remember? I'm from Neptune and all that? And feel free to step in any time."

"Fine," she said, moving next to him. Hell, she'd just stood her ground and fought off giant, hungry Bobzillas. She was pumped. This was nothing. Of course, having a big gun helped. Maybe that's what she'd been doing wrong all her life.

She cleared her throat and spoke loudly. "My name is Lacey," she said, tapping her chest. "And this is Zain." She pointed behind her. "His ship is called Reene."

The sandpoppers stood motionless, captivated but silent.

She turned and whispered to Zain, "They aren't impressed. Do something impressive."

"Just keep talking," he said, looking suspiciously as if he were starting to enjoy this.

She addressed the sandpoppers again. "We are from another planet." She pointed to Zain. "He's a big, pushy alien who sucked me"—she pointed to herself—"the poor, defenseless Earth woman, through space and time and stranded me here."

Zain squinted at her. "Defenseless? Since when?"

She waved him off and continued her monologue. "We were wondering if you knew of a spaceship repair shop nearby? Or better yet, a galactic taxi service."

Hundreds of little heads swiveled and looked at each other, but none answered. Nothing.

"Guess not," she said with a sigh and rubbed her forehead. She was flunking Alien 101 badly. "We're doomed."

Then one of the bigger sandpoppers crawled forward and stood up a few feet from her. It waved two intricate claw hands at her and started making clicking noises, then squealed and prattled in a steady stream. Lacey concentrated on the sounds and realized it was trying to talk to them. The others chimed in and the whole bunch started making noise.

Zain said, "Reene, are you getting this?"

"Yes, sir. They appear to be speaking a crude form of Basic utilizing their vocal limitations. I'm working on the translation now."

"Basic? Where did they pick up Basic?" Zain asked.

"Unknown, sir."

Zain nodded and leaned toward Lacey. "Why don't you talk to them some more?"

She raised her hands. "And say what?"

He shrugged. "You can tell them what a wonderful time you are having on their planet."

"Right," she said with a snort. "It's practically Club Med."

A chirping noise came from Reene. The sandpoppers' heads swiveled in unison toward the ship. The crab in front jabbered back and, after a few seconds, the other sandpoppers took a respectful step from the ship.

Lacey kept her eyes on them and murmured, "What's happening?"

"Communication." Zain turned to the ship. "Reene, tell them who we are."

As Reene and the main crab continued to chat in a gargled string of sounds, the others studied Zain and Lacey. After a few minutes, Reene stopped. The sandpoppers withdrew and amassed in a group about thirty meters away.

"I have apprised them of our situation, sir. They have yet to respond," Reene announced.

Zain nodded. "Who were you talking to?"

"He is Pio, the chief of the *krudo*."

"They have a name?" Lacey asked.

"Yes. The *krudo* have developed a fairly complex hierarchical structure within their race. They have lived on this planet for thousands of years in peace."

Lacey watched them huddle. "So what are they talking about?"

"What to do with us."

*   *   *

Zain eyed the pack of *krudo*. They were at least a thousand strong, and he knew there had to be many more in the surrounding sand. Bad odds. He rubbed his chest absently. He hadn't seen these kinds of odds since . . . His hand paused, bitter memories stealing his thoughts.

"*Now* I see why you aren't the Official Greeter," Lacey muttered. "Is this the way all new species welcome you?"

He shook off the past and checked the power level on his rifle. "I told you to tell them how much you liked the planet."

"If I'd known they were so touchy, I would have," she replied. She drew a deep breath. "So now what?"

Zain caught the tremble in her voice. She was starting to crash from the battle with the Bobzillas.

"Get in the ship. I don't think they can penetrate it."

Her head turned to him. "And leave you alone? I don't think so. I didn't save you from Bobzilla to have you ripped up by the local crab population."

He shook his head and wondered why he even bothered to try. A corner of his mouth rose. "I didn't think you cared."

Her jaw set and she stared straight ahead. "Don't get all excited, cowboy. You're my ticket home."

"Is that why you came out here to help me?" he asked.

She regripped her rifle and hesitated before answering. "I'm not blindly leaving my future in your hands." Then her eyes met his. "Or anyone else's."

He could almost hear the word *again*. "Whatever the reason, I'm sorry you had to use a gun."

She blinked hard, and he knew she was recalling the battle.

"Reene, send that distress message," he said.

"Communications are no longer functioning, sir. I was able to begin transmission. However, it did not complete."

"Hell," he said softly, and caught Lacey's fleeting glance of concern. It couldn't get any worse. "Reene, did they say they were going to kill us?"

"No, sir. They simply will not help us. They understand that we will perish without aid."

Maybe it could get worse.

"Lovely," Lacey whispered. "Left to die by crabs."

"Not if I have a say about it," Zain said, low. "Reene, why are they hostile toward us?"

"They are confused by our presence here, sir. They say a group of humans like you destroyed many of their people when they created this basin."

Zain scanned the immense crater in which they were trapped. "This isn't a natural formation?"

"Not according to the *krudo*. The band of humans detonated an explosion powerful enough to create a hole. Then the "Well" was dropped into it."

Zain froze, an uneasy sensation overwhelming him. " 'The Well?' "

"I believe they are referring to the structure directly below."

"What do you mean 'dropped in'?" Lacey asked.

"It's a ship," Zain said, understanding and disgust

110

weighing in. "That's what we are sitting on." His unease turned to downright dismay and he closed his eyes. They were in bigger trouble than he'd thought. Damn.

"Zain, what's wrong?"

He opened his eyes and looked at her. That was a mistake. Those blue eyes deserved a better answer than he had. "I should have realized it before. That's the only way a structure that big could have been built on this planet. It wasn't. It landed."

Her eyes widened. "That's got to be one hell of a ship, even in your universe."

"It is."

"But if it's a space ship, then we can we fly it out."

Zain shook his head. "Doubtful. These types are usually dropped in place by a starship hauler. Then the engine disconnects, leaving the station behind. At least, that's the way it's normally done. What else did the *krudo* tell you, Reene?"

"They are concerned that we may destroy them again. They still believe it is the fault of the humans that they are attacked by Bobzillas every time the portals eject them from their underground homes. It appears that the *krudo* and Bobzillas are trapped here much like we are."

Lacey shook her head. "Didn't you tell them we won't harm them?"

"Yes, but they are still unsure. The humans before us were reckless and callous. However, the *krudo* are quite impressed that you killed several Bobzillas and

111

that you did not fire upon their people when they first appeared."

"I hope that will be enough," Zain said. He watched the *krudo* disband and move toward his ship. "Are any of your weapons operational?" he asked Reene.

"Negative."

"Please get in the ship, Lacey."

"Nope." She faced the *krudo* with her gun ready and didn't spare him a look.

He gripped his rifle. "How's that translation program coming along, Reene? We could use it right about now."

"Translator on," Reene replied.

The head *krudo* crawled forward on all legs, then rose to his full height and faced them. His saucer head tilted forward as he prattled and Reene translated. "I am Pio of *krudo*. We offer assistance."

Lacey let out an audible sigh of relief and lowered her weapon. Her thank-you translated back.

"Ship broke," Pio stated plainly. "Repair?"

Lacey gaped. "You can repair it? How?"

Pio swiveled his head to her. "Repair station. Fix your broken machines."

Lacey's eyes met Zain's warily. "How very convenient."

"My thoughts exactly," he agreed, but they didn't have many choices.

"Where is this repair station?" Zain asked.

Pio tapped one of his legs into the sand. "In the Well."

Chapter Eleven

"Major Schuler, come in," the booming order rang out.

As Schuler entered, his commanding officer leaned back in his wide chair and inhaled on an expensive smoker. General Lundon's large feet sat atop a desk topped with polished stone. Behind him, a panoramic view of the military city of Jagear on the planet of Kree spread out in all its glory.

Lundon's office walls were lined with luxurious fabric, and the grand space decorated with fine, hand-hewn furnishings. InterGlax spared no expense to keep their top men happy at operations headquarters. Schuler greeted Lundon and sank into the deeply cushioned chair opposite the man's desk.

"So, how's Supplies and Ordnance?" Lundon asked, blowing a stream of cured smoke his way.

Schuler smiled. "Keeping me busy pushing buttons all day. My fingers are killing me."

Lundon bellowed a laugh and then said, "We have it made, don't we, old friend? Who'd have thought we'd still be here after twenty-two years." He heaved himself from his chair and made for a tall cabinet. On command, it produced two glasses of Lundon's custom-blend liquor.

The general brought one to Schuler. They nodded and downed the short drinks in unison. Schuler waited. His superior officer rarely invited him to drink for no reason. A moment of unease flashed through him. Had he been sloppy? Left a clue behind that would lead InterGlax to his covert operation? Re-routed one too many munitions to his installations?

Lundon stared into his empty glass before saying, "Too bad we won't have another twenty years. InterGlax is falling apart, torn from the inside out. Pretty soon we won't be able to keep the crisis under cover."

Schuler took a silent breath. Lundon knew nothing. "You are doing a fine job of soothing CinTerr."

Lundon shook his head slowly and made his way over for a refill. "I had a meeting with CinTerr's top level today. Any more attacks on sector planets and they will drop us as their enforcement branch and find someone who is more competent." He sighed deeply. "They are ready to dismiss us. I never thought I'd see the day. Half a million InterGlax operatives out of work." Lundon cast him a sad look. "Do you know this city was built on InterGlax? If we go down, it will be deserted." He turned back to the view. "I can't even imagine the anarchy that would follow in the sector without any military presence. It'll be like it was a thousand years ago, lawless and violent. Stars help the juveniles."

"We'll find the culprits who are undermining InterGlax. We are getting closer," Schuler offered.

Lundon snorted loudly. "No, we aren't. There's no pattern to these attacks. No clues. No trail to follow." A look of disgust pinched his face. "They are outwitting us from the inside, Schuler. I wish I knew how. We've grown too big, too sluggish, and too complacent. I don't even know whom to trust anymore." He glanced at Schuler. "Except you."

Schuler smiled back at him. He couldn't wait to see Lundon jobless. "Then we'll figure who's behind this together."

Lundon downed his drink. "I'm afraid by the time we find out who, it'll be too late for InterGlax."

Schuler drank to that. Lundon didn't know how right he was.

Lacey held Zain's hard waist on what she hoped would be the last time they rode this hot, dusty trail. The battle with Bobzilla and the confrontation with the *krudo* had wrung her dry, and the remnants of adrenaline had long since vanished.

She buried her face in Zain's strong back and, for the first time since they woke up this morning, she relaxed. He felt solid and safe, and all she wanted to do was curl up against him and forget the rest of the universe. In the back of her weary mind, she heard the words *bad idea*, but her mind was having a hard time convincing her body.

Despite the exhaustion, she smiled in silent triumph. She'd fought off Bobzillas and won. It wasn't on her New Year's list, but it counted for something. It had been a long time since she'd had a victory.

On the downside, the programming fairies weren't finishing her database for her back on Earth. Damn. Four days left. If Zain could get the power cells in, maybe she could be home tonight. She'd still have enough time to finish the database. It wouldn't be perfect but it would be deliverable.

The speeder slowed to a stop next to the dome. Zain swung off the vehicle and lifted his visor to check the *krudo's* progress. "They are stronger than they look."

"Good thing, too, because I'm not up to pulling a spaceship today." She twisted around to where a few hundred *krudo* were dragging Reene on his runners by cables Zain had attached to the ship's hull. It reminded her a tug-of-war gone horribly wrong.

"How are you holding up, Reene?" Zain asked into his comm unit.

"Sir, this is highly unusual. I am not designed to travel in this mode," the reply came back, sounding flustered. "And Oliver is most displeased."

Zain chuckled. "I realize it's uncomfortable, but we need to move to you closer to the dome for repairs. Pio says the entrance is there."

"Sir, I must point out that I have grave concerns.

This arrangement has significant areas of vagueness."

"I'll try to get you a concrete plan once I check out the Well."

There was a split-second pause. "Much appreciated, partner."

Despite her exhaustion, Lacey laughed. "Reene is definitely one of kind. I've never met a computer with a sense of humor. How did you end up with a talking ship—or is he the norm?"

Zain leaned back on the speeder. "No, he's a hybrid model. I had him customized with specialized equipment for long journeys."

She tipped her head back on the seat and watched him. "Reene seems very . . . human. Aren't you afraid that he is going to take over your ship? What if he decides he doesn't like the way you do things?"

"I'm not worried. He takes orders well. You probably didn't notice that."

She ignored the obvious jab. "Well, if he suddenly starts calling you Dave, don't say I didn't warn you."

"Another movie?" Zain asked.

"*2001: A Space Odyssey*. Most appropriate, don't you think?"

He laughed. She liked the sound of it, deep and rumbling. He turned then and caught her staring at him. His eyes narrowed intently and she averted her gaze before he could see the heat rise in her face. It was only a look. What was she so afraid of? "So, you trust the *krudo* to move Reene?"

"I don't know if I trust them, but I doubt they'd

offer to drag the ship and us all this way just to kill us."

She stared at him. "What a lovely thought. One I hadn't even considered until you spelled it out for me."

He tipped his visor. "Glad to be of service, ma'am."

She shook her head. Cowboys. "I still can't believe those . . . beings figured out how to work the dome."

"They had years," Zain reminded her.

"Yes, but how did they do it?"

"Jealous?"

"Damn right," she said, sulking. "And it's making me a little crazy too. Call it an ego thing, but I'd like to think I'm smarter than your average crustacean."

Zain grinned, a wide white flash across his suntanned face, and she was captivated by her space cowboy. He had changed into long tan pants and a black short-sleeved shirt. Finely chiseled pecs pushed against the thin fabric. He wore his silver visor and under it, his jaw was dark with a shadow of a beard.

She suddenly wondered just how much DNA they shared.

No, she thought. Even entertaining carnal thoughts of the man was wrong. And knowing her luck, he'd be a great lover. He'd be slow and careful, thorough and passionate, the kind of man who could spend all day in bed and never tire. A man who paced himself. She nodded to herself in agreement. He didn't seem to rush anything. He approached every task with single-minded concentration. She'd bet anything he would do that with a lover, too. He'd probably kill her with patience.

She, on the other hand, having never been properly seduced by a man, would be putty in his hands. And therein lay the danger. Putty in the hands of a man. She'd done that, and look where it had gotten her.

Still, a voice whispered, *just once*. What would it be like? What was lovemaking like where he came from? Were there wild positions, aphrodisiacs, exotic oils . . . Those big hands had to be good for something besides—

"Are you okay?"

She jumped, ripped from a damn good fantasy in the making. "What?"

His silver gaze fixed on her. "You're smiling."

She could feel the rush of blood to her cheeks. "So?"

He shrugged. "Just checking to make sure you're okay after this morning."

She swallowed and forced her mind to behave. "Oh, you mean shooting Bobzillas and chatting with crabs? No problem. Us W-Ps can boldly go with the best of them."

"W-Ps?"

"Warrior Programmers."

He got a good laugh out of that, which kind of annoyed her. Obviously he didn't think of her as warrior anything.

"Well, W-P, I think I figured out what the dome is for," he said.

119

Her mouth dropped open. "You did?"

"Don't sound so surprised. It happens occasionally."

"I'm just feeling a little left out. So what did you find?"

"I had Reene merge your drawings with our maps last night. The small sample you gave us matched a part of this sector. Each image correlates to a coordinate in space. A planet. The portals work with the locations in the dome."

She shook her head. "For what reason?"

"I'm not sure yet," he said evasively.

"Oh, bullshit."

A corner of his mouth curled up. "You don't believe me? What a surprise."

"You know something. You just don't want to tell me."

Silence.

"Fine," she said, and blew a sticky hair off her face. "Let's see if I can figure it out myself, since I apparently stink at everything else. We have one hot, dry, deadly uninhabited planet. Well, except for the wildlife. So, that means you were shot down by some kind of automatic weapons system because someone didn't want any live bodies snooping around. The dome is the only structure here, inconveniently located in the middle of a desert basin, camouflaged and surrounded by teleportals. Underneath is one big-ass ship, and I'll bet it cost a whole lot of money to set up, and someone went to a lot of trouble to make sure no one finds it. You know, if this were Earth I'd blame drug dealers." She kind of laughed at that until she realized what she was saying. Then it made perfect sense.

Zain was silent, and she didn't need to see his eyes to know she'd nailed it. He pulled out a water bottle and handed it to her.

"I knew it," she huffed, and took the water. "So what are we on top of, Zain?"

"I don't know and I don't want to . . ." He stopped and turned toward the desert. "Get inside," he said and pulled her off the speeder. They ran just as the ground around the circles glowed gold, and then the arches of the portals rose again from the red sand.

They were safely inside the dome before Lacey turned around. The portal sphere was bright, and around it sandpoppers were running for their little crustacean lives.

The floor shook, and a flash of light momentarily blinded Lacey. When she looked again, a shipper was rising from the sand. In a dazzling burst, it disappeared. Another shipper rose and vanished. She watched as more units rose nose-first like bullets from the ground below, faster and faster until it became a steady blur. The other three portals were also working. In less than five minutes, a thousand units must have passed through.

She turned to Zain. "What was that all about?"

He stepped into the center of the room and frowned at the lit images on the wall and ceiling.

"Someone just sent out a very big shipment."

Zain walked around Reene in the late-day sun. On the outside, the ship didn't look any worse for being dragged through the desert, but Reene couldn't take any more. Another attack would do it, and they were now nearly on top of the portals and the Bobzilla feeding grounds.

Lacey was inside, checking to make sure Oliver had survived the trip. Just as well. Zain realized that, for some reason, she could read him too easily. It was an issue he wasn't used to dealing with. Usually, the people around him couldn't read him or didn't care.

He also had a very bad feeling that he wasn't in any mood to share with her. He'd checked the last set of illuminated images in the dome against Reene's computations. That last shipment had gone to a planet in the X445-3 sector, quadrant A-M-3.

After that, he'd done a quick survey of the other planets Reene had matched up. He recognized some of them. All were outer rim, all contained inhabited juvenile planets. So, who was using teleportals to ship to planets that had not achieved space technology outside their own solar systems? It was strictly prohibited by the galactic community of CinTerr and adamantly enforced by InterGlax. *Illegal* didn't even begin to cover this operation. He and Lacey needed to get the hell out of here and soon.

Pio stepped forward and made a series of clicks. The standard issue communications earpiece that Reene had loaded translated in his ear: "We are here."

Zain smiled at Pio's obvious statement. "Thank you. We appreciate your help." His reply translated into *krudo*.

Pio's little head swiveled. "Ship talks much."

Zain laughed. "Yes, he does." He nodded toward the nearby portal. "Can you take me below now? I'd like to see the repair station."

"Yes."

"Yes, what?" Lacey asked, appearing behind Pio, wearing a communications earpiece like Zain's. Between that and the pistol and holster she'd commandeered, she was beginning to look more like Crista all the time. Bad for both of them.

"I'm going below," Zain said. "Stay here with Reene."

She raised her chin. "I'm coming with you."

He set his jaw. "I'd rather handle the initial investigation alone. It could be dangerous."

Pio's head swiveled back and forth between them.

"Dangerous? *Now* you're worried about danger? It's a little late for that, don't you think?"

"It's safer here," he insisted.

"Well, let me think about that. Would I rather be inside Reene playing Lacey-in-a-Can for the Bobzillas, or follow you into the dark unknown? Decisions, decisions." She stared at him and he knew he'd lost.

"Fine," he muttered, brushing by her to enter the ship. "We need to pack a few things."

He made his way through the disheveled corridor to the forward cabin. "Systems check," he said to Reene as he took his seat. Reene rolled through the stats in a holo-image that faded in and out above the console. Half the controls weren't even lit, and the other half didn't look at all healthy. He needed to get enough power to run the perimeter alarm tonight. And weapons might be nice.

"Sir, the nanos have stopped working. They repaired as much as they are capable of, but we had significant internal disruption. The power cells are nearly depleted, the aft fin is bent, all sensors are inoperable, life support is unavailable, core systems are below twenty percent . . ."

Reene continued his depressing report. Zain hoped Pio was right about the underground maintenance facility. Without replacement parts, Reene would not make it through tonight. "Reene, prioritize and download to my datapad a list of parts you need. Power and weapons come first."

"Data . . . downloaded." Zain frowned at Reene's hesitation. The power levels dropped appreciably, barely above the dead zone.

"Reene?" he asked.

"Sir, I am switching to auxiliary now."

Lacey sat down next to Zain. "What does that mean?"

He turned to look at her. "It means Reene's in trouble."

Her eyes grew huge. Then she stared at the console. "Reene, can you store your working memory anywhere?"

"My start-up routine is not designed to—"

She moved forward. "Just do it."

"Transfer initiating." After a few seconds, Reene announced, "I will be shutting down now."

Next to him, Lacey gasped. "No."

Zain hit the controls to open the back hatch, then all the lights on the his panel went dark. He waited, hoping they would come back on. They didn't. He'd just lost Reene.

Lacey watched him, her eyes full of compassion. "We'll get him back, Zain."

He shook his head, feeling the frustration and anger of helplessness. He hated it more than anything. No matter how hard he tried to control his world, he always ended up losing. Crista, and now Reene. Would Lacey be next?

"We need to get underground," he rasped.

He rose abruptly, grabbed his pack and knelt to load it up with their gear. New priority list: secure parts, repair Reene and bring him back, shut down the automatic laser cover, send Lacey and cat home, finish mapping this bloody system, all the while avoiding the owners of this lovely facility, InterGlax, and a handful of persistent bounty hunters. How had things gotten so complicated?

He shoved a food ration into the pack and looked up to find the medkit in front of his face. Lacey held it and peered down at him.

"We might need this," she said evenly, but the words went right to his gut. He closed his eyes. She shouldn't have to worry about carrying a weapon, or requiring medical attention, or searching the landscape for the next predator. She should be home safe. He wanted to tell her how sorry he was, but the words seemed inadequate. He deserved to be hated and sworn at, but she didn't. She just handed him a kit he might have to use on her.

"Zain?"

He opened his eyes to find her kneeling in front of him. In her blue eyes was compassion like he'd never imagined. Not pity, not anger. Just concern and worry. She cared about him. He wanted to tell her that he wasn't worth it; she deserved better than she'd gotten from Bob, but he wasn't her answer.

Her soft hand pressed against his face. "Zain, I'm sorry about Reene. Are you okay?"

"I'm . . ." he started as her palm slid along his cheek and she moved closer. The power of her skin against his robbed him of speech and subverted his control. *Don't come any closer, Lacey.* But whatever his mind was trying to say was lost in the blue of her eyes. Her face was like a new day, fresh and innocent, before his memories clouded it; that split second of peace he felt until reality smothered it. When Lacey filled his vision, nothing else mattered.

"Talk to me," she whispered, her eyes searching his.

Whatever control he'd had vanished. The medkit hit the floor. His hands gripped her shoulders and drew her to him until all he could see was the promise of peace. He heard her small gasp as his mouth closed over hers. So soft, so tender. He took more and she gave it to him, opening her mouth. He delved deep into her sweet heat and felt her fingers on his face pull him in. Her tongue found his and she moaned, fueling an escalating fire, and his body began to tremble. It had been too long, and she was too close. He should back off, but there was little hope of that. Even less with her nibbling at him that way.

Passion roared through him and he knew he couldn't tame it. He wanted her. Wanted to toss her on his bunk and take everything her actions promised. Drive into her, bury himself over and over again until she obliterated the past completely. He wanted to save himself . . .

Even as the thought formed, he froze. *No!*

He pushed her away. She blinked at him in confusion, her lips swollen and still parted.

He swore in his native language, a phrase he normally reserved for the most heinous of crimes. The phrase fit. He shoved himself to his feet and turned his back on Lacey. He couldn't face her. Not after taking something he had no right to. He should apologize but it would have to wait. He was too angry with himself. Any words would be filled with disgust.

As he returned to filling his pack, he heard Lacey stand up behind him and shuffle over to her seat. In his peripheral vision, she sat down and crossed her arms. She didn't speak, didn't yell, didn't fight him. She should be giving him hell; hurt him like he'd just hurt her. So why didn't she?

He shoved the last of the supplies into his pack. The medkit lay at his feet, and he grabbed it and stuffed it in.

"Oliver will have to stay here," he said, pulling on the pack.

Zain turned to find Lacey standing next to him, her rifle slung over her shoulder. She wouldn't look him in the eye, but he didn't need to see into her soul to know what he'd done. He was no better than that bastard, Bob. But at least she understood that now.

He turned to walk to the back of the ship. "Let's go."

Chapter Twelve

Zain went first and she fell a few paces behind. Outside the dome, a waiting Pio raised up on four legs. "Follow."

If she hadn't made such a damn big deal about going underground, she could just stay in the ship. But no. *She* had to be independent. *She* had to be in control. Right up until the moment when she made a complete and utter fool of herself.

Dammit, *he* was the one who kissed *her*. She was just offering a little compassion after Reene shut down. Next thing she knew, she was swept into Zain's passionate vortex, riding a wave of passion she'd never dreamed possible. There was so much power and desperation in that kiss; he couldn't fake that and she wouldn't believe he didn't mean it. So why did he push her away? To humiliate her? To teach her some twisted lesson? Whatever the reason, he wasn't getting another chance. She'd already done her time. Her one priority was to get off this planet—alive and soon.

Inside the dome, Pio sprang off the stone floor and landed on top of the center island. Then he turned around and pointed one bony leg to the other side. "Here."

Lacey and Zain stepped around to where Pio indicated. That's when she noticed the circle carved into the stone floor around them.

Pio carefully placed each of his six legs on various spots on the black surface of the island. Beneath him, the entire top burst into a bright array of circles and squares. Lacey gasped. Underneath that film of sand was a control panel just like in Zain's ship. Then the ground moved.

"What—" She yelled as the floor lowered beneath her feet. Zain's arm lashed out and grabbed her. Pio and the counter dropped with them, and they all descended into a dark well. Smooth metal walls engulfed them.

Lacey latched on to Zain for dear life until she realized what she was doing. She tried to pull away, but he held her fast. She peered up at him, backlit by the circle of light above. In the distance, the opening sealed itself, plunging them into black except for the control console's glow. There was a loud whoosh as they passed a band of light in the walls.

Lacey gazed into Zain's briefly lit face, and her breath caught at the sadness in his eyes. Pain and guilt. For whom? Then he closed up on her and looked at Pio.

"How long?"

"Short ride," Pio clicked, rocking slowly atop the counter.

Another whoosh, a band of light, and silence.

Lacey studied the widely-spaced, colored sections on the island that controlled the elevator, and noted Pio's six legs were carefully placed on six small red spots.

"How did you figure out how it worked?" she asked.

Pio chirped, "By playing."

"I don't believe it," she said, shaking her head. "All that work, and all along I didn't have enough extremities."

The elevator slowed and Zain held up his rifle. "Get ready, Lacey."

She readied her weapon and waited.

"Done," Pio chirped.

Suddenly the walls disappeared, and they were lowered onto a round platform surrounded by a bank of consoles. The elevator locked into the floor with a dull click. Gone was the barren desert. Gone were the sun and its warmth. All were replaced by miles of metal. Air whistled around the solitary platform, which was about fifty feet in diameter. The lights were dim and ambient, casting shadows around the vast structure surrounding her.

Lacey untangled herself from Zain and walked to the edge of the platform, looked down and couldn't see bottom. On the other side of the hundred-foot-wide abyss, a wall of technology encircled them. There were cables, conduits, boxes, and lights—all meshed tightly together and weaving around level upon level of giant holes twenty feet high. The holes opened into tunnels, and inside she could just make out storage containers packed end to end. She turned around slowly, counting four columns of tunnels and even more containers.

"It's the freakin' Borg," she whispered.

Zain surveyed the complex with grave concern. He'd never seen so much hardware in one place, even in all his years with InterGlax. This was worse than he'd imagined.

If each tunnel ran several klicks, and Reene was right about the twenty levels, this was no ordinary storage facility. This was too big, too expensive, and too damn powerful. He knew one of those containers could hold lot more than supplies and cargo. He'd seen them in action, popping open and sprouting troops, ships, and ground tanks. With the speed and throughput they'd witnessed earlier, all those containers could be dumped anywhere in a matter of minutes. No ordinary customer needed a delivery that fast.

He scanned the platform and the ring of control panels, and noted one small teleportal arch on the floor. Damn. That was a definite problem. He checked the area, looking for cameras. They would be here, of course. Even a station like this couldn't be one hundred percent autonomous. Unfortunately for him, there was no place to hide. However, if their entry had been detected, they'd probably be dead by now. And Pio seemed to move down here freely. Perhaps the sensors only detected certain types of activity. It would help greatly if he knew which kind.

"What the hell have you dragged me into?" Lacey said, frustration filling her voice.

He clenched his jaw. "I hope we won't be on this planet long enough to find out. Do you want the bad news?"

She huffed and made her way over to him. "You mean there's good news?"

"We already had our good news: We haven't been disintegrated yet."

"You aliens have a really warped sense of humor, you know that?" she replied.

He nodded to the circle on the floor. "Another portal."

"So? What's one more portal?"

"This one is specifically designed for humans."

She looked perplexed for a few seconds, and then her expression lit up. "So we can go home?"

"Not quite," he said slowly. "I'm assuming it leads directly to whoever owns this lovely facility. A service entrance."

"But that would get us out of *here*," she said, sweeping a hand around.

"Maybe," he noted, walking over to one of the consoles.

She huffed. "Don't you want to get off this rock?"

"Passionately." He scoured the layout of the panel.

"Then what's the problem?" she asked, an edge to her voice.

"Problems. Plural," he said as he read the controls. "One, we don't know who the owners are." He pressed a button on the panel. The monitor in front of it lit up with the message: "Access Denied."

"Two, we've already established they don't want guests." He punched another button. Another "Access Denied."

"And three, we have no idea how to control this damn thing."

He pressed another button, and the monitor in front of them displayed a descending time sequence.

Lacey moved up beside him. "What is it?"

"A countdown. Four days and counting."

"To what?" she asked.

"An excellent question," he murmured. One he'd rather not be around to find out the answer to. He gave a quiet sigh. "I need Reene in order access to these systems."

Her reply was swift. "We'll fix Reene, Zain."

Her determination surprised him. Their eyes locked and for a split second, he wasn't alone. Lacey was right there, by his side like she'd been with the Bobzillas. She might be fragile and small and soft, but she also had an unshakable spirit.

Next to him, Pio clicked. "They are back."

"Back?" Zain asked with a frown.

Pio turned and looked up. The entire chamber darkened. The console panel lights came to colorful life. Zain lifted his rifle with one hand and reached for Lacey with the other. Pio didn't move or appear alarmed, so Zain could only hope for the best.

The floor rumbled and, above them, four giant semitransparent tubes dropped from four circles in the ceiling—the teleportals around the dome. One dropped past the platform and locked into a hole below them, forming a conduit. Light brightened the iridescent tube and then a shipper descended. It shot down and into the waiting tunnel, followed closely by another. Zain turned to the other three conduits. They were also accepting shippers at a rapid rate. In short time, the conduits had emptied into the tunnels. Then the tubes disengaged and withdrew into their respective cavities in the ceiling.

As the chamber's lighting powered back to full strength, Lacey asked, "Are those the same units that went out a short while ago?"

"Probably."

"So maybe they are back empty now?" she suggested.

"Right," he said, trying to sound like he meant it. But his sixth sense was thrumming, growing more restless. "Pio, how often do the portals activate?"

The creature tilted its head. "Many times each cycle."

Busy place. "Do they always leave and come back?"

Pio's head tilted the other way. "Yes."

Zain pointed to the teleportal on the floor. "What about that?"

"They come every thirty suns."

"How long before the next visit?"

"Four suns," Pio chirped.

135

Zain studied the countdown. Maybe that's what it was for.

In four days, they were going to have a serious problem. Not that they didn't already, but it was going to be impossible to hide Reene if anyone showed up unannounced. He and Lacey would have no warning and no defense except for their rifles.

Lacey turned to him. "Zain, what is going on?"

"Something big."

Blue eyes narrowed in challenge. He was beginning to enjoy their battles, even if he lost sometimes. He put his hand up. "I'd like some answers, too. But first, we have to get Reene some power cells and work on his weapons." He turned serious. "Preferably before Bobzilla discovers we are vulnerable."

He gazed down into the abyss. Then up at the other side. He addressed Pio. "Where are the parts?"

The creature danced atop the counter and Zain heard a whirring beneath him as a narrow service walkway extended across the void and locked on to the balcony of the first floor of the other side. Pio sprang off the counter, and clicked across the floor and onto the walkway. A pedestal with a control podium sat just inside. He rotated around to face them.

"Other side," was his translation.

Zain turned and grinned at Lacey. Her horrified expression said it all. Her head had already begun to shake back and forth vehemently.

"Don't even *think* about it," she said.

Chapter Thirteen

"I cannot believe I'm doing this," Lacey muttered. Her hands gripped a skinny railing, the only thing keeping her from certain death as the moving walkway drifted down. The metal mesh beneath her slippers gave a perfect view of the bottomless abyss they were sliding into. The flimsy walkway stretched between the center tower and the ring of vertical wall. She took another look over the railing and tried not to barf.

"I still don't understand why I couldn't have just waited back on the platform."

Beside her at the podium, Zain replied, "I don't want you too far away—in case someone enters through that portal up there." He worked his datapad, balanced perfectly on his feet as if he rode these things all the time.

She knew he wasn't telling her everything. He was holding back—for what he thought was her own good, no doubt. One part of her hated it. The other part didn't really want to know. If she knew, what would it change? Nothing. They'd still be stuck on this stupid planet with a dead ship surrounded by Bobzillas. On the other hand, they could just plunge to their deaths right here and now.

She inhaled a deep breath, closed her eyes, and listened to her heartbeat. Think of something else, like Zain and his exceptional DNA.

"Are you all right?"

Zain's soft voice interrupted her panic attack. She nodded a half-dozen times before peering at him. "I've just never experienced so many degrees of terror in such a short period of time. I can't wait to see what else you've got in store for me."

"I'd hate to disappoint you," he said with amusement.

"Please. Disappoint me," she begged, trying to look anywhere but down. Above her, the view wasn't much better. They had dropped at least ten stories, and one of the portal circles was directly overhead. A troubling thought occurred to her.

"So, what do we do if the portals activate again and we are in the way?"

"Duck?" He grinned, not looking up from his datapad.

Smart ass. "Since you seem to have all the answers, just how do we know where we are going?"

"We have to trust Pio. He says the parts storage is located on the center level."

She glanced at the happily bobbing *krudo* who appeared to be enjoying the ride. Was she the only one who sensed danger here?

Endless minutes later, the walkway began to slow. It came to a complete stop and then slid sideways, catching Lacey by surprise, and she stumbled off her feet and into the railing. Zain's hand closed around her arm in a split second. As the walkway rotated around the tower, Lacey felt dizzy. "I'm definitely going to need drugs to get back."

"No, you won't."

She nodded adamantly. "Yes. Yes, I will."

From behind, Zain wrapped his hands around her waist, holding her fast and anchoring her as the walkway continued its sideways glide.

"Better?" he asked softly near her ear.

She could feel his heat on her back and closed her eyes against the insanity around her. She wanted to lean back just a little, just enough to lock herself in his strength and banish the free-floating anxiety she'd had since coming here. Even if he was the cause of it.

Hold me, she wanted to say. *Hold me and keep me sane.*

"All done, Lacey."

Her eyes fluttered open. The walkway had stopped, and she was facing one of the tunnels at the other end. Zain breezed past her toward the other side. Pio was already there. Paralyzing anxiety gripped her as she watched Zain stroll down the length of the catwalk as if it were as wide as a parking lot. About halfway across, he turned and noticed she wasn't following.

"Are you coming?"

She shook her head a little. It was the only part of her body she could move. Was he nuts? That walkway was getting narrower by the second. Hell no, she wasn't going. Her feet wouldn't budge and her mind had shut down altogether. She wasn't moving from this spot.

He returned, his eyes dark with concern. He stopped in front of her, blocking out the sliver of walkway.

"I'll help you across," he said quietly.

She shook her head. That meant "No, I'm not going." He was an intelligent life form, he should be able to figure that out.

Zain took her clenched fists in his hands. He looked down, frowned and carefully pried open one of her fists. She winced and realized blood creased her palm where her fingernails had dug in.

She heard him say something softly, and then he pried open her other hand. Slowly, his gaze rose to hers. She waited for him to tell her that her fears were stupid and ridiculous. To tell her in a lengthy, humiliating lecture how she should be able to conquer them like a normal person. Just like Robert.

Instead, he wrapped her fingers in his and gently pulled her toward him.

"Look at me," he whispered, and she promptly lost herself in his dark eyes. Somehow her right foot slid forward, then her left.

"Breathe," he said. She did. Another step, breathe, step, breathe—the whole time his eyes never left hers, keeping her in his spell.

Who are you? she wondered, marveling at his intense eyes, high cheekbones, chiseled lips. Are you my dream or are you a nightmare? It was hard to tell the difference until it was over. By then it was too late.

His lips moved. "We're here."

She blinked and looked around. Sure enough, she was standing inside the tunnel with the walkway behind her.

"Good job," Zain said with a faint smile. Then he turned into the darkened tunnel.

The parts center was a lot bigger and lot busier than he'd expected. Endless rows of racks were packed with inventory. As Zain stood on the balcony overlooking a cavernous room that stretched hundreds of meters, he wondered what the hell was going on. This housed more than just a few spare parts. There was an entire inventory here as well as a recovery area and repair station, all manned by robots. There wasn't a live body in sight.

He ducked his head at a flutter overhead. An airborne robot sphere flew by, oblivious to them. A set of arms hung below it, grasping what looked like a boring tool.

"A little ship?" Lacey asked, her voice hushed as she stood next to him.

"A runner," he whispered back. "They are designed to perform small tasks like carrying tools and hauling equipment." And for surveillance, although he didn't say it. More runners buzzed by, pulling out parts and tools and then flying off.

"It looks like a Home Depot in here," Lacey said. "Except these guys actually know what they're doing."

He eyed her. The color had finally seeped back into her cheeks. He'd had no idea how truly terrified she was of the bridge. It had taken great courage for her to fight such a deep-seated fear. No wonder she'd wanted to stay up top. But he couldn't leave her alone with the teleportal.

No, she needed to stay with him. For her protection. And it had nothing to do with the fact that he was enjoying her company.

"They don't seem to notice us," she noted.

"And I'd like to keep it that way. Pio, why all the activity?" Zain asked.

"Repairs. Always after they return," Pio bleeped.

"The shippers didn't look damaged," Zain noted.

"Inside they are." Pio swiveled and clicked across the balcony to a floor lift. They all boarded it together and descended to the first level. Zain took the lead, heading for the closest rack. On it, he recognized a diagnostic scanning unit.

"Parts?" Lacey asked, coming up behind him.

"For a spacecraft navigation system."

She swept her hands around. "Is this what's being teleported in?"

"Possibly."

A shadow overhead caught his attention. He looked up just as a charred part of a laser cannon was carried by. He ran down the length of the rack, exiting the row just in time to watch it dropped into a recovery

Dumpster. A sizzling sound followed and the smell of melting metal filled the air.

Lacey came up behind him. "What was that?"

Zain pursed his lips, not wanting to tell her what he was thinking. "Another part."

After a moment, he squatted to the creature's height and asked, "Pio, did that come out of a returning container?"

Pio tilted his head. "Yes. Many."

Weapons. Zain closed his eyes, his worst fears realized. This was no simple repair facility or shipping facility. It was a military armory, and a high-grade one at that. The big question was—what was it doing here?

"I know you are the strong, silent type but I'm getting pretty tired of talking to myself," Lacey muttered as she towed a power cell on a hovering thingie behind her.

Zain walked ahead of her, carrying a serious-looking cannon on his shoulder. This was the third trip they'd made down this tunnel from the repair depot to the bridge, and Zain hadn't said a word. That man's head was like Fort Knox. But the part that worried her most was that he suddenly seemed in a hurry. Something had changed.

She continued, "And I'm boring myself to death."

"You are anything but boring," he called over his shoulder.

"What's the sudden rush, Zain?"

He didn't reply for a moment, then said, "I want to get back to Reene."

She squinted at him. He wouldn't look at her, and she knew he was hiding something. They'd reached the end of the tunnel and the bridge awaited. Lacey stopped her hover thingie as he strolled across the bridge and deposited his item with the others they'd already brought out. He walked back and she held her breath at the sheer commotion his intense gaze could raise in her. His gaze traveled from her eyes down to her lips and stayed there. Nervous, she licked them, which had the immediate effect of darkening Zain's gaze. Then he took the handle of the hover thingie from her and guided the power cell across the bridge.

Lacey closed her eyes, her blood pumping at a rate it was definitely not used to. She was an idiot. She still wanted to kiss him.

"Ready?" His warm hands wrapped around hers and she opened her eyes to find him watching her. "Just look at me," he said softly, pulling her with him as he backed across the bridge.

So she did, losing herself in the dark shadows of his eyes. One step at a time, she let him lead her on, her life in his hands—literally. Tears stung her eyes. Did he have any idea what this one little bit of kindness meant to her?

They stopped where the bridge widened on the other end. Pio waited patiently atop the console beside the spare parts they'd collected. The bridge jerked to the left, and Lacey gasped.

"It's okay. It's just the added weight of the parts,"

Zain said near her ear. He wrapped both hands around her waist and held her steady. The bridge abruptly stopped its horizontal slide and then made a new grinding, whining kind of noise that didn't sound at all good.

Lacey's belly trembled. She couldn't survive another trip. No way. The bridge moaned dreadfully and her entire, boring, fruitless nonlife flashed before her. She grasped Zain's thick forearms, sinking her nails into the skin.

"Easy, Lacey."

She shook her head, fear eating at her. Maybe he could do this but she couldn't. In a blur of terror and panic, she spun in his arms, grabbed his face and kissed him on the lips. Hard. It worked. She forgot all about the bridge. However, a split second later, mortification took hold. What was she doing? She let go of his face. His eyebrows were raised in surprise.

"For luck," she blurted. "I saw it in a movie once."

He looked up at the platform high above them and back down at her. "I think we'll need a *lot* of luck."

Her heart stilled as he leaned over and his lips skimmed hers. She felt the earth move under her feet, and she clutched him like salvation itself. The bridge was still making an awful racket, but she didn't care. Zain was doing something wonderful to her mouth and she didn't want to miss it.

She pressed against him, her hands going to his chest and meeting solid muscle. She sensed more than heard his deep growl. Under her hands, she felt his entire body focus as his rising heat eclipsed hers. He wanted her too; it wasn't just her. Relief vied with passion.

So, why had he pushed her away in the ship? Did he fear passion as much as she did? Was he swept away in the undertow, too? Maybe it was unbridled lust and nothing more, two souls stranded in space and time with nothing left to lose. He nipped at her lip, and she groaned as he dragged her deeper into the depths of a passion she couldn't contain. His hands moved over her—anchoring and caressing at the same time. She pushed against him, coaxing. If she was going under, she was taking him with her.

A sudden, jarring thump interrupted their burning kiss.

"We are here," Pio chirped, and hopped off the console and onto the platform.

Lacey looked up at Zain, who was watching her with enough desire to send her back to Earth on sexual energy alone.

"Why did you do that?" she ventured bravely. She wanted to know—needed to know.

For long seconds, he didn't answer, and she thought he might not. Then he straightened and reached for the handle of the hover thing.

"I figured you could use a distraction until we reached the platform," he said and pulled the cart off the bridge toward the console.

"A distraction?" she repeated. Humiliation burned her face. "How very kind of you."

There was a slight pause before he replied, "No problem."

Chapter Fourteen

Ferretu's image appeared on the holodeck in Schuler's home office. "I have intercepted a partial message from Zain Masters to Rayce Coburne. Masters is stranded on a planet with an inoperative ship."

Schuler steepled his fingers in front of him. So Masters was alive despite having half the galaxy looking for him. Such talent. It would almost be a shame to waste it. In fact, a man of that caliber would be an asset to his operation. The opportunity appealed to Schuler. If he could convince Masters that InterGlax had betrayed and abandoned him, the man might be quite useful.

"Any idea where?" he asked.

"The communication ended before coordinates were relayed. I am following the transmission stream. It went through a complex conduction array and will take some time to trace."

Schuler nodded. "Good. When you find out, contact me. And, Ferretu, I want Masters alive."

Ferretu paused momentarily, and Schuler could sense his intense disapproval. "The deal was I kill him."

"I realize that. But the deal was made five years ago, and since you have failed to produce him in all that time, I am altering our original agreement."

Ferretu straightened in a clear challenge. Schuler could only imagine the sneer on his face beneath his helmet.

"I'm not a bounty hunter. Bringing a man in alive is a lot more trouble than killing him."

And not half as much fun, Schuler bet. "You have kept me waiting a long time, Ferretu. Consider the fact that you are still alive payment enough. Let me know when you have him in custody."

Ferretu nodded stiffly. "Out."

It was dead of night by the time Zain installed one of the power cells, and he was getting damn tired of lying on his belly, hanging over the floor bay of the rear cabin. Even shirtless, sweat poured from him because Reene had turned into a veritable furnace in the hot sun all day. However, his condition probably had more to do with Lacey's kisses than the weather. Leave it up to him to find a beautiful, intelligent woman who was also a hell of a kisser. Although she probably wouldn't be doing it again anytime soon.

Zain closed his eyes for a moment, torturing himself with the memory of her lips. He had hated lying to her. There had been nothing noble about that kiss. He'd wanted it. He'd wanted her. He still did. But he was definitely not the man for her. Bob might be a fool of galactic proportions, but at least he wouldn't get Lacey killed. Zain could, and he had no business being involved with any woman, especially one who was becoming far too tempting for his own good.

He made the last connection on the power cell and then rolled over onto his back with groan. The environment systems kicked on with a healthy hum. He savored the small victory, but they weren't done yet.

He rolled to his feet and walked to the front cabin where Lacey waited. She lifted her head and peered at him with tired eyes.

"We have power." Zain sat at the console next to her and activated a holographic interface that represented Reene's data storage. The image rose from the console's holodeck like a cone. Thousands of tiny balls rotated within it, connected by slender optic lines.

"Each ball is a file. The lines link them together," he explained.

Lacey shook her head. "Wow, so this is Reene. That's what I call a file structure. I'm impressed as hell. Have you ever been in here before?"

"I only know the theory behind it. Reene usually takes care of his own structure." Zain watched the mass of files with little hope. There were just too many variables. "Frankly, I don't think he completed the final memory transfer."

She answered without looking at him. "Core modules must be in the center cluster. He said he stored his working memory in an archive. Just need to make sure he can see those files when he boots up. Can you search for the most recent file saved?"

"Not without Reene's help. But if we don't reinstate his working memory, I don't know how much of him we'll lose. He may be crippled."

"Can we link files ourselves?"

Zain nodded. "It's all manual manipulation. Just drag a link from one box to the next."

She blew out a long breath. "Okay then. Plan B. Archives and infrequently accessed files would be probably on the fringes. Look for a file that appears different from the others."

For a long time, they watched the complex structure rotate and Zain lost more hope. If they couldn't do this, would the friend he'd known be gone forever?

"There it is," she whispered.

He could see the anomaly as it rotated into view. One small oval with a slightly different color and misshapen. It looked as if it hadn't been completed.

Lacey carefully raised her hand. "I'm going to link it to the biggest, baddest file I can find and hope the path gets established." She tapped the anomalous file and an optic line followed her finger to where she touched a massive cluster in the center. She removed her hand—the link complete.

She nodded. "Let's boot him up."

Zain activated the start-up sequence. "Reene?"

Nothing. Then a warbled, "Sir, are you all right?"

Zain took a breath. "We're fine. What's the last thing you remember?"

"You were preparing to investigate the underground structure."

Lacey grinned at Zain triumphantly. Blue eyes sparkled back at him and he was mesmerized by the indomitable spirit that shone from deep within her. Courage he doubted she knew she possessed.

"We have Lacey to thank for bringing you back," he said.

"Much obliged, Lacey," Reene said.

She laughed.

"Thank you, Lacey," Zain added softly.

Her smile faded and uncertainty flashed in her eyes.

"You're welcome," she replied finally.

Zain said, "Prioritize and regulate environment systems for now, Reene. I only have one cell installed and we still need weapons."

"Accessing."

Zain watched the weapons systems power up and felt a whole lot better. Unfortunately, a weapons system wouldn't work with broken guns.

"All weapons-systems software enabled. Perimeter alarms are fully functional," Reene reported, sounding stronger.

Zain headed to the rear compartment. "Release the nanos. They might be able to do a little more now that we have some power. I have to bring the remaining cells up one at a time, so it's going to take a few trips. The lift and bridge aren't designed to carry a lot of weight."

Reene asked, "Did you investigate the facility below?"

"It's big." And bad, but he wasn't going to say that in front of Lacey. "I'm going to install cameras in the dome and on the platform below for a visual feed. There's a human transport portal down there, and a countdown sequence display that I want you to monitor. The good news is that parts we need are also below."

"I realize that my parts are standard, but I find that quite a coincidence," Reene observed.

"I know," Zain said and knelt down to slide the floor panel over the power cell bay. "There's more, and I'll fill you in later." He locked the panel down and got to his feet, stretching his back.

"Bedtime, cowboy," Lacey said, standing in the doorway.

"Go ahead without me."

She crossed her arms, pushing her breasts against the shirt he'd loaned her. She sure knew how to wake him up.

"Not until you do," she replied simply.

He shook his head. Stubborn woman. "The perimeter alarm won't do us any good if I don't get at least one of our main guns working. Bobzilla and friends will be back. I want to be ready."

"I guess we better get moving then."

He didn't have the energy or inclination to argue with her tonight. So he handed her his tool kit. "Take this up front. I'll be right there." She disappeared, and he pulled the parts he needed from the pile behind him and joined her.

"The main guns are in the belly of the ship, but the

access panel is here." He dropped to his knees in the middle of the corridor and released the panel. Lacey knelt across from him and peered into the pit at the mangled gun.

The front of her shirt opened enough for Zain to see the curve of her breasts. They would fit perfectly into his hands. And just like that, he was hard. This wasn't going to work.

"You took care of Reene. I can handle this alone," he said, his voice a little strangled.

She frowned. "I really wish you would stop giving me orders. I'm you're partner, you know."

You're a distraction, he thought. "You need your sleep."

"So do you," she countered.

He pursed his lips, put his imagination on hold, and stuck out his hand. "Give me the flat tool with the knob on the end."

She opened the kit and sorted through. Proudly, she held up the latcher. "This?"

"Thanks," he said, taking it. He wedged his shoulder as far into the weapons bay as possible and began loosening the lockdowns. Lacey lay on the floor across from him with her head near his.

"So, you're pretty good with your hands, huh?"

He nearly dropped the latcher. "What?"

"You know, handy."

Handy. He swallowed. He was a little more than handy at the moment. "The nanos can only do so much. I need to be able to repair everything on the ship."

She sounded very impressed. "A space cowboy *and* a handyman. Women must swoon over you."

He wished. "Not lately."

She was silent for three whole seconds. "So, did you learn this in the military?"

"Some." He twisted around to reach another lockdown. "I was an advance scout for a military organization called InterGlax. I assessed new territories."

She hummed. "So you've always done exploration?"

"For as long as I can remember."

"Why?"

He reached for the last lockdown. "The challenge of the unknown. And I could set my own schedule with no one looking over my shoulder and telling me what to do."

"No wonder you loved it," she muttered. "Was it hazardous?"

"Occasionally. But that's the price you pay for exploration. Every mission was different, every planet an adventure."

"Even this one?"

"This is still better than being tied to a chair in an office surrounded by people who are content to do the same thing every day, every year, for the rest of their lives."

Lacey said, "You mean, like me?"

He released the last lockdown and pulled himself out of the bay. Lacey was on her belly, her shapely legs crossed at the calves, her face in her hands. The long shirt outlined her narrow back and round bottom delicately. He was pretty sure the view was going to kill him.

"I don't see you that way. And I didn't mean it as an insult. Worlds need those people. I'm just not one of them."

She sniffed. "Well, us brainy types will ultimately conquer the universe, so you better be nice to us."

"I'm doing my best to keep you brainy types happy. Us Wild Wild West men have a reputation to uphold," he added with a smile.

She wrinkled her nose. "What else did you learn? Besides how to give orders."

"I learned how to not ask a lot of questions."

"How utterly boring."

"Yes. But safer, trust me."

"Anything else?" Her big, beautiful blue eyes blinked at him.

At this rate, he was never going to sleep, let alone fix the guns. He tossed the latcher on the floor and rolled his stiff shoulder. "Weapons, ops, and about a hundred ways to kill someone in under three seconds." He leaned back against the cabinets and waited for her shocked reaction.

"Sounds like a risky way to make a living," she said simply.

"It was."

"You must have been very good."

He clenched his jaw. "Not always."

Her eyes narrowed. "Once?"

Zain stilled. Had Reene told her? No, the computer wouldn't do that. He knew better.

"Maybe twice," he said lightly, trying to throw her off.

She stared at his bare chest and, for a few seconds, his ego was really happy. And then Lacey said, "Is that when you got those?"

He frowned and rubbed the three thick scars with his fingers. So much for his ego.

"I had an off day," he conceded. "It happens."

"Bobzillas?"

He pursed his lips. He really didn't want to be having this conversation. "Sort of. Give me a little help here."

He leaned over the bay and braced himself with one hand. Lacey scooted up on her knees and moved across from him, giving him a hell of a look down her shirt. He groaned. Her face lifted to his.

"Are you okay?"

He shook his head. "Fine. I'm going to ease the barrel of the gun out. Just hold it steady so it doesn't bang around too much.

"What happens if it bangs around?" she asked.

He reached a hand in and gripped the gun barrel. "It's full of live ammo."

She gasped. "It's a bomb?"

He clenched his teeth as he lifted the gun out of the tight confines of the bay. "Bomb is such a strong word." The gun hit the side wall with a loud bang, and he winced.

"If you blow us up, I'm going to kill you," Lacey said, peering at what he was doing.

"I can do this," Zain told her.

She grabbed the gun shaft with one hand. "Are you sure this thing is going to fit?"

"It'll fit," Zain insisted, turning it the other way while Lacey held on to one end.

"It's too big. It's not coming out."

"They got it in, I can get it out."

He twisted the gun, and it clanked against the opening.

She glared at him. "I thought you said you knew how to repair everything on this ship."

"I do." He rapped his knuckles against the lip of the bay as he wrenched the mangled gun out. He set it down carefully and shook his battered hand. "Damn."

Lacey reached for his bloodied hand, but he pulled it away. "Don't."

His bark startled her. She blinked and withdrew to a safe distance. Anger returned: her protection.

"Don't worry, I won't." Her words were like ice.

He wanted to explain that every time she touched him, he lost control. And when he lost control, he took. He wanted. Didn't she understand that he was a dangerous man?

So he just sat there and said, "I can install another power cell in the ship tomorrow. After that, I should be able to send you and Oliver home in the VirtuWav."

She nodded, refusing to meet his gaze. "Fine. Well, I'm sure you can handle the rest of this job." Then she stood up and climbed into her bed without a word.

Zain closed his eyes. He was such a bastard.

* * *

An hour later, he finished locking down the hatch and leaned back against the corridor wall. "Give it a test shot, Reene."

He heard the laser gun fire as it lit up the night outside the viewport.

"Good," he said and pulled himself to his feet, coming up beside a sleeping Lacey. For a moment, he just stood there and watched her sleep. Maybe it wasn't the right thing to do to watch a woman without her permission. A good man wouldn't be standing in the dark, wondering what she was dreaming about, or who. A good man wouldn't be wondering what it would be like to watch her wake up and be the first one to see her eyes light up in the morning.

Then again, he wasn't a good man.

She was going home tomorrow, back to where she belonged. With a pang, he knew that her sweet promise would haunt him forever—more than stolen kisses, more than the sexual desire she unfurled in him. In her, he saw the peace he'd always sought. She'd brought laughter back to his silent world, reminding him that life was about more than a job and what was beyond the next star.

It would be much better once it was back to just him and Reene again. He could explore the galaxy like he loved to with no one to question him. No one to challenge him. No one to laugh with. No one to make him forget. No one to keep his dreams alive.

From his perch on Lacey's chest, Oliver made a little chirping noise. Zain reached out and stroked his fur. "I'm beginning to think you're a genius," he told the cat.

He took one last look and headed to the back room. "Reene, all weapons systems on full. I'm going to grab a few hours sleep."

"Yes, sir. Happy trails."

Zain smiled and tossed a mat on the floor. "You, too."

He placed a rifle next to him and stretched out on the floor. They were sitting on a bomb, all right. The biggest damn bomb there was—an illegal armory. There were few organizations who could afford this type of operation, and almost none of those were legitimate. He didn't want to be here long enough to find out for sure. In fewer than four days, they'd have company. Somehow, he'd be gone by then—even if he had to take his chances trying to shoot his way out.

A faint noise came from the front of the ship, and he turned to see Oliver sitting at the door watching him.

"You want something?" Zain asked.

The cat's eyes flashed in the darkness, bobbing up and down as Oliver padded. Zain and the animal regarded each other with uncertainty, and then, to Zain's utter surprise, the cat turned around a few times before curling up next to his head. A soft purr shook its warm, furry body as it relaxed and went to sleep.

Zain listened to the soothing sound and stared at the ceiling, memories weighing heavier than any blanket. He shook them off and crushed them under his mental foot. It was a trick he'd learned long ago. The only time they surfaced to haunt him was when he slept. Sleep was a necessary evil, and dreams a price to be paid for past mistakes. But even as he fought it, exhaustion swamped him. Sleep prevailed.

As he drifted toward it, he heard the laughter and voices of his family: his father's bellowing laugh, the relentless jabs from seven brothers to their only sister, her quick retorts. Theirs was a house that rocked all the time with meals that inevitably turned into political debates, and as always, discussion of the almighty family shipping business.

And then, amid it all, the name 'Qomoti-Rul' echoed in his mind. *No.* He clung to the warmth and safety of his youth and family.

Zain! There are too many of them! Crista's shout hurled to him through the darkness, leaving him vulnerable, exposed, and ensnared. The sulfurous odor of the Qomoti-Rul swamp replaced the memories of family meals, and his feet were already trapped in the thick mud. He slid into terror. Shadows descended and attacked. Crista screamed behind him. Metal slashed across his chest. He felt the warm spray of his own blood, heard his grunt of pain, and knew what was to happen next. The outcome was inevitable, but he could never bring himself to abandon Crista.

This time, though, just as he reached out in a vain attempt to fight for Crista's life, Lacey's voice came to him. The nightmare wavered, the shadows halted. His breath stilled, hope transcending fear. Lacey whispered to him again and he held onto the sweet sound.

He didn't care what happened to him, as long as he could hear her. Let the shadows take him. Let death be merciful and quick. Let this nightmare end.

She became stronger, and the swamp, the shadows, and the fear withdrew. In their place was Lacey's smiling face. Her lips moved as she soothed him. He felt her hands on his chest, healing. Her lips were on his, infusing him with passion like a breath of fresh air. He growled, pushing himself into her softness. Peace wrapped around him—a sensation he hadn't felt in so long, he shuddered with the power of it. Lacey intertwined with his mind and body. He could taste her, feel her, hear her. Everything he needed was right there.

"Lacey," he whispered, hearing his own voice, and the dream shattered.

Suddenly, he jerked fully awake. His thoughts scrambled. What happened? Had he made a noise? Had he said her name? He forced his heart to slow, his ears to listen. The only sounds were those of the ship. Lacey was still asleep.

Zain checked the time. He'd slept four hours straight, longer than he could ever remember in the last five years. He looked at his hands. They were fine, no blood, and no marks. He closed his eyes, the dream still lingering.

What was Lacey doing in his dreams about Crista? How could he allow that to happen? Do that to Crista's memory? Especially the sex. He'd never dreamed about sex with Crista.

He blew out a long breath. Well, apparently he did with Lacey, and he had the erection to prove it.

Chapter Fifteen

T minus three days and counting . . .

Lacey woke slowly to sunlight streaming through the ship's viewport. Another day on an alien planet and one less day to work on her database. There was no hope of finishing it in time now, but if she returned today, she could at least contact Marquet and try to get a short extension. She'd tell them there were extenuating circumstances. Elaborating probably wouldn't be a good idea.

She closed her eyes. She wanted to go home, back to where her life was her own. Where she could choose whom she wanted to let in. Where she succeeded or failed on her own, without any domineering space cowboy telling her what to do all the time.

Don't. She swallowed, recalling Zain's word last night; Robert's favorite word. Don't laugh so loud,

Lacey. Don't tell that story to my friends, Lacey. Don't wear that dress, don't hold my hand in public, don't bother me when I'm working. Don't be yourself. Yes, she understood fully what "don't" meant. Even out here.

It dawned on her that Oliver was MIA. She glanced around. No sign of Zain, either. Had he left already for the next load of parts?

"Reene?" she whispered.

"Yes, Lacey," the computer replied in his soft voice that still creeped her out, though she was getting a little more used to it.

"Where is Zain?"

"In the back."

She frowned at the bright sunlight. "It's late."

"Yes. I did not wake him. He rarely sleeps this agreeably."

"Does he always have nightmares?" she asked, leaning up on one elbow.

"Yes. Although, they have not been as bad since you arrived."

"Why is that?"

Reene paused. "I do not know. However, you are the first person to spend this much time with Zain in 3.1 years."

She shouldn't be surprised. He'd told her his life was solitary, and he obviously preferred it that way. He could have any woman he wanted—she was sure of it. This was the life he chose. She couldn't help but wonder why.

"Does he ever tell you what the nightmares are about?"

Another hesitation. "Not specifically."

"Are they always so violent?"

"Yes."

She wondered how many times he'd woken up to only a computer, even one as sophisticated as Reene, and how many times he'd bandaged his own hands. What would make him thrash with enough desperation to injure himself like that? When she left, would his nightmares come back?

Yeah, so he'd been a jerk to her last night. Maybe he was just tired and cranky. Even she had her moments. It didn't mean she wished him misery in his sleep. She scooted off her bunk and stepped quietly to the back of the ship. The door was open and two golden eyes peered at her. Oliver was lying on Zain's chest.

"What time is it?" Zain's gruff question startled her.

"I'm sorry. I didn't mean to wake you."

"No problem. I have to get moving anyway."

Oliver jumped off him as Zain rolled to a sitting position and leaned back against the wall, his face lit by a beam of light. He didn't look tired. He looked rumpled and relaxed and sexy.

Just what she needed.

Above his head hung one of the paintings, a dull brown landscape with a bloodred sun.

"Are those your paintings?"

He smiled. "Afraid so."

She shook her head. "No, they're good. Really

165

good. A little on the Goth side maybe. Freud would have a field day. Have you been to these places?"

He nodded. "Planets I've visited over the years."

She recalled the other paintings she'd seen. All landscapes. "Do you ever paint people?"

He was slow to reply. "No."

"Why not?"

He leaned his head back against the wall. "I guess there's no one I want to immortalize."

"I bet you could sell them if you wanted. Might be a safer occupation than stellar cartography."

"Not my style," he said, getting to his feet. "But I'm glad you like them."

She watched as he stretched and the muscles in his back bunched and flexed. Then he strolled to within a foot of her. His heat engulfed her senses. Maybe it was her heat; she didn't know and really didn't care. It felt good and dangerous and exciting—and damn it, a woman deserved a little excitement once in a while.

"I'm sorry about last night," he said softly.

She blinked, lost in her fantasy. "You were tired."

"No excuse." As he spoke, she realized that he had a beautiful mouth. His lips were just right. Chiseled but soft and firm. She liked the way his stubble framed them and his rare smiles.

"You can stay up here while I go underground for the next power cell. Once that's installed, I should have enough power to send you back. Today."

Today. She blinked. By this time tomorrow, he'd be out of her life forever, and she'd be alone with her

NAME: _____

ADDRESS: _____

_____

_____

TELEPHONE: _____

E-MAIL: _____

_____ I want to pay by credit card.

__ Visa   __ MasterCard   __ Discover

Account Number: _____

Expiration date: _____

SIGNATURE: _____

Send this form, along with $2.00 shipping and handling for your FREE books, to:

Love Spell Romance Book Club
20 Academy Street
Norwalk, CT 06850-4032

Or fax (must include credit card information!) to: 610.995.9274. You can also sign up on the Web at www.dorchesterpub.com.

Offer open to residents of the U.S. and Canada only. Canadian residents, please call 1.800.481.9191 for pricing information.

database and her New Year's resolutions list.

"I'm coming with you." The words popped out of her mouth.

His eyes narrowed. "I thought you hated that bridge."

"I'll be fine," she insisted. The thought of never seeing him again seemed to dull the fear that crept inside her. "Besides, you could use someone to help you bring that power cell up. It's heavy."

He watched her for a few seconds. "You have a point."

Zain scoured the desert through his visor.

"Where do you think Pio is?" Lacey asked.

"Maybe looking for food or sleeping. I think we're on our own."

Zain joined her, and they headed for the dome. He couldn't believe how late he'd slept this morning. He tried to tell himself that it had nothing to do with Lacey, but the nightmares had changed for the first time in years. And when she was gone, he was sure the much more depressing version would return. He'd take these few nights of peace, even if they meant waking up fully aroused. It was a condition he was getting accustomed to.

He entered the interior of the dome first. Lacey followed, and they stopped at the counter. Zain brushed the sand off the top. "Do you remember the six areas Pio pressed?"

Lacey concentrated, a little crease forming between her eyebrows. She moved around the other side of the counter. Zain loved watching her brain work.

She stood in the same location they had yesterday and made six little Xs, one by one. They were spread out across the surface. After a few seconds, she nodded. "I think that's it." She cocked her head. "You know, it would take three people to operate this thing."

That had occurred to him yesterday. "Not very practical or efficient, but good for security. What are the odds of guessing the exact combination?"

"Almost nil. So, how are two of us going to do this? I only have one pair of hands." She looked him over. "I don't suppose you are hiding a couple extras?"

Zain chuckled. "Sorry, no." He moved up next to her and studied her marks. He leaned over and placed an elbow on one and then lowered his arm to reach another 'X' with his fingers. It fit, and he could stretch enough to touch one more with his free hand.

Then he stood back. "See if you can do what I just did."

Lacey moved in front of him and placed an elbow down and then her fingers. "This is a little like Twister," she said with a laugh. With her free hand, she touched one more near the center. "I have three. You'll have to get the others."

Zain noted two on her left and one on her right. The logistics were interesting. Not that he was complaining. He stood behind her and placed an elbow and hand. Then he leaned forward, pressing against her back to stretch himself over to get the last spot.

It was all he could do not to groan as her soft body made contact with his.

"Do you have it?"

He couldn't answer her, not until he could get his control back. Three years was a long time without a woman, especially one who was already interrupting his dreams. He indulged himself and breathed her in. She smelled clean and sweet and sexy. Raw desire swept through him. Not controlled and civilized like with Crista, this was volatile, swift and merciless. His imagination took over, the possibilities flooding all reason. He wanted to run his hands over Lacey's body, to remember what it felt like to hold a woman. Being a fugitive had some really lousy side effects.

"I'm set," he managed somehow.

"Nothing is happening," she said, and moved her bottom just enough to make him hiss through his teeth.

"Hold still," he warned, his body temperature jumping sharply. It took supreme effort not to grind her into the console.

"Well, nothing is going to happen if we don't move. Maybe this," she mumbled and slid her fingers over a little. The entire console lit up and there was a great rush of air as the floor lowered into the Well.

As soon as the lift was underway, Zain pushed off the console and away from Lacey. He sucked in a healthy breath and pulled out his rifle. The metal felt cold in his hands—a welcome return to reality. Lacey turned and leaned back against the counter, looking a little flushed.

"Are you okay?" he asked.

She nodded and smoothed her hair. "I suppose we'll have to do that again to get back up."

He decided not to think about it.

Lacey squinted at him. "How are you going to operate this when I'm gone?"

"I'll have to get Pio to help me."

The lift opened to the armory below and clicked into the floor. Zain swept his eyes and rifle along the platform. No threats. Except of course, Lacey.

He stepped to the monitor. The countdown showed three days.

"Still running," Lacey noted, coming up next to him. She gave an audible sigh. "How are you going to get out of here, Zain? Even if you fix Reene, you still don't know how to shut down those lasers."

"Reene and I will find a way, don't worry," he said. He made his way over to the touch pad panel of the bridge. More controls. Just what he needed. If he didn't have Pio here, he'd never get anywhere, but he didn't want to tell Lacey that. It wasn't her problem.

She walked up behind him and activated the controls. The bridge lowered. Zain stepped behind her and wrapped his free hand around her waist. As he pulled her back against him, he told himself it was only to soothe her fears. But as her heat seeped into him, he knew better.

Then the bridge hesitated markedly, and his warrior senses took over. High above, he heard a sound that chilled him, and he automatically swung his rifle up. He swore silently at what happened next.

The portal tubes were descending.

Chapter Sixteen

Lacey's gaze lifted to the sound of certain doom.

Zain's hand gripped her hard around the waist and pushed her back in front of the bridge controls. "Stop this thing, Lacey. We need to get off. Now."

"Stop it? Easy for you to say, Mister I'll-let-Pio-do-it," she said, trying to calm her nerves enough to think straight. "I'm just copying him. It's not like I actually *know* how to work this damn thing."

"Just do something, Lacey," Zain ordered.

"Fine. It's your quarter," she said and hit two boxes on the panel. Nothing. She hit a few more. Nada.

She looked up at the tube coming right at them as loud as a 747. It was like looking into a giant nozzle. Now she understood why Oliver was scared to death of the vacuum cleaner.

She banged her hands across the whole damn control panel. The bridge slowed and then stopped.

"Good job!" Zain shouted.

She shook her head and yelled over the din, "I didn't do anything. It stopped by itself."

"Move." Zain wrenched her arm and dragged her down the bridge.

She wanted to tell him to quit telling her what to do, but frankly, "move" seemed like a good idea at the moment. She let him pull her into a tunnel lined with hundreds of shippers—bumper to bumper like a convoy. The storage units themselves were bigger than she'd originally thought, at least forty feet long and fifteen in diameter.

As they ducked around the first, Zain cast a glance over his shoulder and his expression told her something was very wrong.

He pushed her in front of him. "Run!"

She didn't need to look behind her to see what had happened; the resounding snap said it all. The portal tube had attached to *their* tunnel.

"Of all the tunnels you could have picked!" she yelled over her shoulder, running as fast as her legs could take her.

"You drove," Zain replied, hot on her heels.

The containers made a hissing sound, rose above the ground in unison and lurched forward toward the end of the tunnel. Lacey could feel the suction and power of the portal tube. They ran past a hundred or so moving units—she lost count after a while—and then Zain cursed loudly.

"Now what?" she gasped.

He cast her a quick glance as he sped by to take the

lead. "The end of the tunnel is closing in. We're going to be shoved into the tube and through the portal."

Lacey looked up ahead and saw the end wall moving slowly but steadily toward them, pushing the shippers into the portal tube. "I *hate* this damn planet."

Zain stopped at one of the shippers. "You're going to hate it a lot more if you get sucked through a portal without protection."

He was concentrating fiercely and running his hands over the shipper's midsection when she finally reached him. "What are you doing?"

"Finding protection," he replied, and then she heard a click. The entire side of the capsule opened. Inside she saw a space ship, like Reene but smaller.

"Shit," she heard Zain say softly behind her.

"Good grief, now what?"

"Nothing. Get in."

She scrambled through the hatch and crouched in the small space beside the ship. Zain hopped in after her and hit a panel. The door slid shut, plunging them into the dark except for a few flashing red lights. Seconds later, a floating orb of luminescence lit the interior.

"What is that?"

"A lightball. Here," he said, guiding her to the side of the capsule where harnesses were attached to the wall. "I'll strap you in."

She watched him handle the clips with ease. Then he secured his pack and strapped himself in next to her.

"Reene," he said into his comm unit. "We're trapped in the teleportal activation. I've accessed one of the shippers, and it looks like we're heading out."

Reene answered immediately. "That may not be a wise course of action."

Lacey nodded in full agreement.

"I know. Track us as long as you can. I hope we'll be back."

"Yes, sir. Good luck."

Zain snagged the lightball out of the air and stuffed it into his pack.

Lacey blinked in the darkness. Their container swayed lightly. "The sane part of me knows that you wouldn't do this unless it was safe." She hesitated. "Right?"

"I used to travel this way at InterGlax all the time. An entire team could fit into one of these with all their gear. We ride through the portal and land on the other side. Easy," he answered smoothly.

Lacey gripped her harness and closed her eyes. Her heart beat painfully in her chest. She wasn't up to teleporting today. It just wasn't a good day. Tomorrow would be better. Or never. Never would work, too.

"What's going to happen to us?" she asked, even though she really didn't want to.

"We'll transport from here to the receptor on the other end. I know you find this hard to believe, but it's remarkably safe. In fact, it's basically the same technology I used to bring you here. You weren't afraid that time."

She pursed her lips. "I was an idiot then. I thought I was dreaming, remember? You were nothing more than a figment of my fertile yet celibate imagination."

"Celibate? I find that hard to believe."

She scowled at his amusement. "I really don't want to talk about my sex life right now. And stop changing the subject. I'm about to be split into molecules and shot across to . . ." She stopped. "Where?"

Zain replied soberly, "I don't know."

"Will it hurt?"

"No. It'll be over fast, I promise."

The container lurched forward and nosed up sharply. Panic seized her as they went vertical. Tears rolled down her cheeks. She didn't care if he knew. She didn't care if she made a fool of herself, or if he laughed at her. They were going to die. How much worse could it get?

It occurred to her that every time she used that particular phrase, something worse always happened.

"I'm scared."

When Zain didn't reply, she figured he hadn't heard her. Then she felt his warm palm against her cheek as he guided her lips to his, and kissed her. She felt a sudden rush and then fireworks filled her head, blocking everything out except for the ghost of his lips on hers. She held on to it in terrified desperation. If he lost contact with her, she'd never make it.

Seconds stretched into forever, and then the shipper leveled out.

Zain broke off the kiss. "We landed."

"We're alive?" she asked, patting herself down. All

175

her parts were there in what felt like proper order.

"For the time being," he said, just as she was starting to feel pretty good again.

They slowed to a full stop. The shipper whined, and the top half split open lengthwise, revealing a bright starry night. The small spaceship in the center of the shipper abruptly started, and just as the ceiling opened wide, the ship's wing unfolded. Lacey covered her face as air jetted around them and the ship rose and flew off so fast she couldn't even track it.

Zain released his harness and stood up. Lacey did the same, wobbling a little as she looked around. They were in the middle of a vast meadow, surrounded by a dark, foreboding forest of twisted trees. A thick, swirling mist danced around several hundred shippers just like theirs. Her eyes widened at the small army of capsules laid out across the field. They were all opening. Ships filled the night sky in every direction. The obvious question was why?

"What kind of ships are these, Zain?"

"Short-range, unmanned InterGlax fighter drones."

She turned her head to look at him, stunned. "*Your* InterGlax?"

Zain scanned their vicinity, and then his gaze zeroed in on something in the distance. "There's only one InterGlax."

She raised her hands in utter relief. "This is wonderful. You know them. After we get sent back in this shipper, you can just call them and tell them we're stranded. We'll be home for dinner."

He took his sweet time replying. "I can't do that."

She was getting tired of him saying what they could and couldn't do without good reason. "Why the hell not?"

He turned to her with a look of dread and resignation, almost longing. She had a bad feeling that she wasn't going to like his answer.

"Because InterGlax has a warrant out for my arrest." His gaze was steady. "For the murder of my partner."

She knew he'd said the words but somehow they weren't getting past the churning mist of the alien planet, the fighter spaceships zooming overhead, and the general chaos of life on the edge of sanity. She must have heard him wrong. The eye of her storm, the man she trusted with her life, and the object of a serious amount of lust—he couldn't have just said he'd murdered his partner. He'd held Lacey, fought for her, and helped her. He might be controlling and hardheaded, but he was no cold-blooded murderer.

"You didn't kill your partner. What happened, Zain?"

Before he could reply, a loud rumble erupted in the distance. Lacey dragged her gaze from Zain to where a series of bright lights illuminated the valley below them. Flames flickered through the trees, and the night was filled with gunfire and destruction.

"Oh my God," she whispered. "Are these ships doing all that?"

"Probably."

She shook her head in confusion. "But I thought InterGlax were the good guys."

The distant battle lit up Zain's face and the bitterness there. "Not always. Stay here. I want to investigate," he told her. He jumped out, and she followed. "Contact me as soon as the ships begin to come back for the return to the Well."

A brand-new fear took over—more frightening than all the others, if that was possible. "What happens if you don't get back in time?"

He checked his rifle. "Then return to the planet and tell Reene to call Rayce or Cohl to pick you up. Make sure Reene explains the automatic weapons systems. They will have to deal with them somehow or help you install a new power cell so you can use the VirtuWav. But either way, you need to be off that planet before InterGlax comes for their monthly check in three days, even if it means leaving Reene behind."

She shook her head at the calm way he was telling her all this. If he didn't return, it would mean he was dead. Or as good as.

"I don't want you to go. It's too risky. If we just stay here, the ships will eventually go back through the portal."

His shadowed face turned to her. His words were almost desperate. "I need to know who InterGlax is attacking and why. Please stay here."

The smell of smoke and lasers in the distance did nothing to assail her fears. Yet Zain's plea was more than she could refuse. Whatever the history between him and InterGlax, this was important to him.

"Just get back in time," she relented.

He reached out and pulled her to him for a sizzling kiss. She wrapped her arms around him for what might very well be the last time.

"For luck," he whispered against her lips. A second later, he disappeared into the night.

Zain stepped silently through the light underbrush in a twisted forest. The battle flashed ahead of him, close enough that he could see individual lasers slicing the night. The one-sided siege had been going on for more than an hour as the IG fleet attacked with deadly execution. He didn't recognize the planet they were on, but it was most likely a juvenile. The lack of return fire told him that this was a complete surprise to the inhabitants. They didn't have the manpower or firepower to defend themselves.

He used his goggles to zoom in on a target. Small homes were burning, and he could make out their inhabitants running for cover.

He watched the ships slaughter the defenseless souls in the valley, and fresh anger rolled over him. What the hell was IG doing, attacking civilians? Even if the people of this planet launched a defense, they would only be destroying unmanned drones. Their efforts would put nothing more than an insignificant dent in IG's armor.

Abruptly, one of the ships peeled off and headed over Zain's head, drawing him back to the present. Lacey was alone at the insertion point. He turned and sprinted through the forest as more ships tracked overhead.

179

"Zain, get back *now*," Lacey's voice sounded over his comm, urgent and clear. More ships zipped overhead, and he knew he didn't have much time. They would return to the capsules and head back through the portal. This was like no InterGlax op he'd ever seen. They came, they destroyed, and they left. For what purpose? There was no victory, no surrender, nothing.

He ran harder, crashing through the underbrush, giving up stealth for speed. As he broke into the misty clearing, the attack ships were already reseating into their capsules. Zain scanned the rows looking for Lacey. His goggles picked up her heat signature as she stood on deck, and he headed for her. With fifty meters to go, he watched a ship descend into their shipper and it began to seal up.

"Zain!" Lacey's cry came over the comm at the same time something ripped into his back, just above the shoulder blade with enough force to slam him into one of the capsules. He rolled under the container and went down on a knee, stars flooding his vision from the impact. His night vision picked up several people running toward him with hand weapons. The locals were finally fighting back.

He resisted his trained instincts to return fire. This was their home. They had every right to defend it, and as far as they knew, he was the invader.

"Zain, where are you?" Lacey's plea drove him forward. Using the shipper for cover, he loped toward her location.

Pain seared his back but he blocked it from his

mind. He had to get back to her. He wouldn't fail another partner. He wouldn't fail Lacey. He stumbled over the terrain, surprised by his own clumsiness. The ground around him seemed to heave and roll, and he realized that he was moving more slowly, his body betraying him. *Poison.* The word surfaced through a suffocating fog. Whatever had hit him was doing this.

A smattering of ammunition pelted the metal capsules around him, and he could hear people shouting. He pushed ahead blindly, barely able to stand up. They were right behind him when he reached what he hoped was Lacey's shipper.

The hatch was wide open, and he threw himself in as a salvo of gunfire rattled around him. He laid on the floor, his back burning. Even as his mind spiraled out of control, he knew she was there. She was safe. He hadn't let her down. He was with her.

Lacey hit the panel to close the hatch, overwhelmingly relieved that Zain had made it.

"Are you all right?" she asked frantically, crawling over to him in the dark where he lay on the floor. He wasn't moving and she knew he was hurt. She ran her hands over his face and his chest.

"Zain? Talk to me."

He groaned. "I'm fine."

"Right," she said, trying not to panic but not doing a very good job. Her hands reached beneath him and her fingers sunk into something wet and warm and sticky. She didn't need light to see he was bleeding.

"Harness yourself, Lacey," he rasped. "We're going back through the portal.

"You first, cowboy," she grunted as she tried to push him to the wall. He wouldn't budge. The man was solid muscle.

He moaned. "Don't."

"*Don't*, my ass. You are moving, mister, so get yourself against that wall or we're going to be banging around inside this death trap together."

He hissed in pain and rolled onto his side. His voice was laden with agony and confusion. "Anyone tell you . . . stubborn?" His words slurred.

"My parents, three sisters, all my friends, and every other person who even remotely knows me. Stand in line."

She dragged him with little help to the side. Missiles had stopped rattling the shipper, and it was moving faster now. She and Zain didn't have much time before the return trip.

He leaned back against the wall, and Lacey felt the energy drain out of him. It had taken all he had to get this far. She fumbled with the harness in the darkness. It had just clicked tight when she felt the ship sharply drop.

He grabbed her and pulled her to him. "Hold on."

She wrapped her arms around him as her world came apart, tossing her into the terrifying vortex of teleportation. A soundless scream tore from her lips. Zain's arms tightened like a vise, keeping her grounded.

Seconds turned to minutes, and then the weight of

gravity settled over her like a blanket. The ship went vertical, and she knew they were on the other side. It seemed like an eternity passed before they leveled out, and Lacey almost felt as if she were on solid ground again. They were still moving but at least she could kneel and check on Zain. His arms clamped around her, dead weight.

She reached into his pack that was still strapped to the wall and fumbled around until she found the lightball. It activated the second she tossed it into the air, illuminating the interior.

Zain's head lay back against the wall, his eyes shut. Agony filled his face.

"Stay with me," Lacey whispered, fear making her hands shake as she wiped his sweaty brow. He was hot and flushed and out of his mind with pain.

She felt the shipper slow to a stop. *Now what?* She hit the panel to open the contraption's side panel. Bright light flooded in. She leaned out and looked around. They were in a tunnel again, probably the same as before.

The shipper's ceiling yawned open, and a roar of flutters filled the air. Above her, the robot runners zipped by hauling hover sleds. Three of them dropped into their capsule and began inspecting the ship. She held her breath, but they didn't seem to notice her as they pulled panels off the fighter drone and peered inside. One of the hover sleds was close, and she reached out and tentatively pulled it toward her. Keeping one eye on the robots, she released Zain's harness and shoved the sled in front of him.

He groaned loudly as she muscled his body across the sled, face down. That's when she saw the damage. His shirt was soaked in gore where three metal spikes were wedged in his back. Her first instinct was to pull them out, but what if it worsened the bleeding and she couldn't stop it? She needed to get him back to the ship where Reene could help.

She hopped out and drew the sled carefully behind her. As she made her way down the tunnel with Zain, she noted all the shippers were open and the craft inside being repaired or maintained. For some blessed reason, the runners didn't acknowledge her presence.

At the end of the tunnel, the bridge stretched out before her where they'd left it. Her gaze drifted down through the mesh walkway and into the great void below. She choked back panic. Her body wouldn't move. She couldn't do it.

Zain moaned behind her, reminding her that her fears could kill him. She stared at the control podium that seemed a mile away.

"Come on, Lacey. Don't be such a wimp." She gritted her teeth and stepped onto the mesh. "You've come this far." She took another step. "Gone where no Earthwoman has gone before." Another step, then she checked Zain who wasn't moving. "Survived multiple teleportations to God only knows were, attacking Bobzillas . . ." She kept moving forward. "Talked to aliens, been kissed senseless . . ." The podium was nearly in reach. "What's a little walk on a skeletal bridge over a bottomless abyss?"

She reached the other side and latched on to the podium for dear life.

"There now, that wasn't so bad," she said, barely hearing her voice over her pounding heart. She tapped the panel and the bridge rose slowly. As they rode to the top, she knelt down next to Zain. His eyes were closed and his breathing weak.

"Don't leave me now," she whispered. His eyes opened with great effort, dark and unfocused. He tried to move his mouth, but nothing came out.

"Oh, Zain," she said, tears stinging her eyes. He was bad; she knew that. The bridge was moving too slow, and she didn't know how she was going to activate the lift alone. How was she going to do this?

Then he groaned in pain and renewed resolve settled over her. He needed her and she wasn't going to let him down, no matter what it took. The top of the platform was in sight and she pulled out her pistol. No one was going to stop her from getting him to the ship. She held her weapon ready as the bridge clicked into the edge of the platform. It was empty except for Pio and two of his *krudo* friends.

"You back," Pio chirped.

She grabbed the handle of the sled and pulled Zain off the bridge toward the lift. "You have no idea how happy I am to see you and your many legs. How'd you get down here?"

"We play," he responded. "You play, too?"

"Maybe later," she said with a shake of her head. "Right now, I need you to take us up." She positioned the sled so that it and Zain were within the circle, and knelt to hold him in place. Pio sprang to the controls while the other *krudo* stayed below, and the lift rose into the darkness. Lacey laid her head on Zain's hot body. He was burning up.

Just a little longer, Zain. We're almost there.

Chapter Seventeen

The *krudo* helped her get Zain into the ship and onto his bunk on his stomach. Reene had been grilling her with questions since she set foot in the door, but she was too exhausted to give him any more than the basics. The last thing she felt like doing was reliving the past few hours in graphic detail. Besides, she had other priorities.

Oliver was perched next to Zain, looking as worried as a cat could get. Pio bobbed on the front console. "Zain broken?"

Lacey swallowed the painful lump in her throat. "Yes."

"You fix?"

She stared at Zain's bleeding body. She'd never performed first aid on anyone who was in serious trouble, let alone half-dead. "I'm going to try. Tell me what to do, Reene."

187

"You will require the medkit," the computer said in his monotone voice. Forcing herself to remain calm, Lacey pawed through Zain's pack until she found the box, then dumped the contents on the bunk next to him. His face was gray and his breathing shallow.

"He's not going to make it," she said.

"Unroll the black film and position it above Zain's back," Reene told her.

Her hands shook as she stretched the film. Almost immediately, it displayed statistics, layers of skin, muscle, bones, organs, and three darts embedded about an inch deep.

"He has sustained injury to epidermis and muscle. However, the biggest danger is the toxin," Reene said with maddening composure.

Lacey looked up at the ceiling. "Toxin? How do you know that?"

"The med-vid film is feeding Zain's vital statistics to me. Please retrieve the green cylinder marked 'ZAX-1342' from the kit."

She sorted through thirty slender vials and held up the correct one. At least, she hoped so. God, what if she did this wrong? If he died, she'd never forgive herself. If he survived, she was going to smack him for being such a hardhead and not listening to her in the first place.

"Got it," she said. "Now what?"

"Snap the vial in the center and press one of the ends to Zain's neck."

She did that and watched as the contents of the vial drained into his skin.

"How long before it works?" she asked, holding her fingers against the slow pulse in his neck.

"If the poison has not entirely penetrated his organs, it will work within ten minutes."

She frowned. "And what if it has affected the organs?"

"Then it will not work at all."

Lacey closed her eyes. She couldn't think about it. She had to believe in Zain's strength and his damn stubbornness.

"What about the darts?"

"The tips are barbed, which will cause additional harm to Zain. However, they must be removed."

"Easy for you to say."

"He is unconscious at present. It will be much more difficult when he regains consciousness."

Lacey looked at Zain's peaceful upturned face and knew Reene was right. She had to do it now. If she couldn't get them out, no one would.

Reene continued, "You must wear gloves. The darts are saturated with toxins."

Lacey donned gloves from the kit and took a deep breath. She wrapped her fingers around the end of one dart and slowly pulled out the one-inch cone-shaped plug—along with a healthy chunk of flesh. Blood welled up from the wound. It was all she could do to not pass out. Luckily, Zain didn't move. She removed the others as quickly as possible.

"Discard his shirt," Reene said. "Then swab the puncture wounds with a disinfectant towel. Attach the pads marked Aritrox to the wounds."

Lacey ripped Zain's shirt open and tugged it off his body. "What's Aritrox?"

"A healing accelerant. It uses the body's natural abilities and enhances them. Most effective."

Lacey used a towel to sop up the blood, and applied the pads. Red soaked through them in seconds.

"Now what?" she asked, steadying herself against the bunk.

"We wait."

And pray, she added silently. She glanced out the ship's viewport at the setting sun. Another exciting night in Death Valley. "Are the perimeter alarms on?"

"Affirmative."

"And you have guns."

"Yes."

"Guns are good. I can't believe I just said that." She put her palm on Zain's forehead. The heat was fading and his color looked better. Lacey walked over and collapsed in her chair. She laid her head back to rest.

"Space sucks," she murmured. Playing Warrior Programmer was definitely not all it was cracked up to be. She was tired and scared and shaking from her ride to hell and back. She wanted some answers and, dammit, the computer was going to talk.

"I think it's time you gave me a crash course in InterGlax, Reene. Who are they? What do they do? And how was Zain mixed up with them?"

"I am not sure that I can provide that information. Earthlings are not cleared at that level."

She blew a hair off her face, which was about all

she had energy for. "I think it's a little late to be worrying about the prime directive, Reene."

"Pardon?"

She sighed. "I promise I won't breathe a word of this to another Earthling as long as I live. Granted, that may not be long at the rate I'm going. Besides, if I told anyone about this adventure, I'd be locked up. I just want to know what's going on."

After a moment, he replied, "InterGlax works for the Cartel of Interior Territories, also know as CinTerr, which oversees the political, economic, and humanitarian aspects of the consortium of planetary nations. Once a planet achieves manned space travel outside their solar system, they will be officially welcomed into the cartel and allowed to send a representative to speak on their behalf. Until then, planets are categorized as a juvenile systems under the blanket protection of CinTerr."

"Juvenile," she repeated. "Like Earth?"

"Correct."

She shook her head. This conversation was too bizarre for words. "If Earth is still a juvenile, why do we need CinTerr's protection?"

"From rogue invaders."

She lifted her head. "Good God. Are you serious? You mean like *Independence Day*?"

"The galaxy is full of danger."

"Tell me about it." She ran a hand through her disaster of a bad hair day and finally gave up. "How does InterGlax fit in?"

"InterGlax is the enforcement organization used by

CinTerr. They implement CinTerr policies for member systems and protect juvenile systems."

"Yeah well, I don't think InterGlax is doing a very good job. They were attacking those people."

Reene hesitated. "Please explain."

Lacey stared out into the night sky. "We rode inside one of the shippers through the portal. Our shipper contained an InterGlax fighter drone. So did all the others. When we arrived, the shippers opened and the fighters attacked. I'm pretty sure it was an ambush." She swallowed. "I think a lot of people died."

Reene replied, "That does not sound like Inter-Glax."

"Maybe InterGlax has changed," she said, recalling Zain's comment about InterGlax not always being the good guys. "How long was Zain with them?"

"Zain was an advance scout for over ten years. He followed the cartographers after they mapped each sector and collected military intelligence on the planets for CinTerr. Then CinTerr would categorize the planet."

"He told me that InterGlax wants him for the murder of his partner," she stated.

"That is correct," Reene replied. "There are also independent bounty hunters and assassins who would be rewarded for his capture or death."

She nodded. So Zain was completely alone, isolated, and one step ahead of the people hunting him. An outlaw. It all made sense. His aversion to InterGlax, his solitary lifestyle, and maybe even the nightmares. She wished he'd trusted her enough to tell her before. Of course, being an accused murderer didn't generally come up in casual conversation. She thought about asking Reene if Zain actually killed his last partner, but she wanted those answers from Zain.

She cast a glance to where he lay. The shadow of a beard wrapped around his square jaw and lips. Sadness swept over her at all the living he was missing on the lam. How many times a day did he look over his shoulder?

She stood up and walked over to check him. His head felt much cooler and his breathing steady. Beneath the Aritrox patches, the wounds on his back had stopped bleeding.

"Will he be okay?" she asked Reene.

"Please apply the med-vid film."

Lacey rolled out the film and waited.

"He will be fully recovered in approximately eight hours," Reene replied. "You did mighty fine."

She smiled at the irony of a computer's praise. Zain's mouth twitched, his color getting better with every passing minute. He'd survived near-death, probably an experience he was used to. She wasn't.

He had taken a huge risk, leaving the shipper to check out the action. She hadn't thought he'd make it back once the shooting began, hadn't thought she'd ever see him again. And in those moments when her life lay suspended, she'd experienced anger that he'd put himself at risk and frustration for the whole damn mess she was in. But mostly, she had been scared. Not like the paralyzing fear of heights or going through the portal. This was worse and far more dangerous.

She wanted nothing more than to see his dark eyes open and to hear his voice again. He had become more than her ticket home. Much more. Despite his stubbornness and taste for death-defying missions, she had grown to care about him. Maybe because he cared about her.

In fact, for the first time in her life, she felt like she could do almost anything. Maybe even love. And it wasn't that she didn't want to love. It just took too much out of her and there was so little left as it was. How much more of herself could she afford to lose?

But even as she reminded herself that she had a life back home to rebuild, her heart was doing a little dance. She was hopeless. Apparently, her heart would never learn, never realize how much its mistakes cost the rest of her. She reached out and brushed hair from Zain's face.

New Year's Resolution #8: Do not fall in love with the alien.

Zain awoke with a start, the unwelcome effects of Aritrox resurrecting recent events. As he forced his eyes to focus, he realized he was aboard his ship. The bunk felt warm and comfortable under his belly. There was a soft furry weight against his shoulder that must be Oliver. He lifted his head and spotted Lacey asleep in her chair. She was safe.

"Reene?" he rasped.

"Yes, sir. How do you feel?"

"I hate Aritrox," he grumbled, laying his head back down.

Reene replied, "I am well aware of that, sir. However, you had significant wounds to your body which required immediate treatment."

Zain moved Oliver gently and rolled over on his back with some difficulty. His head took a while to register the change of position and he had to close his eyes to keep from spinning. He hated drugs. They robbed him of his control, leaving him at the mercy of his emotions. No way for a warrior to be.

"Zain?"

Lacey. Immediately, his unchecked body reacted to her voice and raw sexual energy swept over him. All it took was his name on her lips.

He opened his eyes to see her hovering over him. Black hair hung soft around her face. Blue, almond-shaped eyes focused on him and him alone. She cared about him. Still. Even after he'd told her about being a killer.

Gentle hands stroked his face. His mind registered her presence but his body registered her touch. *No,* he thought. Don't come closer. It's not safe.

"Don't," he pleaded, the word torn from his soul. She didn't have any idea what she was doing to him.

Her hand stilled for a moment, and she studied him intently. Then to his utter surprise, she leaned down and kissed him. He took her softness and gentleness as it lingered on his lips after she pulled away. In her compassionate eyes, he saw promise and hope and everything he'd longed for in the past few years. If he could capture it just once . . .

Years of loneliness and solitude rushed back over

him, feeding a fire he knew he had no way of controlling. All the hopes he'd pushed away, all the things he'd been denied . . . Just once, he would like to take hold of one dream and run with it. But if he touched her, he would make her his. There would be no saving her. Desire and desperation mingled in a volatile brew through his blood. Unaware of the danger, Lacey smiled.

"I need you," he said in a harsh whisper.

She blinked at him. "Need me to what?"

Her scent swirled around him, goading him on. He clenched his fists, grappling for control he knew he didn't have. All he could think about was her skin next to his, the freedom she could give him, and the hunger that would not be satisfied without her.

"Touch me," he said, half out of his mind with need.

She gasped a little and stepped back, looking over his body before settling her gaze on his pants. Her eyes widened, and he cursed himself. He couldn't control his reaction to her, even if he tried. The Aritrox had exposed his most primal desire and she'd be wise to run, leaving him alone in his selfishness. It had killed Crista. It was bound to ruin Lacey too.

He closed his eyes and let the Aritrox play inside his head. Thoughts merged and scattered with every breath, refusing to follow orders to behave. Despite his best efforts, his body thrummed with unbridled anticipation, and the ache in his groin was becoming damn annoying.

"You'll have to move over," he heard through his

drugged haze. He opened his eyes and focused on her face. She was back. Why?

She nudged his shoulder. "Move it, cowboy."

He shook his head, finally understanding what she was doing. *No.* He was too out of control and too hot. He didn't want to hurt her with his raging need.

"Don't," he said, managing to conjure the word past his body's impatience.

She crossed her arms under her breasts. "Tell me you don't want me."

He swallowed. Impossible. His body could no more deny it than his mind. But she deserved better, a man who would stay and take care of her. A man she could trust to never destroy her. All he could give her was more danger. Reality filled his mind. If InterGlax found them . . .

"No."

"That's what I thought," she said. Then she drew a deliberate breath and pulled off her tank top.

All the air escaped his lungs in one long, unsteady whoosh. For a moment, he thought he was imagining her beautiful breasts—small and round with dark nipples that beckoned him. Then she slid her pants down and he groaned, his erection becoming torturous even through the painkiller. She had no idea what she was offering him. He should tell her he couldn't accept, right now. But as his gaze swept over her flared hips to the part of her that promised him ecstasy, he realized it was too late. He wasn't giving up this one chance. Hell would still be there tomorrow.

She climbed onto the bunk, straddling his aching

body with hers. Her eyes were dark with desire as she skimmed his lips with hers. Soft fingertips traced his bare chest, exploring and tormenting.

He wanted to tuck her small body beneath his and take her properly, but unfortunately the only part of him paying attention was trapped inside his pants. He ran his drug-clumsy hands up her thighs and sleek skin. She was perfect, just like he knew she'd be. Up over her hips his hands slid, before spanning her waist and cupping her breasts. She took a quick breath as he found her nipples and rolled them gently between his fingers.

He had the strangest urge to say "mine."

She froze, her lips still touching his, while her breath shuddered. His fingers traced the sweet globes that fit impeccably into his palms. He guided one taut nipple to his mouth and wrapped his lips around the tip. He flicked it with his tongue, drawing a long "oh" from her.

"Beautiful," he whispered against her breast. Then his hand slid lower until he reached between her thighs and the fine black hair there. He felt her stiffen as his fingers found her nub and the soft, slick folds around it, parting them with fierce concentration and care.

Lacey's eyes fluttered open, her gaze locking on his. He used the pad of his fingers to press, rub, and circle. He watched her reaction in humble wonder. Her red lips parted and her eyes closed. A soft moan dragged itself from her, and her expression turned positively angelic. Satisfaction swept over him, assuaging his own rampant desire. He could do this to her, bring her such pleasure.

With every stroke, he felt the change in her body and the way she focused on the sensation and the moment. Her face was a veil of awe and agony. He waited, mesmerized by her journey, and driven by her passion. She drew a frantic breath, than another, muscles rigid and her face grimacing. A slow growl emanated from deep in her throat, and she climaxed in waves. Her face and breasts flushed as a look of absolute bliss rolled over her. Gratification swept through Zain, more powerful than any orgasm he'd ever had.

When she couldn't take any more, she collapsed on him. He could feel the shudder of her breath as she relaxed in his arms.

"I'm hurting you," she whispered moments later, and pushed herself off his chest. But he pulled her back down, pressing her breasts to his bare skin.

"Not even close," he said. She sighed against him, and he smiled. He knew he would never tire of watching her climax. He ran his hands down her back and over curved buttocks. Silky skin flowed under his fingers, and he lost himself in the sensation. With a quick move, she rolled her hips against him, mercilessly reminding him that he was uncontrollably aroused.

"Lacey," he growled.

"What happened to 'don't'?" She ground her hips against him again and he forgot what he was trying to say.

"It's been too long," he whispered. "I'm not good for you."

"How long?" she asked, nibbling his lips as if it didn't matter what he said.

"Years."

She pulled back abruptly and looked down at him with a deep frown. "How many?"

He licked his lips to get a taste of her. "Three."

Astonishment lit her face. "You haven't had sex in three years? My God. That's not healthy, Zain. You could—"

He pressed a finger to her lips. "I appreciate your concern but really, can we just—"

She shook her head. "Why so long? I know women must throw themselves at you on a regular basis."

He smiled, ruefully. "My choice. I have my reasons."

"What? Do you have a disease? Saving yourself for marriage?" She glanced down at his pants. "Sexual deformity?"

He gave a chuckle. "No, no, and thank God, no. Other reasons."

Her blue eyes darkened, filled with concern or pity. He didn't need the pity. Lack of sex hadn't killed him. Yet.

"InterGlax," she realized. "I'm sorry, Zain."

She knew, and yet she still wanted him. It humbled him beyond any reasonable thought. Then she kissed him, and his body grew harder. InterGlax was abruptly forgotten in a tangle of tongues and bodies.

"Let me in, Zain," she murmured against his

mouth. In his muzzy, unfocused brain, he still realized that Lacey might not be talking about sex. But he didn't care anymore. His mind was singularly focused.

He felt her hand on his pants, over his erection, fumbling with the unfamiliar clasp before slipping inside and driving him insane.

Aritrox didn't dull the rush of savage hunger he felt when she wrapped her warm hand around him and squeezed gently. He closed his eyes, lost. She pushed the fabric down his legs. Once he was free of the suffocating pants, her fingertips strummed his length, exploring him the way he'd just explored her. He arched his hips. He needed more, needed to drive himself into her and ruin them both.

His body screamed in frustration as he tried to roll her over. But his heavy muscles refused to obey, and all he could do was drag her over his tortured body. He uttered an incoherent curse. Damn the Aritrox.

"Relax," Lacey said. Zain opened his eyes to find her face inches from his, over him. She licked her lips, her concentration complete, and with one hand, she guided him into her.

Impossibly soft heat slid down his length in a tight sheath. Two ragged groans filled the space between them.

"So good," he murmured, and kissed her parted lips. She nipped back as she lifted off him and then sank down again. Instinct drove his hips up, meeting her with a low, guttural growl. *More.* He gripped her hips and drove up into her again. He had to satisfy the need she instilled so effortlessly in him. Let her see the monster he could become; he didn't care anymore.

Hunger took him and fed his frenzied pace as he claimed her time and again. He could hear her gasps and feel her nails digging into his flesh with each powerful thrust. Sweet release taunted him and toyed with the scrap of control he held on to, but the battle was already lost.

A great roar built in his throat, her only warning, and with one last lunge, he surged into Lacey and let loose the animal. Each pulse ripped away at him in a release so great, it stripped him of everything—leaving precious peace, ultimate freedom.

Chapter Eighteen

T minus two days and counting . . .

Schuler stepped through the personal portal that connected his home office on Kree to the heart of his clandestine operations center on the planet of Avakur. The ops center bustled with activity appropriate for the epic event about to take the galaxy by surprise.

In the middle of the room, a floor-to-ceiling holodeck revealed his current progress in the quadrant. Red regions were under CinTerr's domain. The green dots now belonged to him: young planets he'd harvested from under CinTerr's noses. Each represented a political victory and economic bonanza, and further eroded CinTerr's solidarity. Locations in yellow were Schuler's next targets—or opportunities, as he preferred to call them. By this time next cycle, they would all belong to him.

Behind him, he heard, "Welcome."

Schuler turned to his ops chief, Everard. Short-statured and slight, Everard nonetheless commanded the ops base with reasonable competence. At least, he would until Schuler found someone better to replace him. "Everything seems under control, as usual," Schuler told the man.

Everard grinned proudly. "Of course. We are proceeding on schedule. Two days and counting. Are there any new developments at InterGlax I should be aware of?"

Schuler shook his head and stared into the hologrid. "CinTerr continues to badger InterGlax to stop the"—he smiled at Everard—"criminals who are soiling their name."

Everard frowned. "Will they increase their efforts to locate us? Perhaps we should postpone our activities for a bit?"

Schuler replied, "InterGlax is more interested in pointing fingers and keeping their high-paid, low-effort jobs. Random attacks continue to take InterGlax off guard and keep the pressure on CinTerr. I want to make sure every installation is running perfectly before the final assault."

Everard continued to look worried. "Won't they become suspicious of Avakur when we send the teams in after the strike?"

"No," Schuler said. "Over the years, I've made sure they see the Avakurians as simply harmless opportunists. Besides, InterGlax will be a nonissue after we hit every juvenile planet in the sector. Are all the installations tested?"

"We are running through final tests now," Everard said. "Minor issues, but we will be ready."

Schuler nodded. He didn't like surprises. "Where is Ferretu?"

Everard shifted uncomfortably. "He has been working on an assignment in his quarters." He hesitated and then added sullenly, "I have difficulty getting regular status reports from him."

"He isn't military," Schuler noted. "But don't worry. I have him working on a special project." A location inside the grid caught Schuler's attention. "Why is Installation 93 flashing?"

Everard stepped up next to him. "The defense system activated several days ago. We investigated, but the planet was experiencing a sandstorm. There was no problem inside the installation itself. I believe it was simply a misfire incident."

"The installation is fully operational?"

"Yes, sir. We have a reoccurring problem with the indigenous wildlife. However, they cause no real destruction and are simply a nuisance. I occasionally send a squad in to eradicate them."

Schuler watched the marker silently flash.

"You don't really believe anyone could bypass our security?" Everard asked, incredulously.

"If anyone discovers one of our installations, the entire operation will be in jeopardy."

Everard laughed. "Impossible. No one has ever survived the first laser attack. It is inescapable."

Schuler stared at the flashing light. "There's a first time for everything."

Lacey woke up, sprawled on top of Zain like a wanton woman as he slept. It occurred to her vaguely that he didn't need her weight on his injuries, although they hadn't seemed to slow him down. But she rolled off him anyway, her tender muscles protesting enough to remind her just how much fun it was to be wanton.

Zain shifted a little, and she slipped down into the narrow space, trapped between him and the wall. She closed her eyes. What had she done? If only he hadn't sounded so damn desperate, and she hadn't been so happy to see him awake again. Right. That was her excuse and she was sticking to it.

Okay, so the sex was best she'd ever had—and the best she would probably ever have in her life. That was still no reason for throwing herself at him. Even if he was gorgeous and beyond sexy, to say nothing of his extra-extraterrestrial physique.

She rested her cheek against his thick bicep. Who was she kidding? She was in major trouble if she couldn't control the self-destruct side of her brain, the one that couldn't say no to a man she cared deeply about.

And she did. She'd never felt like this for anyone before. She'd put it all on the line for Zain last night, and she'd do it again. He wouldn't even have to ask. So here she was—knowing it was a mistake and knowing she'd do it all over again. A hell of a place for a woman to be.

There was small meow, and she peered over a sleeping Zain's chest. Oliver blinked at her in the darkness.

"Don't look at me like that. I know what I'm doing. Mostly," she added, pushing herself up on one arm. Zain's big, naked body sprawled out, nearly filling the bunk without a hint of modesty or self-consciousness. He was beautiful, from his close beard to his powerful barrel chest, to his long, muscular legs and everything in between. No wonder she couldn't resist him. Her gaze returned to his tempting lips.

She moaned at the sudden stampede of heat to every pore of her body. Robert had never affected her like this, not even in the beginning. Sex with him had always felt carefully choreographed, as if he were performing for a crowd. It made her feel as if she were playing a part in his movie. And like a good director, he'd been the first one to tell her when she miscued.

Zain's lovemaking had been wild and careless and very real. He didn't hold anything back—no games, no analysis, and there was definitely no stopping him. Then her eyes widened as she remembered something really, really important: *Birth control*. She glanced over his body and perished the hopeful thought that he might not be potent.

"Damn," she whispered, and buried her face in her hands. What if she were pregnant? It was a complication she didn't even want to think about. The chances were slim, but the way things were going . . .

Zain turned his head and mumbled something semicoherent. It sounded like a name. His hands flailed a little.

"Zain, are you all right?" she asked, fearing his horrible nightmares.

"Crista," he murmured.

She listened to the very female-sounding name. Crista? Zain's body jerked and he said it again, more urgently this time and much clearer. Then he calmed down and relaxed.

Oh, great, she thought. As if she hadn't already done enough damage on her own, he was talking about another woman. Freud was right. All man's problems *did* stem from sex.

She glared at Zain sleeping peacefully with another woman on his mind. Maybe she could drug him again. Probably not an option, unfortunately. Escape seemed like the only viable choice. So, very slowly and very carefully, she stretched out over him to reach the other side of the bunk. With one hand down, she lifted her leg over him. If she could just sneak . . .

"Where are you going?"

Straddling him on all fours with her butt in the air, she froze. His heavy eyes opened slowly to meet hers. *Caught.*

"Um . . . lav?" She pulled the old escape-to-the-bathroom trick.

His dark eyes narrowed, banked fire behind them.

"I really have to go," she added, just to make sure he wouldn't try to talk her out of it or sidetrack her with sex—because that would probably work. Then she scrambled over him and off the bunk. Snatching her clothes from the floor, she hugged them to her body and scooted into the lav. The door shut, saving her from herself.

She was in trouble. Besides the whole baby thing, getting involved with another man was not what she wanted or needed. Especially a man destined to break her heart in ways she probably couldn't even fathom. And he would, too. She was already in deeper than she'd ever been with Robert. She'd thought it hurt when *he* left.

She rubbed her forehead. If she didn't stop right now, there would be nothing left to rebuild from. She couldn't handle another rejection, and she knew that would happen eventually. Zain would see that she was just ordinary. Look at his life with its technology and exploration and space travel—what chance did a mousy little computer geek have against all that? She couldn't even keep Robert happy on her own planet.

No, sooner or later Zain would get bored with her . . .

She stopped. What was she thinking? There *was* no relationship. He hadn't asked for one. They hadn't talked about one. She was going back home. He was exploring the galaxy and obsessed with some woman named Crista.

So it had just been sex. Fine. She could do sex. Not that she was doing it again. Once was enough to wreck complete havoc on an existence she was trying to make havoc-proof. She didn't need any more help with the slow crash-and-burn she called her life.

She yanked on her clothes. No, if she wanted to survive this brave new world, her head was in charge and her heart would have no say in the matter.

But who the hell was Crista?

Zain watched her run. It was pretty obvious by her quick retreat that she wasn't happy about last night. He tried to tell himself it didn't matter; she was heading home, he was a fugitive, and neither one of them was ready for anything more serious than trying to figure out which new sexual positions to try. Not that that wasn't an excellent idea.

He sat up on his bunk and shook off the spins, courtesy of the Aritrox. On his back, he felt the patches Lacey must have applied last night. Reaching around, he pulled them off and checked his wounds. They were healing nicely, thanks to her. Now that he could think straight again, he wondered how she'd managed to get him up into the ship and on his bunk.

But mostly he wondered why she'd given herself to him. He tried to remember the few words that passed between them before he'd lost control of his body and mind. Soft skin, euphoric release, sweet kisses. The exercise only reminded him how much he wanted her again.

Besides, dawn was breaking outside. It was time to get off this damn planet once and for all. He slid off the bunk and walked past the lav to the back room.

"Reene?"

"Good morning, sir. Would you like me to run a status check on you?"

Zain pulled clean clothes from the wall cabinet. "No, thanks. I feel fine." In fact, he realized he hadn't felt this good in years, despite the remnants of an Aritrox haze. It was amazing what a little mind-blowing sex could do for a man.

He was adding "make love to Lacey" to his priority list. It might even top it.

He glanced at the lav door. Was she ever coming out?

"What planet were we teleported to yesterday, Reene?"

"Maadiar. 135-1-2 Sector, Quadrant D-12. You were gone approximately eighty-nine minutes. What transpired there?"

Zain tossed a shirt over his shoulder and winced at the stab of pain. "InterGlax launched a hell of an attack, that's what happened."

"Yes, Lacey conveyed that to me. However, that is not consistent with InterGlax's policies. I have also determined that the facility below us is not listed in InterGlax files."

"I'm not surprised." Zain pulled on his pants, then asked, "What else did you and Lacey talk about?"

"She asked about InterGlax and your role with them."

He pursed his lips. "And what did you tell her?"

"I explained CinTerr and InterGlax's functions, as well as your former position with InterGlax. I deferred all other questions to you."

Zain nodded. "Good. Scan intelligence reports for Maadiar. I want to know exactly who was hit and why. And check the archives for similar attacks on any of the planets you matched using Lacey's data."

"Are we going to investigate this matter?"

"No. I just want to know how big this op is." And how far he'd have to go to get away from it.

"Yes, sir. It will take some time. I am still not up to full capacity."

"Power cells are first on my to-do list." He glanced at the closed lav door. "Maybe second."

Reene added, "Communications have been reestablished. A message is waiting for you, sir. It is from Rayce Coburne."

"Audio only. Go."

Rayce's voice came over the comm. "Where the hell are you?" Zain smiled at Rayce's opening.

The message played on. "I get half an emergency message from Reene and then nothing. Something about you being stranded on a planet, but no location, no information, and no damn explanation."

This from the man who took more chances than anyone else Zain knew.

"Then I get no reply from you and no reply from Torrie. Anyone ever tell you that your family has a serious communication problem?"

Zain frowned. Where was Torrie?

Rayce continued, "I know you are up to something big and bad when you won't even zap me a clip. If you're off having fun and didn't invite me, I'm going to be mighty pissed. Contact me. I hate to lose a good gun. Besides, if you don't, Torrie won't be the only one looking for you. Out."

Reene asked, "Would you like to reply, sir?"

"No," Zain decided. Especially now. The last thing

he wanted was to bring anyone else into this nightmare. He was still trying to figure out how to get rid of Lacey. Sort of.

"Any contact from Torrie lately?"

"She has been pinging us for the past several days, but nothing in the last twelve hours."

That wasn't good. As much as he loved his sister, she could get into trouble faster than . . . well, than he could. Which was already fast enough. He took a deep breath. He had to know if she was alright.

"Ping her," Zain said. "See if you get a response."

"Sir, I cannot guarantee that the ping won't be traced back to this location."

He nodded. "I know. I'm counting on being out of here before anyone can do so."

"Yes, sir." There were a few seconds of silence before Reene came back. "I have issued a ping. No response yet."

"Keep polling and let me know." He headed to the front of the ship and stopped at the lav door. No singing, no sound. He tapped the door. "Lacey?"

"What?" she snapped on the other side.

He raised an eyebrow. "Are you all right?"

"I'm fine."

He crossed his arms and stared at the door. "You don't sound fine. Open the door."

"No."

"Well, I'm not moving from this spot until you open this damn door." He grinned at the exact same conversation they'd had their first night together.

The door slid out of the way and Lacey's defiant

face appeared. She was also fully dressed, much to his disappointment.

"Happy?" she said crisply.

He pursed his lips. "I guess you don't want to talk about last night."

She blinked a few times. "There's nothing talk about. I was simply curious about your . . ." She paused. "DNA."

A slow smile crossed his face. "I see. So how does it measure up?"

She blushed and then pushed by him. "It's the same as any other human male."

He eyed her as she sat in her chair. He knew he wasn't much help last night but he couldn't have been *that* bad. Next time, he'd get it right. Then he noted her scowl. Assuming there was a next time.

To his surprise, she accessed the system stats and was studying them as they scrolled up the panel. "How did you learn to do that?" he asked, sliding into his seat.

"Reene showed me the ropes while you were out," she answered without looking at him. "I figured you wouldn't, being a control freak and all."

He studied her rigid profile. "Thank you for getting me back to the ship."

She nodded stiffly. "No problem."

"Especially over that bridge."

Her gaze swung to his, and a flicker of trepidation flashed in her eyes. He knew how terrified she was of that bridge, and she had somehow done it alone. She shouldn't have had to. He was supposed to protect her, not the other way around.

"I'm sorry you had to manage it alone. But I'm not going to apologize for the sex. I realize that I wasn't exactly in good condition last night, but you are the one who jumped me."

"You started it," she muttered.

He smirked. "You could have just said *no*."

She was quiet for a minute. "I know. It's not your fault, it's mine."

"That makes me feel a whole lot better," he grumbled and accessed his own side of the control panel. Apparently, a next time was officially out of the question.

"It was fine," she said softly.

He glanced at her. "What?"

She cleared her throat. "I said, the sex was fine."

"*Fine?*" he repeated. "Just what every man wants to hear. Why don't we talk about something else while I still have some of my ego intact." He hammered at the console. "You have that information yet, Reene?"

"My search is nearly complete."

"I didn't mean that in a bad way," Lacey countered, sounding a bit indignant.

" 'Fine' is not how I'd like to categorize my lovemaking skills. In fact, 'fine' isn't how I'd like to categorize anything I ever do again in my life."

She threw up her hands. "Okay, how about 'great'? Is your ego satisfied with 'great'?"

He turned to face her. "My ego would be a lot happier if you said, 'Zain, take me to bed again.' "

Her eyes grew wide, and he could see panic.

"I can't do that," she said.

"That's what I thought," he said and turned back to the computer. "You can save me anytime now, Reene."

"Working."

Lacey shifted next to him in a vacuum of silence and then said, "Just how compatible do you think our DNA is, Zain?"

He muttered, "Very, even if you aren't impressed."

"So, I could be pregnant," she said in a wisp of a voice.

His gaze shot to hers. Her face was drawn and distinctly worried. Like being pregnant by him would be such a bad thing.

"I was sterilized shortly after I joined InterGlax."

Horror registered on her face as she focused on him. "Oh, my God. Did InterGlax make you?"

"It was voluntary. My choice."

She shook her head, looking appalled. "Why would you do that? Don't you want children?"

He shrugged. "I was young. The thought of being trapped in a relationship with a mate and children was a fate worse than living with my parents again." He looked hard at her. "So don't worry. You are safe from bearing my children—unless I get it reversed. But why would I do that?"

She regarded him with disbelief, and something like sympathy. As if his ego wasn't battered enough.

"As soon as Reene gives me some information, I'm heading below to pick up the other power cells. Once they are installed, the VirtuWav will be operable and you can go home," he told her. There. That should make her day.

Her eyes lit with interest. "What information?"

He realized with a flicker of hope that she hadn't reacted to the going-home part. "Who IG hit, and why."

Reene chimed in. "My search is complete, sir. Would you like the results?"

Zain kept his gaze on Lacey. "Go."

"Intercepted communications from their planet confirm your report. I also have found reports of random attacks on several planets in this sector that match the coordinates from the dome. In all cases, attacks were unprovoked, deadly, and swift. The planets targeted were juveniles, and could not immediately identify their assailants. However, the execution is identical to your description of the attack on Maadiar."

Zain told him, "Bring up the star map of this sector and mark the systems that InterGlax has attacked."

A grid appeared on his console, spun, locked, and a hundred or so stars illuminated. He hadn't expected so many and so close. Zain studied the map with growing unease. They were sitting right in the middle of InterGlax's operation. "Show me the juvenile planets identified on the dome that have not been attacked."

Hundreds more stars flashed on.

Lacey said, "I don't get it. Why is InterGlax attacking all these people?"

He shook his head. "I've never seen InterGlax work this way. They are not aggressors." He leaned on the console. "Reene, what kind of contact does InterGlax have with the planets they attack?"

"None. In all cases, the Avakurians have invariably come to the planet's aid, offering assistance, trade, and protection from InterGlax—for a substantial fee."

Disgusted, Zain said, "I'll bet. Since when have the Avakurians ever been humanitarians?"

"I'm lost," Lacey said. "Who are they?"

Zain crossed his arms. "Trade-mongers from the planet Avakur. Mostly pirates and thieves. They are known to sell their own family members for the right amount of credits. The last people you want making first contact with a juvenile system."

"They don't belong to CinTerr?" she asked.

"No, they quit about sixteen years ago. Didn't like anyone giving them rules to follow. Planets are not required to join CinTerr. But the fewer planets who participate, the weaker the cartel becomes."

He asked Reene, "Where is CinTerr during all these attacks?"

"By the time CinTerr discovers that the Avakurians have made contact, it is too late. Avakur has already secured their place. And once the juvenile finds out InterGlax works for CinTerr, they decline membership."

"That must be making CinTerr pretty ticked off," Zain noted.

"Yes, sir. In fact, there is significant friction between InterGlax and CinTerr at present. InterGlax denies any involvement, of course."

The pieces made no sense. Why would InterGlax jeopardize their relationship with CinTerr? It would be professional suicide. Both organizations needed each other.

"Earth," he heard Lacey whisper next to him. He turned to find her staring at the dome, her expression etched with horror.

"Reene," she said softly. "Is Earth a coordinate in the dome?"

"Affirmative."

Zain closed his eyes. Damn.

"Earth is a target," she uttered.

He pursed his lips. "Perhaps at some point. There are a thousand targets here. Chances are slim. Just because they have coordinates, doesn't mean Earth is in danger."

She swung around to face him. "Bullshit. You know damn well it's only a matter of time before they hit Earth. I saw the circle on Maadiar; just like Earth's. Another henge. That's a portal receptor. They will come right through Stonehenge in England."

"Earth has weapons," he reminded her.

"We don't have anything that can handle surprise attacks like the one we witnessed. Earth is fragile enough as it is. An alien attack would cause mass hysteria." She crossed her arms. "You are so worried about protecting me? Then you better save me from InterGlax, because if you don't, my planet is going to end up just like Maadiar. This is your organization—

you know how they work. Figure out a way to stop them."

As if it were that simple, he thought. He gave her a hard look. "Do you have any idea how big InterGlax is? How much territory they cover? Hundreds of thousands of operatives. Thousands of stations. Millions of weapons. What would you have me do? Walk in there and ask them to please cease and desist?" he asked. "How far in the door do think I'd get?"

"*We*," she corrected him. "I'm in this too. It's my planet."

A growl rumbled from his gut. He'd love nothing more than to bring InterGlax to its knees. But he wouldn't sacrifice Lacey to do it. "Then, if InterGlax catches us, *we're* as good as dead."

"Then we won't let them catch us," she countered.

He shook his head. He could foresee a future of never winning an argument again.

She pointed through the viewport. "You can't let InterGlax continue to terrorize the galaxy. Innocent people are dying. I know you don't want that. You hate InterGlax for doing this. So for once, stick around and give it a shot."

He scowled. "I tried to play the hero before. It didn't work."

"Yes, but you were missing one important component."

He eyed her. "And what would that be?"

She raised her chin defiantly. "Me."

He couldn't help it, he laughed. "Lacey, even if I had an army at my disposal, there is no way to stop

220

IG, no one to report them to, and no way to get evidence against them—especially with an op like this. This station is totally automated and virtually untraceable. I tried once to find answers to questions I shouldn't have been asking and it got my partner killed in a swamp." He finished with a snarl.

"So you didn't kill him," she said, not looking the least surprised.

He raked a hand through his hair. "I may as well have. It was my fault. I was the senior officer. I should have followed protocol and waited for backup. We walked right into their trap. They set us up, ambushed us, and left us for dead."

"How did you get out?" she asked.

"I called a couple of friends who are very good at sneaking around. They airlifted me. By the time I was conscious and healthy enough to contact InterGlax with my report, I discovered they had issued a warrant for my arrest—for murdering Crista."

Lacey's eyes widened. "Crista was your wife?"

Pain tightened his face. "My scouting partner."

"And more?" she asked.

He turned his eyes to her. "Does it make any difference? I couldn't save her."

"The nightmares."

He nodded. "I deserve whatever nightmares I get, Lacey. In case you hadn't noticed, I'm not the safest person to spend time with."

She lifted her chin. "Maybe so, but I'm not going anywhere until we figure out a way to stop InterGlax from attacking my planet. I suggest you start thinking about it."

Chapter Nineteen

New Year's Resolution #9: Do not volunteer to save Earth again.

Okay, so maybe it wasn't the smartest thing she'd ever done, but what was she to do? Earth might be a mess, it might have a lot of problems, but it was her home and she wasn't about to hand it over to greedy extraterrestrials. It would be like handing Tombstone over to Johnny Ringo and his gang. Not on her watch, even if it meant her career went down the toilet.

She shoved aside the frustration and swallowed a big chunk of pride. She'd have to confess the situation with Robert to her family and beg a loan to get through the winter. She hoped there would be other contracts. She really didn't have any other choice. If the aliens took Earth, her little piece of it wouldn't matter a hoot. It certainly put the New Year's list in perspective.

Lacey spun her chair around to face the front of the ship where Reene displayed a miniature replica of the dome on the holodeck. Oliver warmed her lap and Pio sat folded up in the corner where he'd been for most of the day. She was beginning to think Pio had a thing for her cat.

Zain cursed from the back room, and she knew he was battling the new power cell into place. Her job was to figure out how to shut down the dome and teleportals before he tried to send her home. Once there, the only recourse she'd have would be to run down the road yelling, "The aliens are coming! The aliens are coming!"—which she seriously doubted would work.

She said to Reene, "The portals must be linked to the images inside the dome and the facility below."

"My sensors indicate a conduit link."

"Could that conduit be severed?" she asked.

"Possibly. However, I do not know what effect that would have. It could bring InterGlax in here or trigger a self-destruct sequence of the facility."

Her eyes widened. So much for that idea.

She leaned back and stroked Oliver's head. The dome's image flickered in front of her. It was the key to this whole puzzle. It was tied to Stonehenges all over the galaxy; she was sure of it. There must be a good reason.

"Any idea how old the building is, Reene?"

"Based on the *krudo* accounts, I'd estimate roughly five thousand years."

That made sense. Stonehenge was about five thousand years old. Then she remembered reading something about a legend of giants dancing at the site where Stonehenge was built. She eyed the tall archways. They were big enough for giants.

"Pio, do you know who built the dome?"

The creature stretched his many legs, one at a time, and stood up on the console. "The travelers," he replied. "They come. They leave. They come. They leave. Like you."

She stared at his shiny red skin and wrestled with his logic. Travelers who came and went. Then it occurred to her. "Did the portals belong to them?"

"Yes."

Finally, something that made sense. "Reene, do you have any information on a race of space travelers in this region five thousand years ago? They would have been very tall, like giants."

"Working." After a minute, he responded, "Affirmative. Archives indicate a species called Narous who fit your description. They averaged five meters in height, with multiple appendages and large craniums. They were indeed well-traveled in this sector and known to have established portal entrances on thousands of planets. They disappeared approximately two thousand years ago."

"Then Stonehenge is definitely a terminal," she concluded. "And this dome must be Grand Central. Amazing. But why would they want to visit a bunch of juveniles?"

"As tourists."

"Be serious," she gasped.

Reene replied, "It is not unusual. Many juveniles are considered rustic and exotic locales."

She shook her head: The aliens had already come. Guess that answered *that* question. "Well, it doesn't seem like the Narous set up the portal system to be used for attacks. They would have done so long ago. Pio, did the travelers build the Well, too?"

"No. Belong to others."

Lacey tapped her fingernails on the chair. "So that means InterGlax figured out how to tie in to the travelers' portal system."

"Still trying to stop IG?" the deep voice came from behind her. Lacey spun to find Zain leaning against the corridor wall, arms folded and looking entirely too tempting.

He shoved off the wall and took the seat next to her. "Check your power levels now, Reene."

"Yes, sir."

She stared him down. "I'm not giving up, even if you are. And I'm not going home, Zain. Why is InterGlax bombing old tourist attractions?"

He checked his ship's stats as he answered, "That part doesn't compute. InterGlax is getting nothing out of this except a bad reputation."

"They didn't have a bad rep before?" Lacey asked.

"If they did, I didn't know about it when I enlisted. And I never saw anything like this while I was in. The trouble didn't begin until Cris . . ." He stopped. "I started poking around where I shouldn't have."

Lacey pounced on the opening. "What was Crista looking for?"

He glanced at her, none too happy. "It was my op."

"What was she looking for?" Lacey persisted.

"Why do I bother?" he muttered. "Stolen ships."

"InterGlax was stealing ships?"

Zain shook his head. "Someone had stolen ships from InterGlax. Crista wanted to look into it. That's when we were ambushed. Someone inside InterGlax betrayed us for getting too close to something big."

She could tell his body was present, but his mind was years away. Then a very disturbing thought occurred to her. "Zain, when were those ships stolen?"

He shrugged. "Crista started noticing them about eight years ago, but she suspected it went back further than—" He stopped and turned slowly to look at her.

"I think we found your missing ships," she said. "And if that's the case, then this is why Crista died."

She could sense the tension fill his body and, when he looked at her, there was a spark of intensity. He knew she was right. Whoever was behind the InterGlax conspiracy was also behind Crista's death.

She crossed her arms. "So. Are you going to help me now?"

Zain stared at Lacey and saw the past. There was no doubt in his mind that the fighters in this armory were the same type he and Crista had chased through the swamp. He had a chance to avenge her. No one knew he was here, or what he knew.

His gaze swept over Lacey's bare shoulders, soft skin, and lithe body. He should have never gotten a taste of her. He was going to crave her every day for the rest of his life. But he wouldn't put her in InterGlax's sights for any reason, let alone his purely selfish one. This was his battle.

"Okay. I'll take care of InterGlax. *You* are going home," he told her—over the clear and present protests of his body.

Anger lit her eyes. "You are *not* shutting me out. You need me."

"I don't need you." Was he trying to convince her or himself? "I am perfectly capable of dealing with this myself. I want you on Earth where it's safe."

"Safe? Don't you think that's a little premature? What if you don't stop InterGlax? Earth will be an easy target."

"And if you and I fail, Earth is in the same predicament. If you want to get killed, wait until then. You don't have the skills, and you aren't trained for combat. I am, so let me handle this my way."

"Forget it," she persisted. "I'm going to fight for my Earth. To you, it's just another juvenile."

"But the women are nice," he pointed out.

"Flattery will get you nowhere. I'm coming along, so just get used to it." She held up her hands. "Besides, you need these."

Giving in, he eyed her fingers. "Do I get to choose where you use them?"

She blushed. "For the Well."

He grinned. "And here I thought you just wanted to do more research on my DNA."

She ignored his comment. "And you need my gun."

"Have you ever killed anyone?"

She winced. "Well, no."

"It's not like shooting Bobzillas, Lacey. And I have Pio for the lift."

Her jaw set and she spoke clearly. "I want to make my own decisions, Zain. I want to control my destiny. If I make mistakes, at least they are mine. That may seem silly to a man who flies wherever he wants, but it's a big deal to me. I won't let you take it away."

The fierceness on her face was familiar. It was the way he used to feel when he escaped an oppressive youth for the stars. It was passion. It was hope. All the things he'd left behind with Crista's body.

"I know you think this will turn out like before, but I trust you," she added, her voice softening. "We won't fail."

He knew he was losing. "I can't guarantee to protect you, Lacey."

"I'm not asking you to. I just want the choice."

He sighed. She had as much right to this operation as he did. He couldn't say *no*, no matter how much he wanted her safe and far away. He'd just have to find a way to keep her sheltered from the action.

"Fine. It's your choice," he conceded. "Any ideas on how we're going to take down the biggest military force in the galaxy with two operatives, a cat, and a few lasers?"

"And Pio," he chirped cheerfully.

Lacey smiled at the creature. "Of course. We wouldn't forget you, Pio. You know this place better than anyone."

Her comment gave him a thought. Zain turned his

attention to the little alien. "Pio, do you know how to operate anything besides the lift and the bridge?"

He tipped his head. "No."

Zain switched tactics. "Do you know where and how the armory communicates with the other humans?"

"Lines," Pio replied.

Lacey's wide-eyed gaze met his. "That would do it."

Zain leaned forward. "Where are these lines?"

The cable closet on Level Twelve was a mess. Bits of wires and shielding littered the floor.

"What's it look like down there?" Lacey asked over Reene's comm. She'd stayed in the ship.

"Like a bomb went off." Zain turned to Pio. "So you were tripping the sensors when you played, and InterGlax would show up and shoot you?"

"Yes."

"So you cut the sensor wires?"

"Yes."

"Didn't they come to fix them?" Lacey asked.

Pio gave a little bounce. "Two thousand and thirty-five times."

Zain heard Lacey burst into laughter. When she recovered, she said, "Don't ever accuse *me* of being stubborn again."

He had to grin. He could only imagine InterGlax's frustration. He examined the mass of conduits. "How did you know which cables to cut?"

Pio scrambled over to the cascade of thick tubes.

"We cut all, then watch them fix." He pointed a bony leg to the red cable. "Eyes. Stop fixing."

"Sensors," Zain said for Lacey's benefit. "That explains why they didn't detect us down here. Probably got sick of all the false alarms. What else do we have?"

Pio waved at the blue cables. "Portals. Always, fix portals." Then the yellow. "Ears. Always fix."

"Ears. Communications maybe?" Lacey asked.

"Would be my guess." Zain dropped his pack and began pulling out items. "Give me a few minutes, and we'll be tapped in."

"Report, Everard."

In the miniature holodeck on Schuler's desk, his ops chief stood at attention. "We are on schedule. All systems are online and operational."

"And Installation 93?"

"Nothing unusual to report. I will send a team in tomorrow for a complete assessment."

"Excellent. I understand that Maadiar has finally accepted our protection and trade opportunities." Schuler leaned back and savored another victory.

"Yes, sir. Our field team did an expeditious job of orienting the Maadiar's juvenile governments. We should have no trouble bringing the rest of the juveniles into our trade agreements after tomorrow's strike."

"Excellent. News of the Maadiar attack has reached CinTerr, and the upper InterGlax leadership is scrambling for excuses. They are on the brink of collapse with no one to save them." Schuler paused. "Unless Zain Masters returns from the dead."

"Zain Masters?" Everard's eyes widened. "He can't still be alive."

"Apparently, the man is quite resourceful. I have Ferretu on his trail. With luck, we won't have to worry about him."

Everard blinked rapidly. "Yes, sir. Out."

Schuler closed the comm. On his monitor, the countdown continued its torturously slow march toward victory. Until now InterGlax had known but a small taste of his power.

He wondered how Lundon would feel if he knew his "old friend" was taking down InterGlax under his nose. Schuler felt no guilt and no regret. InterGlax and CinTerr had outlived their usefulness; they were too slow and blind to the fortune to be made from the untapped and fertile juveniles of the Outer Rim. They were obsolete. And once InterGlax was dissolved, no one would stand in his way of negotiating new trade alliances with mature planets. Eventually, CinTerr would fall and the universe would be free of their oppressive rules.

Schuler savored the sweet taste of a triumph twenty years in the making. He was about to single-handedly bring the most formidable military force in the galaxy to its knees. It would be a feat that would change history.

Nothing could stop him now.

Chapter Twenty

Lacey watched the miniature replica of the underground armory blossom on Reene's console as Zain tapped into more systems. The cables were visible now, looking like a spider web spreading down from the dome into the levels below.

"This is very cool," she said to Reene. "So, now you can see whatever InterGlax sends to the station?"

"Correct," Reene replied. "Zain has tapped all the main cables. When InterGlax communicates with or polls the station, I will be able to interpret the results and build an interface."

Lacey nodded. "Will that give you enough of a sample to be able to control the portals?"

"The odds are favorable."

A blue box lit up on the panel in front of her. She glanced out into the surrounding area looking for trouble. She saw nothing but calm red desert.

"What's that light for, Reene?"

"An incoming transmission," he replied.

"From whom?" she asked.

"Zain's sister, Torrie."

Her eyes widened. He had a sister? It occurred to her that she knew nothing about his family. She watched the light flash. "Don't you think you should answer it?"

"I am not authorized to open transmissions in Zain's absence. The sender may leave a message."

Lacey frowned. If it was *her* sister, she'd want to talk to her. So she leaned forward and pressed the blue square. Immediately, a stunning, redhaired young woman replaced the image of the Well in the holodeck.

"Lacey, you are not authorized to manually override—" Reene objected.

"It's about time someone answered," the redhead said over Reene's protests. She raised her eyebrows when she saw Lacey. "Greetings. I'm Torrie Masters."

Lacey leaned back, fascinated by the interactive holographic communication. "I'm Lacey Garrett. Nice to meet you. You're Zain's sister?"

Reene interrupted. "Lacey, I really must insist you break off this conversation—"

With a smile, Torrie said, "Yes, whether he wants me or not, and despite his nagging computer. I've been trying to contact him for days with no reply."

"The ship crashed and then lost all power. We just brought everything back up."

The woman pursed her lips and looked at something beyond Lacey's range. "Is his ship still inoperable?"

"Not anymore. But we have other problems. Bigger ones if you can believe it," Lacey added with a smile.

Reene interrupted, "Zain is approaching."

Torn from Torrie's image, Lacey frowned. "So?"

"Dammit!"

She jumped at the roar behind her.

"Shut it down, Reene," Zain ordered as he appeared. Lacey spun and sucked in a breath. He was glaring at her with murder in his eyes.

"I can't, sir. Manual override is on."

Zain's eyes narrowed to slits. Lacey sank back into her chair as far as she could.

"Why hello, Zain," Torrie said, looking up at him. "I see you still have a way with women. Don't go blaming her. I just followed your ping."

Lacey was relieved when his homicidal gaze moved to Torrie. She watched a quick succession of emotions play on his face.

"There's a reason why I don't answer your messages, Torrie," he said finally.

"Then you shouldn't have pinged me." His sister smiled. "I figured your buddy Rayce would contact you about me, and sooner or later, you'd start to worry. Anyone ever tell you that you're predictable?"

Zain countered, "Anyone ever tell you that you are relentless?"

She laughed. Brave woman, Lacey thought. She liked Torrie instantly.

Then his sister's expression sobered. "I'm on a serious mission, Zain. You need to come home. Father is not doing well. I know you don't get along but you may not get another chance to see him alive. Let me help you—"

"No," Zain growled. "This isn't a good time."

"I know about the ship," she responded. "I have parts—"

"It's not just the ship, Torrie. This planet is a death trap. We're in a seriously dangerous situation."

"Again?" she replied, rolling her eyes. "How do you get into so much trouble in the middle of nowhere?"

"It's a gift," he muttered. "One I don't want to pass along. So, let me go for now."

She shook her head. "No can do, big brother. I came all the way out here to get you and I'm not going home empty-handed."

Zain stood with his hands on his hips and Lacey sensed him waver. "How bad is Father?"

Torrie's expression softened. "Terrible. His heart is failing, and he's too stubborn to get a replacement. He only has a few months left. Probably less." Torrie leaned forward. "Please, Zain. I'm begging you. If you miss this last chance, you'll never be able to forgive yourself."

Zain closed his eyes and Lacey sensed the sadness that seeped from him. "You know it's not safe for me there. It's not safe for anyone around me."

Torrie replied, "Trust your family, Zain. We'll take care of that."

Lacey frowned. We? There were more of them?

Zain exhaled, hard. "Let me handle this mess first. Then, I promise I'll come home."

Torrie looked skeptical. "I could help. I'm close."

A corner of Zain's mouth twisted. "If we need something blown to hell or general anarchy, I'll call you."

His sister made a face. "That only happened once."

Zain smiled at her warmly. "Don't come find me, Torrie."

She gave him a look of concern, then sighed. "I'll be good—if you stick to your promise."

He nodded. "Give me two days."

"Deal," Torrie said. Then she looked at Lacey. "Perhaps we'll meet?"

Zain's eyes met Lacey's and narrowed.

"Uh, thanks, but I'm only here temporarily."

"Really? That's too bad. Zain could use some human interaction." She winked. "Out."

The blueprints of the armory filled the holodeck once again, leaving a sound vacuum that Lacey tried hard to ignore. But it was impossible to ignore a big, angry man taking up most of your personal space.

Zain spun her chair to face him, placed a hand on its arms, and bent down to look her in the eye.

"What do you think you were doing?" he asked coolly.

She held his gaze. "You shouldn't ignore your family."

"Really?" he asked, his voice dangerously soft. "And what would you know about my family?"

"You have a sister, parents, and brothers," she

guessed. "Who worry about you and want you to come home. And a sick father."

"And I could get them all killed," he said. "Now, thanks to you, Torrie likely has a fix on my location."

She blinked. "She said she wouldn't—"

He pushed from her chair and towered over her. "My sister has never followed the rules. Ever. She'll do whatever she feels like."

Lacey crossed her arms. "So what's wrong with that?"

"I don't want Torrie to be shot down by this planet's defenses. Her ship is nowhere near as sophisticated as Reene."

The thought made Lacey gasp in panic. "I forgot."

Zain's stern expression was unforgiving. "Obviously."

"But this is family, Zain. You can't ignore family, even if you want to. Believe me, I've tried."

"Watch me."

Reene's voice interrupted. "We have portal activation."

At the familiar rumble and blast of lights from the upper portals, Lacey looked through the viewport. Sure enough, all the archways were initiating transfers. She glanced at the holo-image and watched color pump through cables from the dome to the sublevels and back.

"Are you getting all this?" she asked Reene.

"Of course," he replied, and added calmly, "We have an execution interface. And I have pinpointed the source of the commands. Sir, it's Avakur."

"Bastards," Zain growled but he didn't act surprised.

Lacey gazed at him in concern. "Do you think InterGlax and Avakur formed an alliance?"

"It's starting to look that way. Reene, any indication of what the Well's countdown is for?"

There was a pause. "No, sir. However, Pio is correct. A routine maintenance check is scheduled for Installation 93 in approximately thirty-six hours."

"Is Installation 93 the name of this facility?" Zain asked.

"Yes."

Breath caught in Lacey's throat and she turned to look at Zain. His expression was drawn with concern.

"So how many other installations are there?" she asked. "And where the hell are they?"

Lacey hung out in the lav for as long as she could. Eventually, she'd have to come out. She rehearsed the speech that she'd come up with:

"I realize that we had sex last night, and that it may *seem* as if I'm interested. But it'll never work out because we have nothing in common. This will only distract us from our mission, and Reene is here, and the cat, and Pio who has moved in, and it's getting a little bizarre. So I think it would be better if we refrained from sex from now on."

She nodded to herself in the mirror—the picture of cool, calm, and collected. And just to be safe, she had her own clothes on. She was going to stay focused and out of the danger zone.

Feeling in control and fearless, she stepped out of the lav to find Zain's naked body stretched across her bunk, covered by a very thin sheet. He had one muscled arm thrown over his eyes, with those perfect lips and shadow of a beard showing. His chest was wide, sprinkled lightly with hair. It narrowed to his hips and then long, lean, strong legs.

"Oh, damn," she uttered, knowing her plan was ruined already.

He raised his arm and heavy, sensual eyes peered at her. "You spend more time in the lav than any woman I have ever met."

"Beauty isn't easy," she joked.

The brown of his eyes intensified. "You would be beautiful no matter what, Lacey."

She didn't know how to reply to that. She'd never thought of herself as a great beauty and she never would. She wasn't tall or leggy or busty or any of those things that set gorgeous women apart from the mousy variety. She had a slew of geeky friends that she really liked and a cat that got her into all kinds of trouble. In fact, there was nothing special about her other than she was probably the only Earth woman living on another planet at the moment.

He sat up and reached out to pull her to him. As she fell into his arms, she stammered, "I have a speech."

"That's nice. You won't need this." He tugged off her top.

"Zain, you have to listen to me. I have something

important . . . oh." He'd bent and wrapped his lips around one exposed nipple. "To say."

He suckled lightly while his gentle fingers caressed her skin, searing a trail of promise. Her pants were slipped off and disappeared somewhere. Strong arms lifted her onto the bunk and on top of him.

"I'm listening," he said, and kissed her throat until it burned.

What was it she'd wanted to tell him? Zain had left her breathless with his mouth and his hands and his heat. Even her mind refused to follow the plan. She had no excuse for responding to him, none whatsoever. He tongued a nipple, and she sighed. She'd find something to blame this on later.

Zain's patient hands roamed over her body, and his heat enveloped her in a sensual blanket, rich with anticipation. She endured the gentle assault of his mouth and lips on her breasts, neck, and shoulders, unable to recall a single word of her speech. Finally, she surrendered altogether. It was hopeless. She was a slave to her own passion and a puppet to his. Zain had no idea what he'd just unleashed.

She growled low in her throat and rubbed her hips against his. She kissed him, hard, with the force of a hundred failures and as many promises. Dammit, if she was going to crash and burn, she was taking him with her.

She planted her hands on his chest and pushed herself down his waist and hips. His eyes blazed hot into her soul as he watched, knowing what she had planned.

She bent and ran the tip of her tongue along the length of his erection, drawing an audible hiss as he sucked air into his lungs. The next lick brought his hips up, and he closed his eyes. She'd barely begun when he abruptly sat up, threw her on the bunk and rolled on top of her. The speed of the maneuver surprised her, but she really didn't have time to think about it as his mouth came down on hers, urgent and demanding.

She loved him like this—wild and unchecked. He wasn't hiding anything. No games to be won or lost, like with the other men she'd known. Just Zain, stripped down to his passion. If only it could be like this forever. If only the rest of the universe could fend for itself.

Then he whispered something in her ear that sounded so wicked and decadent that she trembled, even though she didn't understand a word. But whatever he'd said was meant for only her. And he thought she was beautiful. No man had ever made her feel this special. Zain's body showed how much he wanted her; it wasn't her imagination.

His hands were driving her crazy in ways she'd only dreamed. She wriggled beneath him, her body overwhelmed and overloaded with sensations.

When he finally slipped inside her, and just before she lost herself in him, it occurred to her that she would probably have to put that speech in writing next time.

* * *

The dream began much like it always did, with the acidic smell of the swamp and a cloud of overpowering failure. Zain stood in water to his knees behind the cover of a tree, peering through his goggles at the target a quarter klick away. Stolen cargo was being loaded into a sprawling warehouse that sat on a raised concrete bed in the middle of the empty swamp. Déjà vu marked the moment, and he remembered they had followed the stolen ships here and were trying to discover how the cargo was to get off the planet.

He eyed the oversized structure as he had years before, but this time with new eyes. One tube-shaped section in the middle was several stories tall, looking oddly out of place with the boxy warehouse. In fact . . . he'd bet a large-scale teleportal would fit nicely inside. It all clicked. So that's how InterGlax had moved the ships around and loaded them into the Well.

He could sense Crista behind him, and he realized that this was the first time his dream had ever started this early—before the attack. Crista was still alive.

He turned to see her, and his heart stopped in alarm. She was standing behind him but she was half Crista, half robot soldier—the same type who had ambushed them. Her eyes peered out at him, but cold technology and hard, sexless steel replaced her body.

Training brought his weapon up but he didn't fire. He couldn't. She smiled at him knowingly.

"You can finish what we started," she said, her voice digital.

He struggled for words. She'd never talked to him

243

in his nightmares before. He lowered his weapon.

"I failed last time," he finally said.

She shook her head, slowly. "*We* didn't fail. We were set up. This time you go in as one of them."

He frowned. "What?"

Her robotic arms lifted to her sides. "One of them. Use the tools you have around you."

He didn't understand. "Tools? What tools? I have a ship and a woman who won't follow orders. A cat, a bunch of crabs—"

She lifted an eyebrow. "You have more, though it is not yours. And Lacey is instrumental. Do not shut her out."

At the mention of Lacey, Zain's heart clenched. He tried to find the words to explain himself to his former lover. "About Lacey—"

Crista interrupted. "I never wished you alone, Zain. She is good for you. Trust her. Follow her."

He closed his eyes, her generous words feeding his guilt and anguish. She was dead now because of him.

"I let you down," he rasped. "I couldn't protect you."

"The decision was mine and I lived as I wanted. We were partners, but I was responsible for myself. You cannot confine the people you love."

He opened his eyes to find Crista whole and beautiful, just the way he remembered her.

"I don't want Lacey to die," he said, the words ripped from his heart.

"She understands the risks. Taking her freedom won't keep her safe. Or happy. She is your partner.

You will need her to stop InterGlax. Let her help you."

And then Crista faded away, back into his memories. Zain woke up, and Lacey started next to him.

His thoughts scrambled back to the present, dragging Crista's words into reality. Stop InterGlax. And she'd mentioned tools. What other tools did he have? Reene, his weapons, Lacey. He glanced out the viewport at the dome backlit by the dawn. The dome, the portals, the *krudo*, the armory . . . A flicker of a plan began to develop.

"Nightmare?" Lacey asked, in a concerned but sleepy voice.

He tucked her back under his arm. "No. Just a very interesting dream."

She nestled in. "Good. I don't like your nightmares. They scare me."

"If you think they're frightening, wait until you hear my plan."

Chapter Twenty-one

Curled up in her chair flanked by Oliver and Pio, Lacey nibbled on a snack made of something resembled crushed nuts and molasses—a really bad galactic granola bar.

New Year's Resolution #10: Bring Twinkies on next space adventure.

Before her, Zain paced the short corridor of the ship, lost in concentration. She loved to watch him walk, and not just because he had a tush to die for. It was the way he moved, like a well-oiled, finely tuned, utterly sexy space cowboy. But he'd also changed. There was a bounce in his step that hadn't been there before, and the gleam in his eye *really* worried her.

He'd been like this the entire day, submerged in thought and plotting something about which she was almost afraid to ask. When he wasn't poring over maps and data from Avakur, he and she were making final repairs to the ship. He was getting ready for something, and she wanted to know what.

"Do I get a say in this plan?" she asked, the suspense killing her.

He stopped dead, as if he had just realized she was there. His dark eyes were thoughtful as he pulled himself back to the here and now. He zeroed in on her with a singular intensity that made her shiver in her slippers. He looked well rested and more relaxed than he had when she'd first met him. Great sex had helped, no doubt. Which, by the way, she was definitely *not* doing again.

She scanned his bare sculpted chest, broad, muscular shoulders, and the way his thighs bulged through his thin pants.

Right.

"You are an important part of the plan," he said.

Her eyes lifted from his torso to his face. He grinned. "You seem distracted. It's my DNA, isn't it?"

She shrugged one shoulder carelessly. "Eh. It's okay."

A smile crossed his face. "I said—you are an important part of the plan."

She lifted her eyebrows. "Uh-huh. Do I get to wear clothes?"

"Unfortunately, yes." He sat down next to her. "Reene, bring up a holo-image of the Well." The image appeared, and Zain took his chair. "Remember Pio told us that InterGlax sends a team in every thirty-three days to check this place?"

"Yes," she said warily.

He pointed to the lower portal. "They should be here tomorrow morning, and we are going to be waiting for them."

Her fingers froze around the granola bar. "Then what do we do? Shoot them?"

"Only if we have no choice. No, I plan to apprehend them and steal one of their uniforms."

She had a bad feeling about this. "Why would you want to do that?"

He grinned devilishly. "Because I'm going to put it on and return to where they came from. InterGlax Command Center. Scared yet?"

"I'm getting there," she conceded. "Don't you think they will notice that you aren't the same guy who left?"

"When they come through the portal, Reene should be able to tell me how many access points are on the other side. I'm hoping I can insert at a different location inside their compound. Depends on the setup. Otherwise, I'll just have to take my chances."

"Now I'm scared."

Zain crossed his arms. "You haven't even heard the best part."

He looked far too happy, she decided. Probably insane. "Do I have to?"

"I'm going to locate the heart of their operation, set a timed charge to destroy it, and return through the portal."

She just looked at him, numbly. It sounded far too risky. "There has to be another way, Zain. A safer and easier way."

He shook his head. "Taking out this one armory is not going to stop them. We have to destroy the central command. Once that's inoperable, we can destroy this one too."

"And what do I do?" she asked.

"You are my link, Lacey. I need you to monitor the armory, the portals, and communication from here."

The horrible experience on Maadiar and the seriousness of the situation occurred to her. That portal would be his lifeline. What if InterGlax caught him, or he was trapped, or the portal wouldn't open?

As if anticipating her fears, Zain smiled and added, "There isn't anyone else I'd rather have watching out for me, partner."

As much as she wanted to stop him from choosing this plan, she couldn't. He'd made up his mind, and somewhere in the back of hers, she realized he needed to do this.

She sighed deeply. "I'll be here."

"Thank you," he said, and rolled his shoulders. "We have twelve hours until they show up." His gaze skimmed over her body. "Want to compare DNA?"

"I've got a better idea."

He laughed. "I doubt it."

She eyed him seriously. "Tell me about your family."

His expression sobered. He didn't want to talk about them, but if anything happened to him, she would be the only one who knew. The phrase "next of kin" kept popping up in her mind.

"You know about Torrie. I also have parents and

six brothers. My family runs a very large, very successful galactic shipping business. I left home when I was sixteen and joined InterGlax. Now you know it all." He reached out and accessed Reene's console.

Lacey shook her head. "You've been alone with your computer too long. A little detail would be nice."

He shrugged. "Not much more to tell. I had a normal family life." Zain turned to her. "Your turn."

"What?"

"I want to hear about your family. Parents? Siblings?"

Lacey looked suddenly uncomfortable, and Zain enjoyed watching her squirm for a change. She obviously didn't want to talk about her family any more than he wanted to talk about his. Finally she said, "I grew up with both parents and three perfect sisters."

Interesting. "And you didn't get along?"

She blinked at him. "Of course we got along. That was never a problem. We were just . . . different."

"How?" he prodded.

She sighed. "Ever hear of a black sheep?"

He shook his head.

"It's someone who doesn't fit in, whether it be in a family or a society."

Yes, he understood exactly what a black sheep was.

"I tried, but I always seemed to do things the hard way. It's like I klutzed my way through life, trying anything once, trusting everyone." She frowned. "Unfortunately, I always picked the wrong people to trust."

"Like Bob?"

Hurt flashed in her eyes. "Exactly."

"What did your family think of him?"

"They thought he was perfect for me."

Zain watched her blink rapidly under a crush of memories. "They didn't know him very well."

"No, they didn't. Look, I know I probably deserve this conversation, but suddenly blissful silence sounds like a terrific idea."

"You deserve better," Zain continued, ignoring her request.

She gave a short, cynical laugh. "You don't understand, Zain. On my world, I'm . . . ordinary. I write software for a living. I hang out online with other geeks. Even the cat gets bored with me." She looked away. "And the worst part is, I like it. I like the simple life. It's not what you have, but it keeps me centered and happy."

"Lacey, you are a beautiful, intelligent, sexy woman. There's nothing wrong with you or your lifestyle."

Her blue eyes widened, and her mouth worked a few seconds. "I'm sexy?"

She had no idea. "Incredibly. You don't need to settle for anyone. Especially some heartless, gutless, senseless bastard who didn't know how lucky he was."

Her eyebrows rose. "I suppose that's one way of looking at it."

"That's the only way of looking at it. Why did you finally get rid him?"

She flinched and he knew he'd hit something big. She seemed to brace herself as she spoke. "He was my development partner before he stole our application, erased my name, and sold it out from under me. When I tried to say it was my creation, he told the client I was an ex-lover who was stalking him. Then I mysteriously started losing my other clients, one by one."

"You lost more than that," Zain noted.

She nodded sadly, her spirit fading from her eyes. "I didn't realize how completely he controlled my life until the day I caught him in our bed with one of my girlfriends." She gave a little laugh. "When he realized I was standing there, he told me to wait for him in the living room until he was done."

Zain swore under his breath. He was tempted to give up on InterGlax, track down Bob, and beat the shit out of him.

"The sad part is that I *did*." She swallowed and Zain could almost feel her pain. "For ten minutes I sat in the other room until I finally realized what I was doing. Then I left. It was only later that I found out he'd stolen my application and most of my savings. By then, he was long gone."

"And you just let him go?"

She closed her eyes. "You have no idea how much work is involved on Earth in suing someone, Zain. Lawyers, trials, paperwork, fees. Not to mention admitting that you were stupid enough to let him do it in the first place. I'm just not up to it."

He wasn't letting her get away with that. "You fought off Bobzillas, talked to aliens, teleported to other planets, crossed a bridge that terrified you, saved my life, figured out the dome, and argued with me for four days straight without letting up. I find it hard to believe that you can't take on one cowardly Earthman."

She stared at him in stunned silence. "It's not the same."

"Tell me why not."

Anger flickered in her eyes, bringing with it her spark. "Because none of this is real. My world—back there on Earth, *that's* real. That's where I have to live. I don't want to sit in a courtroom for hours, days, or weeks while Robert laughs at me for being a fool."

Zain willed himself not to smile as he dragged the fight from her. "So you can be a Warrior Programmer here but not on Earth?"

"I can do whatever the hell I want, and I don't need you telling me what's good for me," she snapped. Then she stood up. "And right now, I'm going . . ." She glanced around. "To the lav."

"Running again?"

She speared him with a stubborn glare. "You should know."

As Zain watched Lacey disappear into the lav, he did grin, wishing he could watch her tear Bob apart. He'd love to see that bastard suffer for all he'd taken away from her.

Then his smile faded. He never would see that though. Regardless of what happened tomorrow, he'd have to let Lacey go. She'd fight without him. That's what she needed to do.

He had a feeling that Bob was just one of many

men who had tried to mold Lacey throughout her lifetime. Not one of them cared about who she really was, or the passions that flared so brightly from inside her. They'd missed her wit and her fierce spirit. They'd ignored her intelligence and her compassion. And they'd likely never been mesmerized by watching her in bed. Idiots. Wasn't there one man on Earth worthy of her?

Then the selfish part of him realized he didn't want that, either.

Only one man saw Lacey's true essence. Unfortunately, he was bound to hurt her, too. There was no way around it. Even if by some miracle they stopped InterGlax's operation, it wouldn't clear him of Crista's death. He could be a fugitive forever—not a life for a woman who deserved more than she thought possible. She needed a good mate, children, and a home, all the things that normal people shared. Zain wasn't qualified to give any of those.

He looked out the viewport at the moonrise and wondered what he *could* give her.

Chapter Twenty-two

For the next twenty minutes, Lacey paced in the tiny lav. She was *not* running. She wasn't afraid of Robert and she didn't have to explain herself to anyone. She had goals and everything.

Her knee whacked the side of the sink and she bit back a profanity as she sat down and rubbed it. There just wasn't enough room in this stupid lav, that was the problem.

Her hand stilled on her knee. Muted images of herself reflected back from the metal walls and it occurred to her that she was hiding in a bathroom. Was this what her world had come down to? A small bit of space that she could call her own, that she could control? Where it was safe and quiet and she could protect her heart and her career and what was left of her self-confidence?

Outside that door, the worlds went on without her,

whether or not she approved. People lived, loved, died. The whole damn universe was rolling along just fine. And she was holed up in a bathroom.

She blinked back the fears and listened to the silence of a non-life crisis. It was a little difficult to control her life when she wasn't part of it anymore. Playing it safe might be the smart thing to do but technically it wasn't living either.

What had she let Robert do to her? He'd made her afraid of everything. Bastard. Then she shook her head. No, it wasn't his fault. She was the one hiding. Bob was out having a ball with her money and her software while she stood by and let him. All because of fear and pride. Would it be so bad to let the world know she'd screwed up? Who would care? The rest of the universe was too busy living.

So what will it be, Lacey? Do you want to dance around the fire or sit petrified in a bathroom for the rest of your life?

Anger and resolve stole over her. Robert had humiliated her because she let him. The only thing worse than what he did to her was letting him get away with it. That was the true failure. It was time to dance. Even as she thought the words, she was filled with great sense of relief. The tantalizing promise of excitement coiled in her belly. It would be risky. She'd have to face Robert again in court and she could lose the case and even more money. It was a gamble that she didn't need to take. It was risk. She wouldn't be able to plot it on a spreadsheet or put it in a nice, neat New Year's resolution.

All her tomorrows opened before her with possibilities and the twinge of hope. If she lost, then so be it. She'd rather feel alive and lose than be dead and safe. She inhaled deeply, to feel the air in her lungs, hear the blood pump in her veins. Energy zinged her senses, suppressed for too long, restless and building by the second.

And she knew just where to use all that newfound energy. She got up, opened the door of the lav, and stepped out into the corridor. To her disappointment, the ship was empty.

"Zain requests your presence outside," Reene announced.

"Is it safe out there?" she asked, casting a quick look out the front viewport into the ominous darkness.

"All my perimeter alarms, scanners, and weapons are at full capacity. I would also deduce that Bobzillas are not nocturnal since they have never attacked at night."

Risk, she reminded herself. Get used to it. She headed to the back. "If you say so."

"Evenin', Lacey."

She exited through the back hatch door. She stepped a few feet from the ship and stopped dead. Light breezes moved over warm sands and swirled around her legs. The distance mountain ridge framed the night sky undulating in hypnotic green waves. Wispy tendrils of green filigree blanketed the sky, gently undulating and changing with ethereal grace. A full, giant, reddish moon peeked above the rim of the basin, washing the harsh landscape in milky shadow. So big and so close, she nearly reached out a hand to touch it.

"I know it's not Earth, but it was the best I could do."

He stood a short distance away, silhouetted against the star-studded sky with his back to her. Then her heart stilled as she saw what he'd done. Wedged in the sand, two artificial light torches illuminated the blanket he'd spread out between them. A bin contained glasses and a bottle, and soft music was playing from somewhere nearby.

She lifted her gaze from the midnight picnic to his approaching form. Soft light warmed his dark features as he walked toward her wearing only dark pants that hugged his hips. He was bare-chested and barefooted.

"You did this for me?" she whispered when he was close enough to hear her.

A smile touched his lips. "Is that so hard to believe?"

Yes, she wanted to tell him. It was. "It's my first picnic."

His smile faded and he reached for her hand. "Then we'll make it a good one."

She let him lead her to the blanket where she settled in next to him and watched him fill two glasses. He handed one to her and lifted his.

"What do you want to drink to, Lacey?"

She said the first thing that popped into her head. "Life."

He frowned slightly. "Got a second choice? I don't know what tomorrow will bring."

"We have tonight," she said and touched her glass to his. "To rejoining the human race, Zain."

He hesitated before nodding. They drank, watching each other over their glasses. The liquid tasted full-bodied and pleasant in her mouth with a little buzz of a finish. She lifted the glass to the light.

"Wine?"

"Something like that." Zain slid closer to her so they were both facing the moon and crossed his long legs. "I was keeping it for a special occasion."

"I'm drinking your private stock? I feel honored."

He chuckled. "I can't think of anyone I'd rather share my private stock with."

"Is that a sex joke?" she said, eyeing him.

"A Freudian one maybe." He looked at her then, his expression turning serious. "But I didn't bring you out here to seduce you."

"Oh," she replied, slightly deflated. This risk business was going to take some work. She drew in a long breath and stared into the swirling liquid.

"So you don't want to seduce me?"

He sipped his drink. "I didn't say that. I'm not an idiot. But this is your night, Lacey. Your call. Your chance to tell me what to do."

"Well, when you put it like that." She took a deep breath. Say it, Lacey. You've never been properly seduced. What are you afraid of? Risk.

"Seduce me." The words cut through the silence.

His head turned to her and she felt the heat of his gaze burn into her profile. It took all the courage she had to look at him. When she did, her breath caught at the fire there.

"What would Freud say about that?" he said.

She watched flames flicker in his eyes. "Freud was probably a lousy lover."

He set his glass down. "What about that speech? I had the distinct impression it was important."

She thought about the one she'd practiced. The one telling him that she wasn't really interested and that sex was a bad idea. But as she looked into his rugged face, she realized that it was too late. She was well past interested.

"It needs work," she said.

He nodded thoughtfully. "I see. Part of seduction is not knowing if it's going to work."

"I can play hard to get," she countered. Probably. If she really tried. She looked into his eyes. Maybe not. "Don't kiss me."

Zain gave her a sexy grin as he captured her chin with a finger while his other hand relieved her of the glass she still clutched. Her breath held as his lips skimmed hers, just barely, a soft brush caressing tender skin. Her body sighed down to her toes.

The seduction of Lacey Garrett had begun.

Warm fingers lingered over her face and neck. She closed her eyes and let her senses flow. No holding back. Firm lips nibbled ever so gently at her mouth and steamy breath stroked her cheek. No second guesses. No fears getting in the way.

"And don't touch me either," she managed.

His hands glided over her shoulders and along the

sides of her rib cage before hooking under the bottom of her top. With excruciating patience, he rolled the fabric up over her breasts and arms. He tossed it aside, his eyes never leaving the skin he'd just exposed to the night air. Her belly quivered at his brazen captivation.

"Don't . . ." she started. His eyes met hers and she inhaled sharply. There were no words for the impact of his reverent gaze, nothing she could say to deny it. No excuse would reason away how much he wanted her.

Risk called with all its promises and dangers. There wasn't anything riskier than being seduced by the man who could take your heart and soul, but she could no more fold her hand than stop breathing. So she leaned back, braced herself with her hands and gave him the access he needed for a proper seduction. Air suspended midbreath, waiting for release as her body trembled in expectation.

The firm pads of his fingers traced a line across her collarbone down the center of her throat and his mouth followed. Her nipples hardened for him, ready for the loving they so desperately needed.

An uneven breath slipped from her lips when he obliged, flicking them with his tongue before capturing them whole. She moaned and arched her back, losing herself in Zain. Hands and mouth stroked dormant skin, awakening it. Hot breath fanned the fledging flames.

Zain leaned over her, supporting himself with one hand and using the other to trace the hollow of her back while his lips claimed her breasts. The dual ministrations split her singular concentration, dragging a shuddering breath from her lungs.

"You don't like that?" she heard Zain say through the haze of a really good seduction.

"Don't . . . stop," she gasped.

He chuckled softly against her breast. Then he slid over her body, straddling her. With a hand behind her neck, he pressed her back on the blanket.

"I *won't* stop, Lacey," he promised. The light from his two torches shone evenly on his face, banishing the shadows that usually resided there.

"No more don'ts," he said, a split second before he kissed her lips, sealing them. *No more don'ts*, she agreed silently, and opened her mouth to his. He took possession, and with that went cohesive thought.

Her hands reached for Zain as he stretched out over her. His lips smoldered against her lips, face, and neck. Under her touch, the solid planes of his muscles tightened as she explored the wonder of his body. He nuzzled her ear, whispered urgently, and ground his hips against her. The language he spoke escaped her, but she understood his desperate desire completely.

She was vaguely aware of him lifting off her for a moment to discard his pants, his lips never breaking from hers. Seconds later, her palms flattened against his belly, sliding lower until she could wrap her fingers around his thick erection.

He groaned, and she reveled in the reaction. With a feathery stroke, she explored the length of him, velvet skin over steely muscle.

His guttural growl sent shivers down her spine. She

wasn't the only one being seduced. He didn't deny her anything, didn't play games, or shun risk. Heat and tension radiated from his body as she caressed him. In her ear, his words had turned edgy and terse.

Had she become the seducer?

Without warning, his hands slipped beneath the waistband of her pants, jerking them down with very little finesse and even less patience, leaving her naked. A demanding thigh wedged between her legs, driving them apart, and was quickly replaced by his fingers. She gasped at the contact, her hands moving to his shoulders for support. Her eyes closed, accepting him with absolute trust. His technique was perfection, as if he knew exactly what she needed, and within minutes, her body—primed and ready—surrendered. A churning climax rolled over her, leaving her breathless in its wake.

"Yes," she heard Zain breathe through the aftershocks. He settled himself between her legs, pushing her thighs further apart. She felt his tip as it pressed against her, teasing and tempting.

She opened her eyes and, through tears that appeared from nowhere, looked at his taut face a few inches from hers. He propped his elbows by her head and wrapped her face in his big hands.

"Zain," she begged, mindless as she struggled to draw more of him inside her.

"Remember this," he said roughly. "This is real. *I'm* real."

His hands tightened around her head, his mouth besieged hers, and he thrust into her with a violent

C. J. Barry

need she matched. The possession was complete, leaving no room for doubt. Hips rammed together, bodies roiled, limbs tangled, and Lacey was lost. No beginning, no end, no rules. Just their fiery passion burning up the night.

A roar erupted from Zain's lips, torn from deep inside, and he drove into her one more time. She clutched him until he collapsed on top of her, gulping air into his lungs.

For a long time, she held him. Above them, gentle green filigree netted the stars. Lacey felt alive, but it wasn't just from the risk she'd taken. Risk didn't make a heart soar. It didn't fill her with this bittersweet kind of joy and anguish that would last forever. Only love could do that.

Did he know that in the end, he hadn't just seduced her body? He'd seduced her heart as well.

Chapter Twenty-three

T minus one day and counting . . .

Schuler was about to shut down his computer for the evening when the chime sounded. He checked to make sure his office door was closed before he accepted the call.

The holodeck sprang to life, sprouting Ferretu's familiar stance. The assassin began. "I have traced Zain Masters's location. Planet P254-334-5 in the Bogeeta Region."

Schuler stared at the holo-image in disbelief. It couldn't be. "Installation 93 is on that planet."

"I know," Ferretu said. "But I don't have an exact fix on his location. Perhaps he hasn't found anything."

Schuler glanced at his monitor and the amount of time remaining: less than a full cycle. "Prepare a team to check the installation. If Masters is inside, I want him. Alive," he reminded the assassin. He knew how much Ferretu enjoyed killing.

"Of course," Ferretu replied, a little too benignly. "Out." The holo-image vaporized.

Schuler hailed Everard, who answered promptly. "Yes, sir?"

"Masters is on the same planet as Installation 93."

Everard looked momentarily stunned. "Are you sure?"

"Positive." He moved closer to the holo-image. "Is he *inside?*"

"I . . . don't think so," Everard stammered. "As I said before, most of the sensors at that installation do not work correctly. However, the chances of him surviving the defense systems to even gain access to the control dome are very slim."

"So are the odds of Masters sitting on the same planet as one of our facilities. I'm sending Ferretu with a crew to apprehend him."

Everard balked. "Apprehend? Why not kill him?"

Schuler leaned back and steepled his fingers. "Because I think Masters would be an excellent addition to our operation."

"He will never agree to work with us. There is too much InterGlax in him. You are wasting your time," Everard sneered.

Schuler controlled his temper, despite his ops chief's blatant insolence. "You let me worry about that. Your job is to make sure there are no more surprises. We have one day left, Everard. I don't need to tell you what will happen if we miss this opportunity."

The man stiffened. "Yes, sir."

Zain placed a ravaged and sated Lacey onto his bunk and watched as she curled up in a dead sleep. For a while he watched her, committing her to memory for all time. Whether or not tomorrow went well, she would be gone.

And that would be a problem.

He moved silently to the back of the ship. Opening a cabinet, he withdrew his painting supplies and set up a canvas.

"Is everything all right, sir?" Reene asked quietly.

"Fine, Reene. You can go on standby." He wasn't in a chatty mood tonight. He wasn't in an introspective mood either, but a man about to be alone again didn't have a lot of choice. Particularly a man who had recently discovered that he'd fallen in love.

He started the painting and, as he worked, his mind drifted to what had just happened. Lacey had asked him to seduce her, and he had. And, if he had his wish, he'd do it every day for the rest of his life. He was addicted to the way she gasped in his arms, the sweet sounds she probably didn't even realize she made, and the perfect fit of her body to his.

Tonight hadn't been simple lovemaking, though, and he knew it. She'd given him the control she was so desperately trying to hold on to. She'd bared her body and her soul. She'd trusted him with everything she had, and offered him a gift he couldn't accept: her love. Yet he didn't know if he had the willpower to refuse.

He worked for hours, his thoughts revolving around Lacey and how he was ever going to forget her. Before he knew it, the painting was finished. It wasn't his usual style or subject matter, but he was convinced it was the best piece he'd ever done. He stowed it away in a cabinet for safekeeping, a stolen moment to remember Lacey by when she was once again on Earth and he was exploring the galaxy—if he wasn't dead.

Reene announced, "Sir, the lower teleportal is activating."

Quickly, Zain looked at his console. The platform holo-cam below captured three men walking through the portal. And they all had guns.

"Damn. They aren't supposed to be here until tomorrow!" He pulled a rifle from the rack and donned his headgear comm. "Open the door." He bounded out the hatch and made his way through the darkness to the dome. He took up a position outside the entrance, where he had a clear shot inside.

"Can you tell what they are doing down there, Reene?" he whispered into his comm.

"They are activating the lift, sir."

Zain went very still as he watched the elevator drop silently away. There was only one explanation for the early check-in and the immediate use of the lift: *They knew he was here.* He readied his rifle, aiming it at the spot where the lift would return. The only advantage he had was that they didn't know he knew.

"Reene, go dark. They are coming after us. I'd like at least one of them alive, but if I give the order, take everyone out."

"Order accepted. Scanners indicate the lift has reached the bottom and is coming back up. It will appear in twenty seconds . . . ten seconds . . ."

Warrior calm stole over him, driving Zain's senses to their peak. Three heads appeared through the hole and he waited. Shoulders, bodies, and weapons lifted into sight. The three men glanced around. Two wore InterGlax uniforms, looking like standard-issue guards. The other one wore street garb and a golden head cover. He gave the orders. That was the man Zain wanted.

The leader spotted Zain's ship through the doorway and led the charge. Zain pressed against the outer wall and watched them. The leader silently signaled to split up. One of the guards shouldered a powerful laser cannon that could eat a hole through Reene's hull in a few short minutes.

"Shields up. They mean business, Reene," Zain warned. He slipped behind his mark and whispered, "Weapons ready. On my command, all lights on and take out the two standard-issue InterGlax stiffs. I'll deal with the helmeted one myself."

Ahead of him, the leader raised his hand and dropped it. All three intruders opened fire on Reene.

"Now," Zain said.

The immediate area was flooded with blinding light, and in a flurry of laser fire, Reene's guns dropped the two standard-issues. The leader was surprised, frozen just long enough for Zain to lunge up behind him. The man spun, nearly catching Zain in the head with a metal-covered hand. Zain deflected the strike and shoved his rifle into Goldie's gut. The man gave a pained oomph and doubled over. Zain brought the end of his rifle up and under the helmet, sending it flying and breaking Goldie's nose. Blood spattered across the man's face and eyes, and he roared. Zain kicked Goldie's weapon from his hands, and it landed with a thump in the sand.

"Hands where I can see them," Zain warned, his rifle ready. "I hate wearing a uniform with holes in it."

A murderous gaze met his, and Zain recognized the face beneath all the blood. This was no InterGlax operative. This was an assassin.

"Welcome to Death Valley, Ferretu," Zain said with a smile. "How's it feel being on the other end of the gun? I know I'm enjoying it."

"You are a dead man, Masters," Ferretu hissed.

"Don't waste all your best lines on me. Who are you working for these days?"

The man just stared. Zain squinted. "I'm not a very patient man, and I really don't think IG is paying you enough to die."

The man scowled, but he wasn't talking. Zain would have liked to interrogate the bastard, but he knew Ferretu wouldn't crack. Besides, Zain needed his clothes clean.

"Reene, can you hear me?"

"Yes, sir."

"Did you catch the lower portal sequence?"

"Affirmative. There are six access points on Avakur for this portal. I have downloaded the commands into your datapad. You should be able to place yourself on Avakur at will."

Excellent news. "From this point on, block Avakur's commands to the portals. I don't want any more un-invited visitors."

"Done."

Zain addressed Ferretu. "I guess if you won't tell me, I'll have to find out for myself." Zain studied his outfit. "Hope you don't mind if I borrow your clothes for a while."

Lacey had never seen a dead man before. Well, except at a wake, but these guys were freshly dead and in big chunks all over the sand. It made a difference.

She helped Zain into his disguise by Reene's lights. She'd slept through the whole mess. Thankfully. Any misgivings she'd had about not going to Avakur with Zain were gone. She was in over her head and she knew it.

"Are you sure this is a good idea?" she asked as he turned to face her.

"No, but it's the only one I've got. And if I don't stop them, no one will."

Out of the corner of her eye, Lacey saw their cap-tive on the ground against the outer wall of the dome. His hard, cold eyes had watched her every move since she'd come outside. This was the kind of man that Zain was about to face hundreds of, all alone.

"Maybe there's another way," she blurted. "We can throw a bomb through the portal or—"

Zain slid his hands around her waist and pulled her close. Her heart jumped, and he leaned down and skimmed her lips with a kiss. "I'll be back."

She clung to him. "You better. You aren't sucking me through space and then deserting me."

He grinned. "Still upset about that, are you?"

"And don't you forget it."

His expression sobered. "Well, just in case I don't make it back, Reene has orders and instructions to send you home through the VirtuWav."

She shook her head. "Forget it. If you don't come back, I'm coming after you."

He sighed. "Lacey, you said it yourself. This isn't your world. You have your own battles to fight. This one is mine." He eased his fingers around her face and lifted her eyes to his. His gaze warmed her soul. "Promise me you will go home if I'm not back in three hours."

She knew he wouldn't be satisfied with anything less. She'd make his promise, but it was one she couldn't keep. "Fine."

He gave her one last kiss that burned her lips. She tightened her grip on his biceps, not wanting to lose contact. He pulled back and pressed his forehead to hers. She heard him say something softly in the alien language she'd come to realize must be his native tongue. The words didn't matter. All that mattered was that those sweet words he uttered were for her and for her alone.

Then he released her, stepped back, and donned Ferretu's helmet. He was a dead ringer for the assassin.

Zain looked at their scowling captive. "Reene, I restrained Ferretu, but if he moves, shoot him."

"Understood. Good luck, sir."

His metal gaze turned back to her for a few moments. She gave him a little smile, just in case it was the last. With her heart twisting in her chest, she watched Zain pull on the gloves and head to the dome. Then tears clouded everything else.

Zain moved through the sleek hallways of the Avakur compound. Some serious funds had gone into this venture, and he really wanted to know who it belonged to before he blew it up.

He flattened against a wall as he neared a corridor intersection and peered around the corner, his weapon ready. It was night at the base, and he'd only seen two other guards since he materialized inside one of the compound's portals. They had both simply nodded at him as he walked by in his borrowed uniform.

A lone metal panel of flashing lights up ahead held promise. He checked the empty hallway before taking a good look at it. InterGlax information console. Excellent.

He holstered his pistol and slipped his datapad from his pocket, activating the transmission function before plugging it directly into the panel. Then he proceeded to access systems using Ferretu's pass, and downloaded the entire base schematics into his unit while simultaneously transmitting the information to Reene.

He scanned the wall panel display. The control center was located on Level One in the heart of the compound. It figured. In his cloak, he carried enough detonators stolen from the Well to take out half the building, and he hoped it would be enough. Then he'd get back to Lacey.

His heart squeezed just a little at the thought of her. She was counting on him to return, and he didn't want to disappoint her. Even though it meant living without her after.

A noise to his left brought his head up. A guard stood ten meters away with a rifle pointed at him. Zain fought the instinct to reach for his weapon.

"What are you doing?" the stone-faced man asked.

Zain tipped his head. "Updating my personal unit," he replied, trying to mimic Ferretu's voice.

The guard didn't look convinced. "You are supposed to be on 93."

"It's clear," Zain told him. As he spoke, he moved his finger a fraction and pressed the button to clear all the information from his datapad, including the way home.

The man listened carefully to his voice. After a few seconds, he raised his rifle and ordered, "Remove your helmet."

Zain clenched his jaw. Failure taunted him. Not again. He wasn't going to let IG win this time. Too many lives were on the line, including Lacey's. InterGlax needed to be stopped, no matter what the sacrifice. The detonators weighed heavy in his cloak. He knew just where they were.

Slowly, he took off the helmet and watched the guard's eyes widen. In that split second of surprise, Zain tossed the helmet at him and reached in his cloak for a detonator.

Lacey rubbed her arms, even though it wasn't cold in the ship. The twin gazes of Pio and Oliver watched her. It beat the inhuman stare of their captive outside. She couldn't take much more of him. No wonder Zain had slept so poorly, with men like that hunting him.

Reene had placed a satellite image of a mottled green-and-brown planet in the holodeck. The image zoomed in to the northern hemisphere, to a particularly dark and desolate region. Details filled in around a sprawling complex wedged in a valley. One mammoth building sat in the center, surrounded by smaller structures and a sizable network of streets. The place was huge, far more complex than Lacey had ever imagined. And Zain was in the middle of it all.

She pushed aside her fear. She trusted his abilities. He promised he'd be back, and that's what she would believe.

"How is he going to return?" she asked.

"The datapad is programmed to initiate a portal activation from one of the portals on Avakur to here."

Simple enough. What could go wrong?

"I have incoming data," Reene announced. "Zain is transmitting the compound's schematics and systems."

Inside the large square building, layers of floors materialized, along with corridors, rooms, and equipment. She watched with growing alarm as the image grew more defined. To her surprise, the center section of the building was completely empty, displaying a sizable courtyard.

"Reene, I could have sworn the main building had a solid roof on the satellite image."

"The roof appears to be an illusion created by an energy field, much like the one that covers this basin."

"Interesting," she said aloud, watching the compound render like a CAD drawing. Six locations flashed red: a large one in the center courtyard, two smaller ones inside the main building, one on the rooftop, and two large locations on opposite ends of the surrounding area.

"What are the red marks?"

"Portals. They are typically used in large installations to facilitate high-speed transportation."

Lacey shook her head. Why anyone would willingly dismember themselves one molecule at a time was beyond her.

Reene continued, "In addition to these, I have applied the dome coordinates to Avakur and detected several dormant portals located outside the IG compound."

That didn't make sense. "What do you think they are for?"

"The number of portals indicates that the Narous may have used Avakur as a main transfer point or even lived there at one time."

Lacey stared at the setup. "This is simply fascinating."

"I have received the security access code to our armory," Reene announced.

Relief swept through her. "So you can shut down the energy field and lasers over us now?"

"Affirmative."

She leaned back in her chair. Excellent. Now all Zain had to do was set the detonators and get back here. It was all going to be okay. InterGlax would be stopped, and Earth and other worlds like it would be safe—for a long time, she hoped. And he and Reene could leave this basin in one piece.

On the downside, she'd be returning to Earth. Until now, she'd been so worried about Zain's safety, InterGlax, and her world, she hadn't thought much about what her life was going to be like without Zain. One word came to mind: lonely.

And the assassin outside reminded her that Zain would still be an outlaw for the rest of his life. It would haunt her as well. Every morning she'd wake up and wonder if this would be the day InterGlax caught up with him.

It wouldn't be so bad if she hadn't fallen in love with him.

Reene spoke up. "I have an explanation for the countdown."

"Go," Lacey said automatically.

"I have analyzed the data Zain sent from the Command Center and confirmed ninety-five other installations identical to this one, each covering a specific part of the galaxy. When the countdown hits zero, all drones are scheduled to launch from armories across the galaxy for as long as five cycles. The preset attack sequence indicates that multiple targets will be hit."

Her eyes widened. "Holy shit. How many targets?"

"Over one hundred thousand," Reene replied.

Lacey gasped. "Earth, too?"

"Affirmative."

"Good Lord," she whispered, overwhelmed. The entire galaxy was about to be attacked, including Earth! How many planets would suffer the fate of Maadiar? How many people were going to die? The launch had to be stopped and Zain was their only hope.

Reene said, "Zain has wiped his datapad. All information has been deleted."

Her heart thudded to a halt in her chest. "Then how will he activate the portals to get back?"

There was a weighty pause. "He won't."

She stared at the holo-image in disbelief. *No.* He couldn't have failed. He was too good, too skilled and he'd *promised* her.

"Is he alive, Reene?"

"Unknown. I must tell you that his final orders were to return you to your planet if anything went wrong."

Fear and hopelessness clawed at her. Home. She wanted nothing more than to escape this nightmare. All she had to do was walk to the back room and she'd be gone, back to where her life was simple and ordinary and safe. But it wouldn't be safe for long. The aliens were coming.

And Zain. Her chest tightened. She wouldn't leave him, no matter what she'd promised. Dammit, she wasn't running, not this time. She took hold of her fear and set it aside. It was time to show the galaxy what Lacey Garrett was capable of.

"I'm not leaving," she replied. "How much time on the countdown?"

"Just under four hours."

"And you have absolute control over the armory, Reene?"

"Affirmative. I now have access to all portals, weapons systems, teleportations, and launch sequences."

"Launch sequences?" she asked. "You can target specific locations? Where they go? What they hit?"

"Yes. The fighter drones operate under one common attack program."

She raised her eyebrows. Did he say program? She leaned forward. "Reene, can you build an interface so I can modify that program?"

"Of course."

A spark of hope ignited a fledgling plan. But she could use some help to pull it off. Preferably someone who knew how to handle a gun. "I don't suppose Zain has anyone he trusts hanging in the general vicinity?"

"Rayce Coburne and Cohl Travers are several days away."

Too far. "What about Torrie?"

"Based on her last transmission, she should be relatively close."

Lacey looked out at the dome before them and embraced risk.

"Contact Torrie. We're going after Zain."

Chapter Twenty-four

T minus zero

Torrie Masters was a tall, striking woman in a blue flight suit that molded to a very physical body. With her thick, wavy cascade of red hair and green eyes, she could have been a stand-in for Maureen O'Hara. A long, light gray duster swept around her as she exited her ship, and walked to where Lacey waited next to Reene. Sizable pistols were strapped to each of her thighs and a packed weapons belt was slung around her waist. Maybe *aliens* had invented cowboys.

Lacey glanced down at her own baggy pajamas and fuzzy purple slippers that had seen one too many stones. For the life of her, she couldn't figure out why Zain had wanted to sleep with her.

"Greetings," Torrie said with a bright smile.

"Thanks for contacting me." Her gaze dropped to Pio, standing next to Lacey.

Lacey motioned to him. "This is Pio, a *krudo*. We'd be dead without them."

Torrie's eyes lit with a passion Lacey recognized only too well; it was in Zain's eyes, too. Obviously, she herself wasn't cut out to live in space. Meeting new aliens didn't do a thing for her. Well, except for Zain himself. And he did all kinds of wonderful things to her.

As they headed to the ship, Lacey nodded toward their captive. Ferretu's head was back against the wall and he squinted at them in the morning light. A half-dozen *krudo* kept watch around him.

"Meet Ferretu, your friendly neighborhood assassin."

Torrie's eyes narrowed. "Can we kill him?"

"Only if he moves," Lacey told her. "I'm still waiting."

"Too bad," she heard Torrie mutter. Lacey led her into Zain's ship. On the way to the front, she caught Torrie eyeing the single rumpled bunk, but Torrie didn't comment. Lacey took Zain's seat and Torrie settled into hers. Sitting on the console, Oliver acknowledged them with a half-second of interest.

"It is a pleasure to finally meet you, Torrie," Reene chimed brightly.

Torrie's eyes met Lacey's with more than a little humor. She said to the computer, "Nice to meet you too, Reene. You disobeyed orders. I think you're in big trouble."

"I did not disobey a direct order," Reene sniffed. "I simply took Zain's requests in the strictest sense. He did not forbid Oliver from contacting you. And clearly, Oliver needs a translator."

Lacey grinned at their cooperative effort. She had a whole new respect for Reene. He could be positively devious when he wanted.

Reene had already briefed Torrie on their situation and she started studying the holo-image of the base. "Any idea where Zain is now?"

"His last transmission was from here." Lacey pointed to a second-story corridor. "Nothing since then. We don't even know if he's still breathing."

Torrie gave a small smile. "What does your gut tell you?"

Lacey crossed her arms. "That he is alive and very pissed for screwing up."

Zain's sister laughed. "You have him figured out. I'm impressed."

"Actually, it's my fault he's there to begin with," Lacey admitted. "I thought we should stop InterGlax from attacking defenseless planets. Obviously, it was a bad idea."

Torrie shook her head. "Zain didn't do it because you *told* him to, trust me. And it's not your fault that something went wrong. But I have to tell you, this isn't going to be easy. That's a big installation with major weaponry protecting it. The four blue locations on the rooftop are remotely controlled turret guns. Very effective, and very hard to take out. Interesting challenge."

Lacey eyed Torrie's pistols. "You seem to know a lot about weapons."

Torrie answered with a big grin. "And I'm not afraid to use them, either."

"I need exactly one sharpshooter," Lacey confessed.

Torrie leaned back and crossed her arms. "I'm your woman. What did you have in mind?"

"I think I have a plan on how to get Zain back *and* stop InterGlax," Lacey said. She looked at Torrie. "We only have a few hours to get ready, and it'll be just the two of us. You with me?"

Torrie smiled. "Are you kidding? And miss the chance to hold a rescue over my brother's head forever? I'm in."

Guards relieved Zain of the detonators and weapons, and bound his hands in restraints before shoving him into a windowless three-meter-by-three-meter confinement cell. A translucent force-field door sealed the room. On the other side, three Avakurian guards dispersed, their duty done. He watched them limp and massage assorted body parts. At least he'd given them a struggle they wouldn't soon forget. Unfortunately, he'd failed to activate even one of his detonators.

He sat on the only chair in the cell to try to sort out the situation. One thing was for certain: This was no InterGlax operation. These guys couldn't fight worth a damn, and no one recognized him. He knew his face was plastered all over IG's Most Wanted lists. That meant the Avakurians were stealing from InterGlax without direct association. The realization made him feel slightly better on several levels, but it blew his theory of the connection to his past. If IG wasn't involved, then how were their fighter drones ending up with the Avakurians?

Zain rested his head against the wall and tasted his own blood. He winced at the pain in his ribs and battered fists. He'd gotten off easy. The Avakurians could have just shot him and been done with it. But, for whatever reason, he was still alive. An interesting turn of events. Maybe they were going to have a special execution ceremony. Something to look forward to.

He closed his eyes. This time, he had not only failed the galaxy he had failed Lacey as well. The thought of her derailed all his other thoughts. She would go back to Earth and wait for the Avakurs to show up someday.

And as if that weren't bad enough, he doubted he'd convinced her of what she was capable. He hoped someday she would find out for herself. He hoped she'd find someone to love. His heart constricted. No, he didn't want that. No other man would treat her right. No other man would love her like he did. Right now, he'd trade anything for one more look at her sweet face, just one more touch of her soft skin, one more kiss.

"Well, well, well." A chuckling voice broke through his thoughts.

Zain turned his head to the familiar inflection from the other side of the force field. A staunchly built man moved closer, his InterGlax uniform filling the doorway. Closely cropped gray hair framed a wide, ruddy face. Blue eyes penetrated the force-field and the man's thin lips broke into a smug grin as he reached out and deactivated the artificial door.

"How you been, Zain?"

"Major Schuler." Sudden insight and anger flashed through him. Last he knew, Schuler was a deskbound twit who pushed through requisitions forms. He'd sucked up to the command level until he pretty much ran inventory and supplies. He was the perfect man to steal ships from IG. The pieces clicked together. "So have you killed any good InterGlax operatives lately?"

Schuler shook his head with great drama. "Not since you and Crista, I'm afraid. And it looks like I didn't do a very good job with you." He eyed Zain's outfit. "Have you killed any good assassins lately?"

"Just one," Zain said simply.

The major nodded. "Pity. So, it is vengeance that brings you to me, Masters?"

"Vengeance never dies. You ambushed us, you bastard." Zain hissed. "And when you couldn't kill me, you set me up for Crista's murder."

Schuler shrugged. "I couldn't have you shutting down my supply channels. Not after all the alliances I'd built. The Avakurians are surprisingly skittish."

"You stole the ships and gave them to Avakur," Zain stated, all the pieces coming together. "Used the armories to launch attacks on defenseless juveniles, and then approached them with promises to keep them safe from big, bad InterGlax . . . for a small price, of course."

Genuine respect registered on Schuler's face. "Very good."

"Did General Lundon know?"

"Your old supervisor? No," Schuler said with a shake of his head. "The man wallows in integrity. Must be why you liked him."

"Also, he never tried to murder me," Zain said. "That has a tendency to sour a working relationship fairly fast."

"True, but he never covered your ass either," Schuler added. "A pity that InterGlax was so much quicker to believe a bunch of no-name locals in a swamp than they were their own field operative."

Zain's jaw worked. He hadn't forgotten that little detail.

"Would you like a tour of my base?" Schuler offered.

Zain frowned at him. "Why?"

The traitor smiled. "Because I think we have much in common."

Zain growled at the implication. "*Before* you kill me?"

One corner of the Major's mouth turned up. "Perhaps we can work an arrangement to avoid that."

What was Schuler trying to pull? "Tell me why I should trust you."

Schuler nodded to the guard to his right, and the man motioned to Zain to exit the cell. Still restrained, Zain followed Schuler past a narrow row of similar rooms.

"I know for a fact that you never approved of

InterGlax's policies. You weren't afraid to defy outdated procedures and guidelines. And neither am I," Schuler said. "We just have a different approach. Mine has proven more . . . effective, don't you think?"

They cleared the cell block and headed down a long corridor with doors along one side and windows open to a large center courtyard on the other. "By attacking juvenile systems and killing innocent people? How do you justify that?"

Schuler replied, "I believe those new systems deserve to see what InterGlax is truly capable of. My armories are no different from the power InterGlax wields."

"Those juveniles aren't ready for first contact," Zain growled. "You have no right to interfere."

"And CinTerr does?" Schuler asked, stepping up to a sealed door. He placed his palm against the security pad. "Who are they to decide when a juvenile is ready? And who are they to represent the sector and dictate with whom juveniles will interact politically and economically?"

"The difference is that InterGlax never terrorized new systems." He glared at Schuler. "And they don't hide behind killing machines like cowards."

The door slid open, and Schuler turned to stare at Zain. "Don't count on it, Captain Masters. InterGlax has had their share of collateral deaths. Twelve hundred killed during the Bruielian uprising. Thirty-five hundred lives lost in Kqui-jo region. Countless economies devastated and ruined through InterGlax policies. You know I'm right."

Zain pursed his lips. "They aren't perfect, but then again, they aren't impersonating another group and slaughtering people under a false identity, either."

"There is a dark side to InterGlax that you have never seen," Schuler pointed out. "I have."

Zain narrowed his eyes. "So have I. In that swamp."

Schuler led him into a dark round room lit only by control panels and thin rings of light. Men huddled over consoles, barely giving them notice. In the center of the room was a holodeck displaying the star systems of the quadrant, each color-coded.

A weasely-looking man scurried over. Schuler scowled at him. "Another surprise for you, Everard. Meet Zain Masters."

The man's eyes widened in horror as he stared at Zain. Then he swallowed. "I see."

Schuler brushed him aside and stepped up to the holodeck. "We control ninety-five munitions installations from this base. They are designated in blue. Yellow systems are targets that have not yet been contacted. Green systems are under our protection."

Zain chuckled. " 'Protection.' That's an interesting definition for extortion."

"We offer the juveniles the same options as InterGlax. InterGlax's protection also comes at a price. We just got there first," Schuler countered.

"You used the Narous's system to locate juvenile systems," Zain observed.

Schuler grinned. "An auspicious opportunity. The first dome was discovered here twenty years ago. Through Avakur's ancient archives, I ascertained the origin and built the interface. Once that was accomplished, I was able to locate the rest of the domes and receptors in the network. Then it was just a matter of acquiring armories and weapons. In a partnership, Avakurians supplied the armories—"

"And as Head of Procurement, *you* stole the ships from InterGlax," Zain interjected.

"It worked well enough. I would simply point a finger at careless suppliers or inventory personnel. A few here and there from a massive inventory like InterGlax's hardly made a stir."

"Until Crista noticed."

Schuler nodded. "Yes. Most unfortunate. She was a good operative. I hated to kill her. But at the time, I was not in a position to offer an alliance to either of you and for that I am sorry." His gaze met Zain's. "However, I am now. Juveniles should have the opportunity to choose their alliances, just like mature systems do. Don't you agree?"

His sense of justice was twisted, and Zain fought the urge to head-butt him. The man was more dangerous than ever imagined. He needed to be stopped.

"You have a point," Zain conceded.

"How much time do we have left?" Schuler asked Everard.

"Two hours and counting," Everard replied. "On schedule."

Schuler smiled at Zain. "You are just in time to witness the biggest conquest in history. In two hours, we will launch a simultaneous attack from all installations to all targets that will last several cycles. By the time we are done, InterGlax and CinTerr will be history."

Zain stared at the targets in the holodeck as the full extent of Schuler's insanity took hold. *Damn.*

Schuler crossed his arms. "So, what do you say? I could use a good man to approach juveniles and encourage them to make the right choices. Think of it as a diplomatic opportunity. You will be well compensated for your position."

Zain realized that once the attacks were launched, he wouldn't be able to stop them unless he was on the inside. Then, he could notify InterGlax. If there was an InterGlax left to notify. But it would be the only way. One double cross deserved another. "I'll think about it."

Schuler nodded. "Good."

Zain noticed that one of the blue lights in the holodeck began to flash.

"We have lost control of Installation 93," Everard said, panic in his voice. "The main systems are not responding."

Schuler turned and studied Zain. "I don't suppose you have an idea of what happened to 93?"

Zain remained silent. *Lacey.*

"Would you like to send a ship to check out the planet, sir?" Everard asked.

Schuler kept his gaze on Zain. "No. Blow it up. We'll get by without it."

The man blinked. "Sir?"

Schuler swung his head around. "Contact our closest ship and have them destroy the station and surrounding area." Schuler looked at Zain. "Unless, of course, you would like to consider my offer."

Zain would love to think that Lacey had followed orders and gone back to Earth, but he knew better. If she were still on the planet, she'd be dead. And even if she weren't, Reene was, and the *krudo*.

"That won't be necessary," Zain replied. "No one else knows about your operation except me. I work alone. For obvious reasons."

Schuler regarded him for a few moments. "So you will accept my offer?"

Zain clenched his fists behind him. "Yes."

Chapter Twenty-five

"Does everyone have their orders?" Lacey asked her alien posse assembled in the armory.

"I'm all set," Torrie said, her pistol trained on Ferretu sitting on the floor.

Through Lacey's earpiece, Reene spoke up. "I await your signal. However, I must say that I have calculated the probability of success on this mission. It is quite low."

"You heard from Zain lately?" she asked, adjusting the weapons belt she'd borrowed from Torrie. She didn't know how to use half the stuff, but it looked threatening enough.

"No."

"Well then, our odds can't be worse than his. And remember, timing is everything. You are responsible for executing each step on my command."

"I am prepared to kick buttocks in a most efficient manner," Reene replied.

Lacey laughed, despite the tension that filled her. Computer humor. How perfectly apropos.

She turned to Pio, standing on the island top. "Are your people in position?"

The little creature, of whom she'd grown quite fond, tilted his red saucerlike head. "Yes. We help save Zain."

She nodded. "As soon as your work is done on Avakur, get back here. Oliver will never forgive me if anything happens to you."

Then her gaze met Ferretu's. The assassin smirked, mocking her and her plan. She gave him her brightest smile and enjoyed watching his confusion. Not even he could stop her from rescuing the man she loved.

"Begin Phase One, Reene," she ordered. Around her, the armory came alive. Portal tubes descended into the first level of tunnels. The ends attached and capsules began to float upward.

"How long to complete the transfer, Reene?" she asked through her comm unit.

"Approximately thirty minutes to empty the tunnels and move the shippers into position."

Lacey watched the capsules getting ready to make their way to Avakur. "You are sure IG won't see them coming in?"

Reene replied, "I have selected portals just beyond the compound's detection capabilities."

"Let's hope so," she said softly. Then she stepped over to Ferretu and pointed her rifle at him. "Up."

He snorted. "You won't shoot me. You almost puked when you saw what your ship did to my men."

Torrie's two pistols came into Lacey's peripheral vision. She smiled wickedly. "Get up or *I'll* shoot you. And I promise I won't puke."

His face puckered in a sneer but he didn't move.

Lacey turned her head and said, "Pio."

The little creature moved to her side. She hitched her head at Ferretu. "Eat him."

The assassin's eyes widened in horror as Pio took several steps forward and snapped his claws. The man just about killed himself getting to his feet, then backed away from Pio as far as he could.

"Now, see? That wasn't so hard," Lacey said.

While Lacey covered him, Torrie wrapped tape around Ferretu's mouth and head. "That'll keep him quiet. We don't want him ruining any of our surprises. I just hate when that happens."

Lacey nodded at the assassin and swung her rifle to the portal. "Let's go say hi to all your drinking buddies."

He took a wide berth around Pio until he stood at the platform portal.

Lacey looked down at Pio. "Good luck. And thank you for all your help." She paused and added, "If we don't return, please help Reene send Oliver to Earth."

The creature bobbed his head in understanding. Lacey glanced at the countdown monitor. Thirty minutes before all hell broke loose. Everything hinged on her success. She blinked back any misgivings. Now was not the time to second-guess her decision.

Torrie stepped up behind her. "I've got handsome here covered. Go get Zain."

"See you on the other side." Lacey gave Torrie a final smile, then told Reene, "Activate the lower portal."

The portal opened with a flash of light. When she walked through it, there would be no turning back. No chance to run home and hide. No safety net. No second chances. But Zain was on the other side and that's all she needed to know. She'd spent her life letting other people make her decisions. No more.

With unwavering determination, she stepped through and felt the familiar pull of teleportation. She fought the urge to flee for her fragile Earth life. A moment later, she found herself in the center of a large portal area in a football-field-sized courtyard. A quick look around confirmed this was the building from the holo-image. Arched balconies lined each floor, including the bottom level where she could see guards standing in the shade of a high noonday sun. Overhead was the familiar sheen of holographic camouflage.

She turned just as Ferretu stumbled through the portal behind her, doubled over and clutching his stomach. Torrie must have given him a hell of a send-off. Lacey pushed him a short distance from the portal and trained her rifle on him, while three guards crossed the courtyard with weapons drawn.

Hold your ground, she told herself, even as more guards materialized and the empty courtyard filled up.

The first man reached her and aimed his rifle at her

head. "Freeze." His command translated through her earpiece. And since he wore more junk on his uniform than the others, she figured he must be the top dog.

"You freeze," she countered, and dipped her gun at Ferretu. "Or your pal will be silenced permanently and I'll disappear faster than you can say Shazam."

The guards had completely surrounded her, and she could feel the sweat trickle down between her breasts.

"I want Zain Masters," she said clearly.

One of the guards stepped forward menacingly, and a laser flashed mere inches from his face. He fell back in surprise. The rest shielded their eyes from the sunlight and gazed to the rooftop from where the shot had come. Several guards turned their gun sights from her to the rooftop sniper. More lasers backed them away from her.

Little did they know that this was part of her plan: Torrie sat up there with her pistols while the *krudo* were disabling the turret guns and running nonstop through the portal to keep it from being accessed from the inside by InterGlax.

"I have friends in high places," Lacey told the now more respectful crowd. "Bring Zain here."

The head guard pursed his lips and spoke into his comm unit. As the minutes ticked by, Lacey tried not to focus on the arsenal pointed at her.

Gunfight at the O.K. Corral. She might never watch that movie again, even if she did get back to Earth in one piece. From one corner of the courtyard, a small group of men marched toward her. She searched for Zain's face. *Please be here. Please be alive.*

The guards parted as a single man walked up to her. Not Zain. The man walked military-straight with a bearing and weight that told her she was dealing with the head honcho. As he drew near, he scanned the situation with sharp eyes.

He stopped, bowed, and gave her a disarming smile. "I am Major Schuler. And you would be?"

"Lacey Garrett."

He glanced at her pajamas and purple slippers, and smiled smugly, condescendingly like Robert would have. She tightened her grip on her rifle.

"And what can I do for you, Lacey Garrett?"

"Oh, I don't know," she said in her own patronizing voice. "I was thinking we could make a trade. You give me Zain, and I'll give you back your assassin. He's a little banged up, but I'm sure he'll be as good as new by morning."

Schuler cast a rather dismissive look at Ferretu. "And what of the others?"

"I shot them," she said.

One eyebrow went up on Schuler's face. "Zain does find some interesting partners."

"Where is he?"

Schuler studied her for a moment, giving her an amused look that told her he was toying with her. She was tempted to shoot him on the spot.

Then he turned and nodded at the head guard. Seconds later, she spotted Zain. Several guards flanked him, but he wasn't otherwise restrained.

On the downside, he looked pretty pissed.

"What the hell are you doing here?" he asked as soon as he was within yelling range.

"I was in the neighborhood," she snapped. Dammit, didn't he know a rescue when he saw one?

He stopped just short of her. "I told you to go home. Just once couldn't you follow orders?"

"I'm saving your ass," she growled in a low voice.

He looked around at all the guns pointed at them, and his eyes narrowed. "Have you told *them* that?"

Schuler stepped in, looking quite entertained. "Zain, perhaps *this* partner might like to join our operation as well. I'd be willing to give you an . . ." He looked her over. "Assistant."

She blinked at Schuler and then into Zain's hard stare. "Assistant? You're joining these bastards?"

"I was thinking about it," he said with a grumble.

She shook her head, bewildered by his sudden change. What was he saying? He couldn't have turned against her. The Zain she loved would die before he'd turn on his partners and principles. "How can you even consider that after what they've done to you and Crista? After all those innocent people killed in the attacks? You know damn well IG will never stop."

"You are right, but the Avakurians are trying to save the galaxy from InterGlax's brutal policies," Zain replied firmly. "I've seen the entire operation."

She stared into his dark eyes and they softened, almost pleading. "Join me," he whispered, his tone persuasive. "We'll be fine *together*."

Together? What was he doing? Trying to protect

her again? Well, not this time. Dammit, she had a plan.

She leaned forward until she was inches away from him. "No. *You* join *me*." Then she said into her comm gear. "Reene, launch Phase Two."

A chorus of high-pitched whines filled the air, and the sky darkened. Thousands of InterGlax fighters swarmed down, hovering over the rooftops. All the guards looked up, some running for cover as ships blanketed the sky.

"There's about ten thousand fighters up there, in case you were trying to count them all," she told Schuler. "They should look quite familiar to you. I reprogrammed them to level this base. I also rerouted your other ninety-four armories to attack each other instead of all those poor planets."

Zain raised a single inquisitive eyebrow, and a slow smile crossed his face. She could see the relief in his eyes. He hadn't turned on her.

"I love you," he said.

She batted her eyelashes. "You haven't seen the best part yet."

Schuler pressed his wristband. "Everard, status."

A man's voice came back, "Sir, we have lost control of all the armories. The program appears to have been modi—" Schuler cut off the comm.

Lacey smiled. "This town ain't big enough for the two of us, Schuler. Surrender or be blown to bits."

Schuler's face reddened with rage, but there was no offer of surrender.

Lacey raised her chin. She wasn't leaving without

Zain and that was final. "Phase Three, Reene," she said. Nothing happened. Lacey began to wonder if she'd asked too much of Pio and his people. Maybe they hadn't had enough time to dig back up the dead guards and drag them to the portals.

"Execute them," Schuler snarled. The head guard raised his rifle, only to have it shot from his hands by Torrie. A volley of shots followed that scattered the other guards.

There was a sudden burst of light in the center of the courtyard, about twenty feet away, followed quickly by another, and then a deafening and terrifying bellow.

For a split second, everyone froze. Their collective gazes were drawn to several new additions. Then the ground shook with thundering footsteps and, like a bad B-movie, all decorum disappeared; guards scattered for their lives.

Lacey had to admit, the pair of Bobzillas didn't look at all happy about being tricked through the portal to another planet. However, they quickly adapted and started snapping at the plentiful morsels with their massive jaws. The challenge, of course, was keeping Zain and herself away from those teeth.

"Stop them!" Schuler called out, but the guards were panicked, completely ignoring him. Chaos reigned as most of them fled for the safety of the building. Some remained around her and Zain. Luckily, they had more important things to shoot at.

"Phase Four, Reene," Lacey said into her comm.

Engine noise joined the roars and screams as lasers

rained down. The hovering fighter drones started pummeling the base, and the courtyard filled with dust and rubble. Lacey had reprogrammed the fighters to avoid humans and target critical systems, but there were no guarantees. Balconies crashed to the ground, and windows shattered from the heat and battery. Schuler was racing around, trying to organize his troops as the Bobzillas continued to chomp them at will.

Zain took out a nearby guard with one punch, then relieved him of his rifle.

"I assume you have a plan for getting us out of here," he said over his shoulder as he began firing.

"Phase Five," Lacey called above the insanity.

Reene appeared through the portal and landed close by. His guns lit up, providing cover fire so Zain and Lacey could reach the safety of the ship.

"Go," she yelled to Zain. He ran ahead of her, both of them shooting at anything that looked dangerous, which was pretty much everything.

Halfway to the ship, Schuler stepped between them, forcing a halt. He pointed a gun at Lacey but kept his eyes on Zain. Lacey glanced at the rooftop. Where was Torrie?

He called out, "Stop this attack now, or I'll kill her."

Years of frustration overtook her. "I am *not* invisible!" she yelled. "The name is Lacey Garrett!"

She raised her gun, but before she could pull the trigger, a colossal head knocked Schuler to the ground. Then she watched as foot-long teeth picked him up, threw him in the air screaming, and snapped him in two. Pieces of Schuler thumped to the ground. Lacey stared at them, too horrified to move.

"Lacey!" Zain yelled, and she looked up to find a Bobzilla eyeing them. Her rifle was up and firing before she even realized she was the one shooting. Bobzilla roared in anger, backed off, and went looking for easier prey.

"To the ship," Zain called out. They ran the short distance across the yard and into Reene's open rear hatch.

"Where's Torrie, Reene?" Lacey asked, heading to the front.

"I believe she is still on the roof. I have notified her to leave now. The *krudo* have already returned home. What would you like to do about the Bobzillas?"

Lacey tossed her rifle aside and took a seat. "Leave them."

Her hands were shaking, and she was out of breath but felt damn good. Zain wedged into the seat next to her. Out the viewport, the courtyard looked like a war zone.

"I am detecting incoming ships," Reene reported.

Damn, she thought. Schuler must have called in local reinforcements. "Time to say good-bye. Keep those fighters away from us until we can run through the portal. And make sure Torrie gets back before you let them level this place."

The lasers outside ceased seconds later, and Lacey heard Reene's engines whine as the ship began to lift. They were almost free.

"Was this your plan?" Zain asked. She turned to find him watching her with a wide grin.

She frowned. "Are you surprised?"

He leaned over and kissed her. "No. I'm just wondering why it took you so long." He murmured against her lips, "I always believed in you."

A blast rocked the ship, separating them. Reene listed hard to the right, sending Oliver yowling across the floor. The ship compensated to the left before dropping to the ground with an earth-shattering crunch. Laser fire rained on the courtyard from above.

"What the—?" Lacey started. "Reene, I thought we called off the drones off until we were clear."

There was heavy static, and then Reene's voice— "You must evacuate now."

Zain said, "Reene, bring your console up. I can't see anything."

"Good-bye, sir," his garbled computerized voice responded.

"Reene, no!" Lacey cried.

Then another blast shattered the viewport, sending bits of glass flying.

"Get out!" Zain shouted, and Lacey dove from her seat. Another laser flashed a foot away, and the console exploded. Lacey crawled on the floor with Zain behind her. The cabin filled with thick, black, acidic smoke.

"Oliver," she coughed. A pair of incandescent eyes peered at her from under the bunk, and she scooped his trembling body into her arms. They stumbled, coughing and blind, to the rear cabin where sparks hissed and fire lapped at Reene's ceiling. The heat drove them to their knees, and Lacey crawled, hanging on to Oliver with one hand.

The back hatch was already open, and they half-staggered, half-fell from the ship into the courtyard. She moved forward, pushed from behind by Zain. Smoke billowed around her as she twisted to take in Reene's charred, misshapen hull.

"Oh God, Reene," she cried.

Past her burning lungs and eyes, she realized she'd left her rifle inside, but she was retching too hard to do anything about it. She could hear Zain next to her, fighting for air. Oliver was somewhere nearby sneezing.

That was when a rifle barrel came into her line of vision. Through her tears, she gazed up to find a wall of uniforms surrounding them.

Oh, no. She'd failed. She'd let everyone down.

The rifleman moved forward and jabbered a bunch of words in a language she didn't understand. But one word came through loud and clear: "InterGlax."

Chapter Twenty-six

Lacey paced near Oliver, who was curled up on a bed in a room on a world where they didn't belong. They were inside one of InterGlax's big ships that had landed outside the Avakur compound. This ship *was* along the lines of a Death Star. Or at least an Imperial Destroyer. After seeing the massive ship with all its technology, she felt like she was holding on to a thin wisp of reality that could go poof at any moment.

Every once in a while, one of the InterGlax doctors would check on her with the kind of smile that made her feel as if she were a specimen in a zoo. None of them spoke English, and since she didn't speak alien, they had communicated via hand gestures and expressions. But there was one question she couldn't seem to get through: Where was Zain?

She hadn't seen him since InterGlax separated them in the courtyard, with Reene burning behind them and her plan to get them free a disastrous failure. Poor Reene. The way he'd looked . . . She stopped pacing and rubbed her forehead. He hadn't made it, she was sure. His data storage must have been destroyed. No system could survive that kind of destruction. He'd coordinated the entire rescue and sacrificed himself to save them. He should be the hero and no one even knew he existed.

Tears stung her eyes, but they didn't fall. She was too numb and too lost to cry anymore.

Zain had been taken away, surrounded by a small InterGlax army—the last thing in the universe he needed. She recalled what he'd said and how badly they wanted him.

Dammit, what had gone wrong? Her plan was perfect. She'd thought of everything—even the *krudo* luring the Bobzillas to the portal pads with the bodies of the dead guards and then disabling the roof turrets, giving her and Zain a chance to escape. And it had been executed flawlessly.

She must have screwed up somewhere. And now Zain was in worse danger than if she'd just left him alone. She hoped he wasn't seriously hurt. With luck, he was being treated well.

He had said he loved her. Of course, it didn't exactly count, because he just loved her devious mind for planning the rescue. That was, until it had all fallen apart. But still, those three little words and his proud grin had replayed in her mind until they were a permanent memory—which was very well how they might stay. Where was he?

"I want to go home, Oliver," she whispered.

The door to her room opened, and an InterGlax guard walked in. He was the same one who had initially arrested them. This time, however, he was wearing a translator.

"My name is Major Wyatt of InterGlax. Please come with me," he said.

"Where's Zain?" she asked, not moving.

"I'll take you to him now."

So he was alive. Thank God. "What about my cat?"

Wyatt eyed Oliver with a mix of apprehension and distrust. "You may leave it here. You will be returning after we finish our meeting."

They exited the small room into a long, empty corridor. Metal walls gleamed, and fluorescent light flooded the ceiling and floor. Wyatt stopped at a doorway, pressed his palm to a panel, and the door opened. He and Lacey stepped into a large round chamber ringed by a long, curved table. Only the center of the room was lit, casting a silent row of men in a ghostly glow. Lacey stepped into the chamber, aware of the numerous strangers who focused on her. Straight ahead, alone in a pool of light at a round table, sat Zain. His dark, cool eyes gazed at her indifferently.

This was no meeting. This was a trial.

"Have a seat, please," Wyatt said. She sat in the empty chair he pointed to, and he moved behind her.

Another man stood up, drawing her attention. He said, "I am General Lundon of InterGlax. Please identify yourself and your planet of origin."

"Lacey Garrett," she answered. "Earth."

He walked behind the other men at the table. "Do you know this man?" he asked, sweeping a hand to Zain.

Her gaze flicked to Zain's, but he still didn't acknowledge her. Was he drugged?

"Yes. Zain Masters."

"And how long have you known him?"

She squinted at Lundon, who walked around the table toward her. "A few days. Why?"

Lundon stopped in front of her. "During that time, did he have any contact with the Avakurians or a man named Schuler?"

"No," she snapped. "Why are you asking me this?"

"Please state your involvement and knowledge in this matter," he continued stoically.

Her voice rose in frustration. "I helped Zain uncover *your* operation to attack juvenile planets. And don't even think about messing with Earth." She stabbed a finger at him.

His thick eyebrows lifted for a brief moment. "I am happy to report that InterGlax was never part of that operation. The Avakurians, with the help of a traitor within our organization, stole our ships and impersonated us. Schuler's operation would have killed many more people and wreaked untold havoc across the quadrant. InterGlax will be forever grateful for your help in stopping them."

Was this for real? Lacey's gaze moved to Zain, who was now watching her intently.

"Then how did you know to find us on Avakur?"

Lundon widened his stance and placed his hands

behind his back. "We have been watching multiple suspects for some time, including several Avakurians. The recent massive portal activity gave us what we needed to move."

She eyed him skeptically. Maybe InterGlax really was innocent. And if they were the good guys, that meant Zain was safe with them. Relief trickled into her.

"What about the allegations against Zain?"

Lundon cast a quick glace in his direction. "He will be given a fair trial."

"Trial?" she gasped. "He just saved your butts with CinTerr, and you want to put him through a trial?"

"It is our standard procedure," Lundon said, his face dark. "In addition to a complete statement, Zain has agreed to cooperate with the continuing investigation and cleanup in exchange for your freedom. He has informed us that you are an accidental transport from a juvenile system. Therefore, you are no longer under custody and are scheduled to return to your own planet."

As Lundon talked, Zain watched Lacey's expression harden. She gaped at the general in disbelief and then turned to him. He watched the flash of pain in her eyes. She knew what he was doing. He was dismissing her. Without a discussion, without an argument, without any input from her.

He folded his hands on the table and kept his head down. It was too tempting to look her in the eye and give away that he wanted nothing more than to walk over and scoop her into his arms. She'd faced untold fears to save his life, unleashed a complex plan that astonished him, and given him a chance to reclaim his honor. He owed her everything, but instead he had to pretend she didn't exist. It was the hardest thing he'd ever done, but it was the only way to set her free.

Her tone was steely. "How very kind of you, Zain, to determine my fate without my input."

Zain lifted his gaze, careful to keep an indifferent facade. "Your presence here was a mistake from the beginning."

"A mistake," she repeated slowly. More pain. He hoped it faded fast.

"How bluntly put. So, I guess that my rescuing you was a mistake, too?" she continued icily.

Lundon's turned to her, apparently intrigued. "*You* launched the rescue?"

Zain laughed to cover his unease. "Look at her. Do you really think she is capable of coordinating a multifaceted attack like that?"

A chorus of laughter reverberated through the room, and Zain watched Lacey flinch. "No, she was simply a spectator. I planned the attack on Avakur, as well as the recovery operation if I were captured. That backup plan went into effect."

She speared him with angry eyes. "That's not true and you know it!"

Zain's hard gaze met hers, and he prepared to finish her off. If he didn't, InterGlax would keep her here and put her on trial. Knowing InterGlax's sluggish procedures, it could take months for her to get back to Earth, and he wouldn't put her through that. He'd already taken enough from her. She didn't belong here, she never did, and she never would. She was destined for a life that she desperately needed to get back to. He knew she had her own battles waiting there. Everyone deserved their chance to stand and fight. He was about to get his chance. He wouldn't stand in the way of hers.

He braced himself and uttered, "I let you think you came up with that plan, but it was all programmed before I left. Reene was following my orders. You had *no effect on the operation*." Zain looked at Lundon. "She's incidental. Send her home."

Then their gazes locked one more time. He saw the moment when the light snuffed out in her eyes, when he'd lost her forever.

Lundon finally seemed convinced. He motioned Lacey out the door. She didn't say good-bye, didn't give Zain even one final look. The door slid shut behind her, and his world became very small and very lonely.

There was no forgiving him for what he'd just done. But there was forgiveness, and then there was freedom. He'd just given her freedom.

Lacey sat on Torrie's ship, stroking Oliver's head as the planet of Avakur fell away below them. It would have been a spectacular sight for most Earthlings, but not for her. This Earthling didn't care. She just wanted to go home to her own little world with all its little problems. The rest of the galaxy could go to hell.

And Zain could, too.

Her eyes stung with the threat of tears, but she vowed she wouldn't cry because the only person she could cry for was herself. Even if she wanted to hate him, she couldn't. There was no reason. He had promised he'd come back. He'd promised he would protect her. But he had never once promised to love her when it was all over.

Pain seared a path through her chest: the sorrowful, silent wail of a heart in mourning. Whatever pain she felt, she deserved—justice for a risk she had taken with eyes wide open.

"The *krudo* said good-bye," Torrie remarked, interrupting her thoughts. "Cute little critters. They were very happy to be rid of a few more Bobzillas."

Lacey shook off her self-pity. "Thanks. I lost track of everyone after InterGlax showed up. What happened to the two Bobzillas in the compound?"

Torrie checked her readings. "IG packed them up and shipped them back to their home planet. They will be dumped far away from the crater. Pio and the *krudo* will be safe from them."

"Good," Lacey said wearily. "I hope Earth is as safe."

"IG will shut down what's left of the other installations, now that they know where they are and how to access them." Torrie grinned. "You put on one hell of a show, Lacey. In case no one's said it, thanks for saving the galaxy."

Lacey gave a weak laugh. "No problem. But I think I'll leave the galaxy in your hands from here on in. I've decided that I really hate space."

"Really?" Torrie asked, looking utterly shocked.

"Don't you want to explore the great unknowns? To see what is waiting to be discovered?"

"No." She was positive. "By the way, thanks for the lift home. I've had enough teleportation to last my lifetime."

"After InterGlax finished interrogating me and cut me loose, I had a chance to talk to Zain. I promised him I'd get you home safely," she replied. "He's going to be busy for a while."

But happy, Lacey thought. He'd finally got what he wanted. Honor. Freedom. InterGlax. No more looking over his shoulder, or the slow death of a prison cell. He could play space cowboy into the sunset.

Torrie glanced at her and added, "He'll be okay. InterGlax may be a bunch of arrogant idiots but they will give him a fair trial for Crista's death—once they gather all the information from Schuler's operation."

"I'm sure he'll be fine," Lacey said quietly.

"You do realize that he lied about who masterminded the rescue to protect you."

Lacey stared into the spectacular view of deep space. Even it wasn't enough to move her. "I know. But I didn't want his protection. I wanted respect."

Torrie pursed her lips. "That was all you wanted from him?"

"He didn't offer any more."

Torrie was quiet for a while, then she said, "I think you need to see something."

She rose and walked to the back of her ship. Lacey petted Oliver's head and pushed her heartache back. Zain would be better off without her, she was sure.

But would she be better off without him?

Torrie returned with a flat board and took her seat. When she flipped it over, Lacey gasped.

"I salvaged it from Reene."

Lacey reached out and touched the painting. The edges of the canvas were slightly singed, but the image was unmistakable. It was her, sleeping in Zain's bunk. The colors were ethereal and delicate, the stroke gentle. Gone were his dark, violent colors and slashing style. But it was more than that. He'd painted her, a person. Not a landscape, not some place he'd visited. He'd immortalized her for himself. She couldn't believe it.

If a painting could say a thousand words, then this one said three little ones. He *did* love her.

Tears rolled down her face. "Take me back."

Torrie's lips pursed. "I'm sorry. I can't. He'll be in InterGlax custody for months. You wouldn't get near him. But once Zain is cleared, he won't have to hide anymore. He'll be free."

"What about your father?"

Torrie's eyes met hers. "Zain will probably want to see him for a while too. But that won't be forever. Then he can come after you."

Lacey looked out the viewport to where the whole galaxy awaited him—more planets to explore, more new species to discover, and a freedom she couldn't compete with. No, he wouldn't come after her. Maybe he did love her, but a man like him needed adventure and excitement. Nothing she offered could match that.

"Give him the painting," she told Torrie. "Tell him not to forget me."

Chapter Twenty-seven

Zain's home planet of Dun Galle hadn't changed much in fifteen years. The sun still set in red glory over the hills surrounding his parents' home. When he was a younger man, that sunset had reminded him of yet another day trapped on a planet in a family business he'd never be free of. Looking at it now, the sunset reminded him of how very many years had passed without him.

For all their faults, he was grateful to InterGlax for allowing him to stay here for the duration of the trial. It had helped to fill the gaping hole in his soul.

Inside the house, he could hear the family gathered—brothers, a sister, sister-in-laws he'd never met, and children he didn't know existed. His family had grown without him. And he'd missed it all. The last few months had been filled with laughter, dinners, and love—a life he'd forgotten about. One that he wanted desperately to have again.

And he'd discovered that his father was human after all. The disease had eaten away at him, stealing his strength but never his fight. Every day, the man had told his wife, Zain's mother, how he was getting better and that he was winning. It was a hard-fought battle to the end, and during that time, Zain had rediscovered the parent he'd grown up to avoid.

Now his father was dead. It had taken longer than predicted but was faster than Zain had hoped. There wasn't enough time, and he'd had so much to catch up on. It was too late now, and that time he couldn't get back.

Zain watched the last sliver of sun dip below the horizon and the moon take its rightful place overhead. There was an emptiness in his heart, and it was more than just the loss of his father. Reene was gone too, unsalvageable after the fire. He could get another ship, but it could never replace Reene, and he didn't want to. There was no replacement for a friend who'd given his life for you. As Zain stared into the waning light, he knew that Reene would have forgiven him in a second. Forgiving himself would take a lot more time than that. He finally had his freedom, but the cost had been great.

Today, he'd been officially cleared of all charges in Crista's death. Today, he now had the independence of which he'd dreamed. But the burning desire he'd once had to explore the galaxy had fizzled. The adventurist spirit, which had been so much a part of him for so long, was gone with no sign of returning. All these years, had he been running toward his future, or simply from his past? Now there was nothing to run from, and nothing to run to.

In the silence of the hills around him, Lacey's face flashed in his mind—as it did every time he let his mind wander. His actions taunted him. He'd hurt her so badly, and she didn't deserve it.

"I thought I'd find you hiding out here."

Zain smiled and turned to his sister as she strolled up behind him. She leaned against the balcony railing and gazed out over their family's land.

"Carmon is never going to let you have your own delivery run. No matter how hard you work him over," Zain said casually.

"How do you know I even asked?"

Zain shrugged. "I overheard you corner him in the hallway."

Her eyes narrowed. "I'm sick of minding the office. Sooner or later I'll wear him down—you'll see. He may be running the company now, but he's nowhere as tough as Father. I have my eye on the Galcuta run."

"Too dangerous," Zain said with a frown.

"Ha! You sound like Father. I can handle that run as well as Carmon."

Zain shook his head. "It's right through the heart of the Dead Zone, Torrie. Carmon has been attacked by pirates a handful of times, blown three engines, and lost two crewmen."

"Yes, but *I* know how to use a gun." She grinned.

Zain eyed his sister. "I noticed. Where'd you learn

that skill? Certainly not from anyone in the family."

She humphed. "I've been sneaking out of the house for the past ten years learning weapons use, hand-to-hand combat techniques, piloting. I even devised my own tracking technology. I'm in a better position to handle a run than anyone in this house."

"I don't doubt your ability to take care of yourself, Torrie. Just choose a different run."

Green eyes speared him. "I don't want another run. I want that one."

"Why?"

"Because it's the hardest," she told him, her voice firm. "That's where the adventure is."

He caught the gleam in her eye, one he understood completely. "Adventure is not all it's cut out to be, Torrie. I know. I've been there."

"You had your chance. I just want mine," she countered. "Besides, I have Mother on my side."

She grinned knowingly and Zain shook his head. Seven full-grown men were no match for the two Masters women, and he knew it. Torrie would get her run.

"I think you miss Lacey."

"Yes," he replied simply. How could he explain how she had taken all the light with her when she left? His heart was cold, black, and lifeless.

"So . . . are you going to stick around here forever, or get on with your life?"

"Trying to get rid of me?"

"Unless you're going to convince Carmon to give

me the run, yes." She shrugged. "Besides, I thought InterGlax just cleared you?"

"They did," he said. "And they offered me a new assignment."

Torrie looked at him, surprised. "Really? Doing what?"

"Troubleshooting. I would work alone, with complete discretion handling any internal investigations. Basically keeping InterGlax clean."

"No bureaucratic red tape?"

He shook his head. "No. I would report to senior command only. I'd be a free independent. Nice ship, anything I want."

"Sounds like the perfect job."

"You don't sound happy for me," he said.

She gave him a half-hearted glare. "I just thought you had other priorities. Like, maybe a vacation on a juvenile planet. Let's say, Earth, for example."

He stuffed his hands in his pockets. "She doesn't need me."

"Oh, I wouldn't be too sure about that."

He watched stars fill the night sky. "I can pretty much guarantee that I'm the last man she ever wants to see again."

Torrie turned and leaned against the railing. "She *loves* you."

He laughed at that. "Maybe she did once but not anymore. There are some things that can't be forgiven."

"So?"

He looked at his stubborn sister. "She has to fight

a few battles for herself, without my help."

"So?" Torrie grinned.

"Isn't there someone else in this house you can bother?"

She laughed. "No. Besides, you're miserable without her. Go see her. What can it hurt?"

As if it were that simple. "She would throw me out," he said softly. "There's nothing I can say to give her back what I took from her on Avakur."

"Tell her you love her," Torrie urged. "Tell her how you feel."

"And then what?" he replied sharply. "Ask her to give up everything she's worked for and fly away with me on a little ship traveling across the galaxy into untold dangers?"

Torrie grimaced. "Actually, I have it on good authority that she hates space."

"No wonder. I ruined her," he muttered. "She's spent her life with men who didn't know how to treat her right. Men who controlled her every move. I'm not going to be another name on her list. I have nothing to offer her."

"How about love?"

His heart pumped cold blood through his veins. "I'm not sure I know how to do that without locking her up to keep her safe."

Torrie's expression softened. "You can't tell her how to live her life any more than Father could to you."

Her words sunk in slowly. She was right. Somewhere in the past ten years, he'd become his father—

the controller of all, the man he most wanted to escape. How did that happen?

"Wait here," she said, and disappeared into the house. A few minutes later, she emerged carrying a canvas. It looked like one of his.

"I wanted to wait until IG cleared you. Lacey told me to give this to you to keep, and to never forget her."

He swallowed hard as she turned the painting over to reveal a sleeping Lacey. And everything came back in a flash. The sweet sound of her laugh, the smile on her lips, courage in her heart, love in her eyes—the wave of memories threatened to bring him to his knees.

"It's just too bad that InterGlax offered you the job of a lifetime. If you didn't have anything better to do, you could settle down with a good woman."

Zain's entire body stilled, and he lifted his gaze to his sister. "What?"

She waved a hand. "You know: a house, family, kids, sunsets. Quiet dinners. Long nights staring at the stars. Arguments over what color the house should be. But that would probably be too tedious for an otherworldly explorer like yourself. I mean, there wouldn't be any life-threatening situations to survive or InterGlax to save on a daily basis."

She handed him the painting, then walked back toward the house. Just before she stepped inside, she said over her shoulder, "Besides, how much everlasting love and happiness could one man stand?"

* * *

The sand was blistering beneath her feet as Lacey trekked the forbidding desert. She'd been walking endless hours toward the red hills in the distance, which seemed to be moving farther away with each torturous moment. Tired and thirsty, she wanted to rest. But Zain was in those hills, and he needed her. So she took another heavy step, struggling with her own body for every inch.

An alarm sounded beside her. Dread and panic followed. She tried to run, but the sand was swallowing her up. She screamed and lunged—and sat straight up in her bed. Early morning sun streamed into the room amid the gentle flutter of curtains. Oliver lifted his sleepy head and blinked at her.

Next to the bed, the phone rang.

"I hate that damn dream," she whispered, brushing hair from her face.

She fumbled for the cordless phone before it rang again.

"Hello," she murmured, and laid her head in her hand.

"Lacey?" her mother said. "Did I wake you?"

Lacey glanced at the clock. 6:21 A.M. Obviously her mother didn't want her sleeping her life away.

"I worked late last night," Lacey said with a yawn.

There was an audible sigh on the other end. "You work late every night, sweetie. You can't keep running yourself ragged like this. Don't you think it's time to take a break? Maybe a vacation?"

Lacey smiled at her mother's poor attempt at concealing ulterior motives. A vacation—so she could leave her solitary confinement and meet a nice new young man who would break her heart. As if she had a heart left.

She stretched and swung her feet onto the floor. "I'll take a break after I finish testing the Simmons project, I promise. I have to work on the house anyway."

"That's not much of break. You need to get out and have some fun."

"I just joined the local gardening club. That's getting out."

She could almost visualize her mother's eyes rolling. "Lacey, I meant something exciting. A little adventure," the woman added with enthusiasm.

Lacey laughed to herself. Just what she needed. "I've discovered that I'm not the adventurous type, Mom. Fixing this place up will be excitement enough."

"Well, I hope you don't plan on doing all the work on that house yourself," her mother continued, disapproval edging her voice.

Lacey glanced down the hallway, where she'd stripped off the old lathe and plaster, leaving bare studs and new possibilities. She thought it best not to tell her mother that she'd already done significant demolition. It was the rebuilding part she hadn't figured out yet. Not that that minor fact was going to stop her. She might not be adventurous, but she was persistent.

"Don't be silly," she said. "I just placed an ad in the local paper for a handyman."

"I'm so glad to hear that. Before she sold you the house, Glo always hired a handyman from town. I can't remember who. You could ask the neighbors."

"I will," Lacey said, now that she'd actually met the neighbors. Nice people. Nice little town down the road. Nice, quiet, peaceful place with nary a Bobzilla in sight.

As if her mother could read her mind, she asked, "Have you heard from Robert lately?"

Maybe just one Bobzilla. "I drove to Baltimore and had a short talk with him. He's going to give me a fight for my software ownership." Even as she told her mother, she smiled. The look of utter shock on Robert's face when she showed up on his doorstep and told him to hand over her application or she'd kick his sorry ass from here to the next star system had been worth everything. After a whole lot of stammering, he'd finally regained his lethal tongue and told her she'd have to sue him for it. Fine with her. She'd been threatened by the best. There was nothing Robert could do that would scare her now.

"I wish you'd told us when it happened sooner," her mother said, her disgust clear. "We could have helped you. We're family. We stick together. Your sisters and I would have come out to be with you."

Lacey's eye's widened at the horror of her mother and sisters underfoot. Nothing could save her from that. "I appreciate the sentiment, but Robert is my problem. I can handle him."

"We really did think he was perfect for you," her mother added sadly.

"I know. Don't feel bad. I used to think so, too."

"I hope you find a good man who will make you happy, Lacey."

The heart she'd thought was dead squeezed in her chest. She already had found a good man. She just couldn't compete with the universe.

"I have to go now," she said, trying to keep the emotion from her voice. "I'll talk to you later."

"Bye, sweetie." Her mom hung up.

Lacey turned off the phone and put it back in the cradle. She walked to the window. Outside, spring had finally beat back winter. All was green and fresh and real. Death Valley seemed like a distant memory. A low shrub waved at her in the breeze. It probably needed pruning. Everything needed something in this house. But that was okay. After this contract went out, she would have the time and money to do it right.

Maybe she'd even put a vegetable garden in this year. The gentlemen in the gardening club had been so sweet and encouraging. How hard could it be to get something to grow? And flowers, too. Perennials. Roses perhaps, along the back fence. And a swing on the porch. Like a real home.

She turned to Oliver. "So what do we do today? How about we go hog-wild and rip out the lav?" She winced at the terminology. "Bathroom, I mean." Oliver just yawned and laid his head back down.

"Smart cat."

Lacey went to her PC to check her E-mail. While her uplink tried to connect, she looked up at the poster of Stonehenge hanging over her computer.

Above the familiar stone megaliths hung a single, bright moon that penetrated the night. Behind it, the sliver of a sunset. She'd never realized how very fragile her little world was before. The wars and skirmishes and everyday problems seemed trivial in the grand galactic scheme of things. But Earth was safe now. She'd helped to save it, even if no one would ever know that except for a handful of aliens and Zain.

At the thought of him, a familiar ache swept through her. Maybe it *was* better to have loved and lost, but it made for long nights and a desolate heart.

A message flashed, and she noticed that the connection attempts had timed out. She shook her head. Her satellite dish had probably fallen off the roof, which had rotted out because of neglect. Unfortunately, she needed that uplink. It was her livelihood. So she headed to the back door.

She was halfway to the kitchen when a sharp knock startled her. Who was at her front door at 6:30 A.M.?

She pulled the door open and froze. Her hand on the doorknob was the only thing that kept her from falling over. A man stood on her wraparound porch, his back to her as he scanned her front yard. She took one step onto the porch and let the door close behind her.

He spun to face her. The hair had been cut short, and he appeared tired, but he still had the power to stop her heart. In a denim shirt and jeans, he looked as if he almost belonged here. Still, her mind struggled to place him in her world. For a long time, he just stood there and watched her—studied her, as if memorizing every inch. The world could have ended and she wouldn't have known.

After an eternity, he held the local paper up and said, "I'm here about your ad." When she didn't answer, he raised an eyebrow and added, "It says you need a handyman."

"Handyman?" she parroted. He was standing on her porch. Her porch in her world. In reality. On Earth. Where space cowboys didn't reside. Why?

"Why?" She said the word aloud.

Zain grinned. "I've been told I have great hands." Then he nodded at the house. "Looks like this is going to be quite a job. It might take me awhile." His dark eyes met hers. "Unless you already have another candidate."

She shook her head, careful not to dislodge it from her fragile body. "Why are you here?"

His dark eyes softened enough for her to see torment behind them. They probably looked a lot like hers.

"I want what's mine," he said in a voice raw with feeling. "You took something from me when you left."

"I gave you back the painting," she said, confused.

He stepped toward her. The singular move brought him within a touch of her body, which responded with a sensual sigh.

"I'm not talking about the painting," he said gently. He leaned closer. "You stole my heart, Lacey."

She'd stolen *his* heart? "You stole mine!"

A small smile touched his lips. "Then I guess we

only have one choice. You keep mine and I'll keep yours."

"How?" she asked. He wasn't making sense. He didn't belong on Earth, and she couldn't survive in his world.

He reached out and stroked her cheek. Just a touch, but it zinged her senses like an electric current. "Here with you."

Her mouth dropped open. Was he serious? How could he ever be happy here? Give up everything he'd always wanted just for her? Impossible. Did he really think this through? She needed to know before she could unleash her heart.

She clenched her fists. "This is a permanent position. I can't take anyone who's not willing to commit one hundred percent."

He nodded silently and looked off into the woods. "I see."

"Don't start something you can't finish," she added. Her heart was pounding.

"Well, in that case . . ." He put his hands on his hips. "I guess I'd better tell you what my long-term plans are."

She waited, holding her breath. One false move and she was sure she'd crumble into a million pieces on the floor.

"I plan to fix your house just the way you want it, take you to bed at every possible opportunity, and tell you I love you in all the languages I know until the day I die." His gaze locked onto hers with riveting power. "But only if that's okay with you."

332

Emotions flooded her, swamping every attempt she was making to regain control, but she didn't care. Tears rolled down her cheeks unchecked. "And when you get tired of the job, will you up and leave?"

His gaze intensified as he watched the tears. "I won't run if you don't."

"What about adventure? Exploration? Freedom?"

Zain gazed up into the sky, and she waited for the wistful look. It never came. His voice was clear and sure. "Freedom doesn't just mean you can run when you want to. It means you can stay if you choose."

She still couldn't believe he would give up everything for her. "You'll be doing the same thing every day, every year, for the rest of your life."

When he turned to face her, she saw it—the yearning, love and commitment. A flicker of hope welled up between the cracks in her heart like rays of sunlight after a storm.

With a smile, he said, "I know. I get to spend the rest of my days *with you.* I love you, Lacey. You're all the adventure I ever need. But the choice is yours."

Her choice. And she could see without a doubt that he'd let her decide their fates. If she said no, he'd leave forever even though he wanted to stay. Even if it hurt him as much as it hurt her, he'd give her the power and the freedom to make the biggest decision in their lives. The truth was right there in front of her in his eyes.

She watched them narrow in concern as she took a step toward him. Her fingers stroked his cheek, felt the jaw muscles clench, and the warmth of his skin.

He was real, he was here, and he was hers. No force in the universe could keep them apart now. She gave it all—her heart, her soul, and her dreams—as she wrapped her arms around his neck, binding them in reality.

"Hang up your spurs, cowboy."

Epilogue

"It's so . . . spatial," Mrs. Curry said with a wave of her hand. "The colors, the technique, the balance are all very masculine, but there's an exotically primitive quality to your abstracts."

Zain stood next to her and tried to keep one eye on his best client and the other on the door to his barn studio. Lacey was late. She'd promised to be back in time for dinner. He tried not to worry, but old habits died hard.

Mrs. Curry pulled him along to his next painting: a churning mass of blue flames at the peak of their explosive fury. It still amazed him that his paintings had generated enough interest to draw buyers from the nearby cities and rack up a loyal clientele in such a short amount of time. To him, they were simply captured memories of a life left behind.

"Such savage beauty. Simply marvelous. I just love

your work," the matronly woman said and her perfectly coiffed head turned to Zain. "Where do you get your inspiration, Mr. Masters?"

He smiled benignly. "I've traveled some."

Her etched eyebrows rose. "I see." Then she looked at the painting of the Great Burning Forests on the planet Rrrhan again. "I'll take this one."

"Thank you," Zain said. "I hope you enjoy it." A flash of movement caught his eye and his heart quickened. Lacey stood in the doorway in a light gray button-up suit dress and formed a kiss with her lips. Then she gave him a long, sexy, dangerous look, which didn't help his concentration at all, before disappearing toward the house.

Try as he might, it still took him another thirty minutes to arrange delivery and to escort Mrs. Curry to her car. Then he turned toward the house where Lacey was waiting for him on the porch. She had changed into a short, silky summer dress that matched her eyes and fluttered against her thighs. Around her, the house gleamed from fresh paint and hard work.

A warm rush of satisfaction rolled over him. All the blessings, all the richness of his new life overwhelmed and humbled him. It had even made him consider having his sterilization reversed. The idea of kids running around—his and Lacey's—made him long for something he never before had longed for.

"Hey there, cowboy. Lookin' for a good time?" she said in a lazy voice that he recognized from the old westerns they'd watched together.

He grinned as he ascended the two steps and tipped

an imaginary hat. "What did you have in mind, miss?" he drawled.

She gave him a seductive look. "How about you and me go inside and talk about it?"

He reached out and lashed a hand around her waist. She inhaled sharply as he pulled her to his chest. "I have a better idea."

For a moment, she looked stunned. "You do?"

He chuckled at her confusion. Distracting Lacey had become his favorite pastime. "How about we stay out here and talk about it?"

A look of genuine alarm lit in her eyes and she peered over his shoulder at the roadway. "Are you serious?"

"Maybe," he murmured against her lips.

"You better be careful. I'm the adventuring type, you know." Then she rubbed her body against his, pulling a low growl from his throat. He wasn't the only one skilled at distraction.

"Did I ever tell you how much I love your DNA?" he said, nuzzling her ear.

A soft sigh emanated from her and filled his heart. "A time or two." He felt her hands sculpt his back, then she added, "Yours isn't bad either."

He pulled back and drew her hand to his lips. He nibbled at the soft knuckles. "How did the appointment go?"

She licked her lips and watched him kiss her fingertips one by one.

"Well," she said, her voice a little unsteady. "Robert agreed to settle out of court. I should have my software and back royalties in a few months."

Zain turned her hand over and pressed his lips to her wrist. "So I guess I can't kill him?"

Her eyes narrowed. "I know how disappointed you are but believe me, he's not worth it. And I don't want to find out he's been teleported across the galaxy either, Zain."

He feigned indignation. "Would I do that?"

"In a nanosecond."

He chuckled. It was only because he wanted Lacey to handle her own fight that Robert wasn't outrunning Bobzillas on a desert planet right now. He wouldn't ruin her victory for anything.

A little meow sounded next to them, and Zain glanced over to where Oliver rubbed affectionately against a box near the front door. The B1-series shipping container raised immediate and genuine concern—an uninvited galactic intrusion into his perfect world.

He released Lacey and walked over to it. "Where did this come from?"

She moved next to him. "I don't know. I found it in the middle of the lawn. It must have been delivered when I was out and you were with Mrs. Curry. But there's no label. I figured you ordered something."

"I didn't." Zain picked up the storage container and set it on a nearby table. Oliver jumped up to watch as Zain popped the release. A lightball zoomed out.

"A lightball?" Lacey asked, voicing his thoughts.

He found a holo card inside and set it on the table, while the lightball bobbed in front of them. "There's a message." He tapped the card to activate it, and the image of his sister popped up.

"Greetings, you two," Torrie started. "I hope mated life is sheer bliss. I finally have a gift for you. Sorry it took so long to finish. Had a hell of a time getting the interface right. See you in a few months for the family gathering." She flashed a big smile. "And I'm expecting to hear about some new additions by then, so get to work." She winked and the image faded.

Zain crossed his arms and stared at the bobbing light. "Why a lightball?"

"Because a spaceship would draw too much attention," replied the orb.

Zain froze in disbelief at the familiar voice. It couldn't be! Hope rolled over him, even as he told himself it was impossible.

Lacey recovered first. "Oh my God. Reene? Is that you?"

The lightball bounced up and down. "Greetings, Lacey. Greetings, sir. Meow, Oliver. It is nice to see you all again."

"Reene, old friend," Zain managed after he swallowed the lump of emotion in his throat. The final remnants of guilt relinquished their hold. "It's good to have you back. What happened?"

"Before I went through the portal to Avakur, Torrie replicated my working memory into her ship's databanks. It was her idea. A most auspicious exercise."

Zain scowled at the holo card. "She didn't tell us that."

The lightball glowed softly. "She was not sure the

transfer to another shell would work. It took several months to simplify my program enough to fit inside this unit." Reene executed a few impressive loops. "I rather like this form. I have great freedom. However, I do lack weapons, sir."

Zain chuckled at how far they had come. "I think we'll be okay."

Two fat tears rolled down Lacey's face. "You look smashing." Then she frowned slightly. "You *are* here to stay, right?"

"Yes, ma'am," Reene replied.

Lacey laughed. "Welcome to the family."

She slipped her arms around Zain's waist, and her eyes shone with a love that had endured across the galaxy.

How much everlasting love and happiness could one man stand?

Exactly this much.

UNRAVELED

C.J. BARRY

To continue her father's life's quest, Tru Van Dye has to leave the insular colony of Majj scientists where she was raised and find Rayce Coburne. Yet the virtual-reality program she acquires to gird herself against the man's touch is for naught—his presence overwhelms her. Tru's clever plans, her control, everything is coming unraveled.

Rayce Coburne tried to give up treasure acquisition. He despises dealing with icy customers. And Tru Van Dye is worse than usual—a prissy woman who will blackmail him with all his hopes and dreams. Still, there is a way he can fight back: A kiss a day is the perfect strategy. Unless the spinning he feels inside is Tru unwrapping his heart.
